Dragon Airways

DISCARD

BRIAN RATHBONE

DEDICATION

For Dad. You are missed.

CHAPTER ONE

Without connection, energy cannot flow. To be disconnected is to be lost.
—Gemino, sorcerer and artist

* * *

Cold fingers clutched a warm blade. Distorted shouts echoed through snowy fog. Danger was everywhere, but the lure of magic was irresistible. Whatever enchantment the dead man's knife possessed, it hadn't been enough to save him. It was, however, enough to lure Emmet Pickette from his bed and into the night—barefoot and in his pajamas.

Time stretched. Fat snowflakes hung nearly motionless, suspended in air. Halos around gas street lamps looked like unshaken snow globes. Wild and uncontrollable, elongation of time was a rare thing usually experienced in only fleeting glimpses. Emmet was different, had been all his life; people told his sister so. He experienced time differently than everyone else. Sometimes his life was almost normal—time seemingly passing at the same speed for him as it did for others, but when time compressed, it felt as if everything were happening at once. Memories of what people called "episodes" haunted him, but he was just an ordinary boy on the inside. In some ways, though, he felt incomplete. Always he'd yearned for something without understanding exactly what, knowing only that it would be magic. Like a scent on the wind, it would come to him. And on this night, he'd traced it to the source.

Removing the dagger from the dead man's icy grip gave Emmet chills, but he could not leave behind the magic he'd desired for so long. A lifetime of deprivation and anticipation ended when he pulled the knife free and gripped it for the first time. There was no sense of invincibility as he'd hoped, but finally holding an object with magical properties was exhilarating. Even unidentified and dormant, tangible magic still existed in the world. It validated things most considered myths and legends, and in some ways, Emmet's own existence.

Only minutes before, he'd been sleeping. The presence of magic had grown strong enough to draw him out from under warm blankets. His need deep and insistent, he'd risked Riette's wrath and slipped outside. Always he had known, had sensed magic on the breeze but never so nearby. He was dizzy with it. Never had he expected to find a dead man in the courtyard. The cause of death was not readily apparent, save a small hole in his heavy wool coat.

Running slender fingers along the dagger's rounded edge, Emmet wondered how he could have been fooled into thinking it was something so crude as a knife. Riette would not understand, and he could not explain it.

Words were his enemy; those he did find caused no end of trouble. He was not supposed to make a spectacle of himself. He was to appear as normal as possible, lest the wrong people come looking for him.

Snowflakes gathered on the dead man. Voices drew nearer. Every shadow had the potential to hold the "wrong people." Emmet had seen them before. Shivering, he stashed the dull blade within the hem of his coat. Noises from behind elevated his senses. Snowflakes fell with increasing speed. While he considered every possible escape route, the courtyard closed in around him. If anyone saw him, Riette would find out and he'd be in trouble—again. Holding up his pajama bottoms to keep them well above the dusting of snow, Emmet padded barefoot along the covered walkway where he would not leave such distinct footprints. Those he'd left in the snow already made him feel vulnerable and foolish, but it was done.

Harsh voices grew louder. Shadows across the courtyard shifted. Emmet sprang like the Fae kind he so closely resembled. After slipping silently through the doorway, he was tempted to watch and see what happened next, but shuffling within the small apartment he shared with his sister urged him to move.

Darkness and the sound of Riette talking in her sleep greeted him. Guessing what was to come, Emmet slipped back into bed and tried to get some rest, but his imagination conjured frightening images and scenarios. Panic rose within him. An unstoppable wave, it made his heart race. No words could truly explain what he experienced when time compressed. His convincing his mouth to utter such words was even less likely. Images, sounds, and feelings assaulted him in a relentless deluge, making it feel as if someone had picked him up and hurled him through time. A barrage of thoughts and senses came in a single, overwhelming rush, stacked atop each other until whispering wind felt as if it might crush him.

Mom was gone.
Cold.
Alone.
Dad was gone.
Grief.
Fear.

It was too much. Only then did Emmet realize he was rocking violently, holding his ears. Heart and breath racing, his muscles trembled, the effects lingering like the last vestiges of nightmares. Doing as his mother had taught him, he took slow, deep breaths until the waves of energy grew larger and less frequent.

Time once again expanded, the world now moving with what seemed exaggerated slowness. From where his coat hung, the dagger called to him, promising to change everything, but he could not afford to be caught with it. Riette would not understand. He couldn't make her understand. Emmet Pickette was a boy lost in time, and he was afraid.

* * *

Riette Pickette woke with a start. Disturbing dreams lingered. Something had woken her, and she looked around, waiting for the shadows to move, but nothing did. Creeping to Emmet's room, she found him curled up beneath all his blankets, bathed in moonlight and the dull glow of street lamps streaming through the window. She'd never get back to sleep.

Her brother had been up late and would likely sleep for at least a few more hours. There was no need to check the cupboards to know precious few scraps remained. The thought of taking Emmet to the bakery again made her blush. While Baker Millman tolerated him well enough, Emmet was especially unpredictable in the bakery, surrounded by so many of his favorite things. Twice he'd been caught helping himself to whatever struck his fancy. No one had ever seen him go behind the counter and take a sweet roll, but there he would be, suddenly eating the very thing they had come to get. He had a certain knack.

Riette was grateful Baker Millman found Emmet's "tricks," as he called them, amusing. Others called it theft. The number of places Riette could shop was becoming limited. Provided she was by herself, most left her alone, but Emmet drew stares wherever he went. Recent sewing work left her with enough coin to keep them fed and housed, for which she was grateful. It had been, at times, a close thing.

Dressing quickly, Riette made the decision to slip out to the bakery while Emmet slept. It was something she felt guilty for doing, but her life no longer afforded her the luxuries it once had. Now she was lucky to make a few coppers here and there from folks who knew she did quality work at a cut-rate price. This was another reason the number of places she could shop was shrinking. It pained her to be an outcast among her own community, but mostly she just wanted to be ignored and left alone.

After lighting a lantern, Riette looked back to make sure she hadn't woken Emmet. He did not appear in his bedroom doorway, and Riette heard nothing. When she turned back, the light reflected from faint footprints along the tile floor, visible only when she held the lantern at a certain angle. Riette's blood went cold. The footprints were from small, bare feet and led all the way to the front door. To her knowledge, Emmet had not been outside all day and had been wearing thick socks before finally going to bed. Winter was not yet finished with them, and the evening air bore a chill. Her mind racing, considering all the ways Emmet could have gotten into trouble while she slept, Riette accepted the fact that she might never know. Rarely did her brother answer a direct question, and even less often were his answers helpful. She loved her little brother, but he did make her life a challenge. She pushed thoughts of her parents aside. That line of thinking usually led to tears and solved nothing. Better to go to the bakery before Emmet awoke and avoid any more trouble.

After closing the door silently behind herself and easing the lock into place, Riette walked the cobbled streets of Sparrowport, her breath visible in the chill air. Her guard up, Riette heard the men before she saw them. They were close by—too close. She would not be alone in rising early, but most who did lived in the merchant district. Folks in the residential district tended to rise with the sun. Keeping to the shadows, Riette approached the intersection closest to where the men currently stood talking beneath a streetlight. For a moment she stood still, listening. The fact that these men stood in the light and were well dressed did not speak of danger, but Riette had a bad feeling in her gut.

The two men stopped talking and walked back into the courtyard her apartment shared with a dozen others. One of the men spoke, his voice clearly audible. It was the magistrate. She recognized his voice from when he had scolded her and her brother. No matter that she'd offered to pay for anything Emmet had taken, some could not find forgiveness in their hearts. Riette was not perfect, but she felt sorry for those who couldn't recognize how special and harmless Emmet truly was. No matter what mischief he'd ever gotten into, he'd never hurt anyone.

Sparrowport's merchant district exuded an aroma that drew Riette on; even at night, when the shops were closed, the fragrance lingered. There was something magical about the mixture of the fires burning at the bakery and the smithy, the baked goods, and the tangy sea air. Historic architecture lent to a feeling of timelessness, as if Sparrowport had always been there in that state while the world around it continued to change.

Riette's stomach rumbled by the time she reached the bakery, but she couldn't help sneaking a look into the smithy as she passed. It was dark, the coals in the forge still banked for the night. In some ways, Riette was relieved. Next door, Baker Millman worked hard while most slept. Three loaves of bread waited in the day-old bread bin, which was where Riette usually shopped. On that day, though, she also hoped to get something fresh. Without saying a word, she watched the baker work, hoping to see sweet rolls emerge from the ovens.

"Can I get you anything else?" Baker Millman asked, obviously not expecting her to ask for anything. She rarely did.

"Do you have any sweet rolls coming out soon?"

"They'll be a little while longer," he said. "And they have to cool before I can ice them."

"I see. Thank you. This will be all, then. I must be going."

The man gave a knowing nod, having no doubt noticed Emmet's absence and the early hour of her visit. A moment later, the door opened and Brick walked in, making the bakery suddenly appear much smaller. Dear, sweet, persistent Brick.

He grinned at her and leaned on the counter. "Morning, Millman."

The baker grunted and tossed two wax-wrapped packages on the counter. "That hinge is coming loose again."

"Again?" Brick sighed. Sometimes Riette wondered if he really wanted to be a smith. "I'll come back later with a bigger hammer."

Baker Millman waved him off and went back to work pulling, among other things, sweet rolls from the ovens.

"What are you doing here, anyway?" Brick asked Riette without waiting an instant. "Didn't you hear what happened up your way last night?"

"No. What?" she asked, her bad feeling growing worse.

"Someone was killed not far from your place, and people were seen snooping around. I think it's the Zjhon, but I'm not allowed to investigate any further. Father told me to stay out of it. He's afraid I'll get myself killed. If there really are Zjhon sneaking around killing people . . ." his thick brow furrowed. "Where's Emmet?"

"I have to go," Riette said.

"Here. I'll go with you."

Before she could say no, Baker Millman interrupted. "Just one more minute," he said, working with icing on rolls not yet at the right temperature. But he was determined. A moment later, he handed Riette a wrapped package with two sweet rolls that warmed her hands through the paper. After paying Baker Millman and settling the purchases in her bag, Riette turned to leave.

Brick followed. She held a hand up to his chest to stop him. Physical contact always worked to his advantage; he was so strong and handsome. "Stay here," she said, knowing her face was flushed. "Do as your father says. He's right."

Brick's expression soured. "You let me know if you need anything," he said, now resigned to going back to work at the forge instead of out adventuring and battling the Zjhon.

"Good morning, my little Ri Ri," Joren called from within the smithy.

Waving in return, Riette hurried on. Part of her regretted telling Brick not to come, but a bigger part knew he stuck out anywhere but at the forge, and she didn't want to be noticed. If a man truly had been killed, there would be questions, and she didn't want any of those questions coming back to Emmet, who was poorly prepared to answer them.

Footprints.

The thought slammed into Riette like a hammer. Emmet was in no way capable of killing anyone; he'd never been anything but peaceful and sweet with the exception of his ill-timed outbursts. What connection could he possibly have to this? And if the Zjhon truly were here, looking for people, then the war was perhaps not so far away after all. Riette quickened her step.

When she turned the last corner, she wasn't truly surprised to see the magistrate and a few others still looking about, though she had hoped to avoid them. Had she known they would be at that spot, she would have come in a different way. It was the very reason she and Emmet lived where they did: multiple points of egress.

"You're off to an early start this morning, Miss Riette," the magistrate said, tipping his hat.

The simple statement was both observation and accusation, and Riette recognized it for what it was. It was everything she could do to keep the tremor from her voice when she answered. "Yes, sir."

Saying nothing more, she did her best not to meet his gaze. Though guilty of nothing, she felt like a thief trying to escape from beneath the arm of the law. There was no way to know if Emmet had done anything wrong or not, and she presumed him innocent. Feeling eyes on her and drawn by irresistible need, she looked back. The magistrate and several others watched, knowing exactly who she was and that she was almost never without Emmet by her side. So much for not attracting attention. Riette's breath caught on seeing another pair of eyes watching from the shadows not far away.

Once inside, she bolted the door, knowing it would do little to stop the magistrate and his men. As Brick always told her, "Locks are just there to keep the honest people out. Anyone truly determined will find a way to get past a lock."

She found Emmet sitting on the side of his bed, wide awake. Riette was about to ask if he was all right when the banging on the door started. "I'll be right there," she shouted in response. Had it been the magistrate, he would have identified himself, but no one spoke.

Emmet didn't even look surprised. Dressed warmly in knickers with boots laced up over his calves, he wore a buttoned shirt, woven vest, and a flat cap that made him look like a miniature version of older boys. All the years living with a renowned seamstress had ingrained certain values in Riette and Emmet as well. That thought always threatened to bring her to tears, but she held them back, something at which she'd become adept.

Swallowing hard, Riette took Emmet's hand. With a final glance back at all the things she'd worked for and that remained of what her parents had left behind, she led him through the basement tunnel. It would at least give them a head start.

CHAPTER TWO

Flying is but a temporary reprieve from gravity's persistent embrace.
—Barabas DeGuiere, dragon rider

* * *

Riette had planned for this. Talk of trouble had been dribbling in for months, mostly centering on those who were special or different. Such people were simply disappearing. She'd had to plan for every eventuality and do everything for Emmet until there was nothing left for her. It had been the nature of her life for some time, but she remained determined to keep her brother safe. It was the last thing her mother had asked of her, and she could not let her down. The very idea left her awash in guilt, and the current circumstances didn't help. Shadows moved and shifted. Even on a normal night, it was dangerous to walk the dark side streets and mist-filled alleys of Sparrowport. Here strangers poured in with every ship, balloon, and now airplanes. It was as if time had accelerated and every day brought new machines and inventions—perhaps too much change too fast.

While Riette had planned for this, she was far from truly prepared. A few supplies and a meager stash of coin were all she'd been able to set aside in the event someone came looking for them. Now she wished she'd done a great deal more. Emmet had always been different, and it was a matter of time until the Zjhon came looking for him.

Across the land, news spread of pariahs and outcasts disappearing. No one had done a thing to protect these people or even to investigate what had befallen those who disappeared. Some families had been relieved, a burden removed from their lives, and this made Riette angry, partly because she detested the idea and partly because she longed for that same relief. The last part made her feel dirty and weak. Her mother would not have approved. Squeezing Emmet's hand, she pulled him along through the night, using her knowledge of the streets to get them closer to the port proper and the landing strips without attracting notice. The swishing of her skirts was enough for someone to follow them in the darkness, and Emmet's occasional outbursts made it impossible for them to hide in the shadows as so many did. She could feel their eyes upon her and Emmet, peering through the mists and measuring them. Many had gone into those mists, never to be seen again. Riette quickened her pace in spite of her sturdy leather boots making her footsteps echo in the relative silence.

A shift in the wind brought the pungent tang of the shoreline and the faint rumble of breakers. The mists parted, revealing an old dock rat watching them. Wearing things her mother would not have used for rags, the man was more desperate than most, which made him absolutely terrifying. Like an alley cat stalking port mice, he watched. Riette quickened her step even more and squeezed Emmet's hand tighter. It was a mistake. He'd been silent until that moment but then let out a squeak and pulled his hand away.

Stopping, he pointed to the dock rat. "He's dirty."

Even with a heavy pack already over one shoulder and a few things she just couldn't bear to leave behind clutched to her chest, Riette bent and scooped Emmet from the cobbled stones. Shuffling sounds from behind told Riette all she needed to know and she fled. Running along shiny, mist-slicked cobblestone was inadvisable under the best circumstances, but Riette knew what fate would befall her and her brother if they dawdled.

An angry shout cut the stillness. Boots rang against stone—too many boots from multiple directions. Dark shadows danced and moved even as first light threatened to clear the mists altogether. Though it hampered their movements, Riette would have much preferred to remain hidden within the fog. It wouldn't take long, though, she knew. Soon Sparrowport would come to life, sending the dock rats scurrying into the remaining shadows, disappearing along with the night. Her home—their home—would wake. In spite of desperate effort, she could move only so far so fast. The noises from behind ceased along with the shouts. Merchants opened their shops, greeting those early to market, and she considered just going back home or taking the alley. This was no time for polite conversation.

Her breathing rapid and her back sore, Riette lowered Emmet back to the roadway. He remained utterly silent, for which she was grateful. There were moments it seemed as if he knew exactly what was going on around him and understood the dangers they faced. Other times he was unable to cope with the world. That was when she did her best to understand. The times when Emmet's condition conspired against them both were more difficult to accept. His outbursts had cost them dearly just in the feelings he'd hurt among the people of Sparrowport. Many local families had been there since the area was first settled. Feelings, once hurt, were all but impossible to soothe. Riette had done her best. What separated Sparrowport from other small towns was the constant influx of new people. By air and sea, people converged on what had begun as a simple fishing village but was now among the most powerful economies in the Midlands.

Riette resigned herself to walking the streets of Sparrowport and risking seeing those who would want to talk with her and say the usual things about poor Emmet. She knew some of what they said behind her back. Never were such vile words said to her face, but it was in their eyes. Mostly, though, she did not want to see Brick. The time had come for Riette and Emmet to leave Sparrowport, and she could not have him making a fuss over it.

The light brought warmth, and the fog cleared, with the exception of a blanket that clung to the ground, threatening to turn an ankle with every step. Walking with exaggerated care and casualness when Heiress Davenport passed, Riette simply nodded to the woman, who averted her gaze and gave a furtive nod. The cold emanating from the woman was palpable and made Riette shiver.

Then there he was, already well into his workday. Brick stopped when he saw her. Putting down the hand bellows he'd been using, he approached, looking much like an anvil. Knowing Brick was among the few reasons people left her and Emmet alone increased her guilt. Her role in life seemed to be letting people down. That thought would have brought tears to her eyes, but she held them back.

"Hi, Brick," Emmet said.

"Hi, Emmet," Brick said "It's good to see you again . . . and your sister twice in one day." The muscle-bound man was aptly named, but beneath his furrowed brow was a fully functional brain, and in his chest, a huge heart. He said nothing while looking over just how much she carried. "Where do you think you're going?"

"We're going to see the widow Bernard," Riette responded. "She needs linens stitched and hemmed and new curtains."

Brick nodded and peered at the items she still clutched to her chest. The awl kit and thimble collection he'd made her could be explained away by the stitching work, but he gave her belongings more than a cursory inspection. "You're not coming back this time."

That was Brick. He spoke his truth. Riette envied him. "Someday," she said, the tears no longer obeying her.

"I'm coming with you."

"No," Riette responded, placing her hand on his chest. It was a mistake. The attraction had always been present between them, but physical contact magnified it. He gazed into her eyes, and she wanted to stay, to believe he could protect her. She had believed once, before her father had gone off to save them and never returned. No. Brick could no more save them all than her father could. And she did not want to be the one responsible for getting him killed. He was a good man, even if he'd only just become one and he was perhaps a bit clumsy at it. It was part of what she loved about him. That thought was heartbreaking, and she considered running away rather than face him.

"She loves you," Emmet said.

Riette choked, her eyes bulging, and she glared at Emmet before looking back to Brick, who wore an expression of shock and wonder.

"I'm coming with you," he said. "Wait *right here*." Standing in the doorway, he looked over his shoulder and wagged his finger. *"Wait right here."* Again, he gave her a knowing look.

She waited for five breaths after he'd disappeared into the smithy before picking up Emmet and running. Tears streamed down her cheeks. Past the bakery and butcher shop, she kept her eyes straight ahead, not giving anyone the chance to stop her.

"He loves you," Emmet whispered in her ear.

She gripped him tighter as she cried and ran. Emmet held on to his cap and said nothing else, fascinated by the sights and sounds as the airfields drew near. The strips themselves weren't actually visible yet, but hulking shapes filled the air above them.

Some balloons were still strewn across the meadows, but others were well into the inflation process. She'd already thought this over, and balloons would be her final resort. Diesel engines roared, promising the fastest travel by far, though a bit more restrictive with regard to destinations.

A dirigible was the second best choice with regard to speed but would be much more difficult to trace due to the variety of possible destinations. Most holds had airship docks, while few had runways. Airships were farther down the airfields. While balloons and dirigibles did not need airstrips to land, airstrips proved excellent places to interchange passengers. The three competing industries had come together at last to provide the ability to travel almost anywhere in comfort and relative safety. Aircraft hawkers were known to say air travel was four times safer than travel by roadway. Riette wasn't certain how true that statement was, but the journey there lent it credence.

Brick would eventually follow her, and she hoped to catch the next departing flight, no matter where it was going.

"Fly Midlands Airways, where we treat our passengers like family," said a bright-eyed female hawker. Her manner was polished and practiced to the point of being unauthentic, but Riette didn't care. Approaching the woman, she asked, "What's the next flight out?"

"What's your destination?" the woman asked, her expression a mask of servitude.

"Away from here," Riette said with an edge to her voice. "What's the next flight out?"

"Forest's Edge," the hawker said, the hint of a smirk reaching her practiced expression.

"How soon does it leave?" Riette asked immediately, knowing her desperation showed. No one in their right mind went to Forest's Edge unless headed to war or part of the logging crews.

"Won't be too much longer now. We just need to finish refueling."

"How much?"

"Two silvers each," the hawker said with a completely flat expression in spite of the outrageous cost. While it was among the longer flights, the airways seemed to take advantage of those with few other options. Riette reconsidered her first choice. Airship travel was considerably less expensive than airplane. She and Emmet could eat for a winter on the coin they'd save.

Brick was coming. Whoever had been knocking on her door was coming. Those thoughts drove her to desperate action. "I'll take it."

"Thank you for flying Midlands Airways," the woman said, wearing a manufactured smile. "Please enjoy your wait on the benches provided."

Waiting was the last thing in the world Riette would enjoy. She'd hoped to take off before Brick arrived. Doing her best to appear calm, Riette sat and watched another plane approach. In the distance, other hawkers extolled the virtues of their enterprise. Young men, presumably headed to war, occupied the benches opposite her. Riette avoided their gazes. They might not see another girl again for some time, and their stares lingered.

Emmet sensed it as well. "Scared," he said, pointing at the young men. Riette could have thought of no more effective way to discourage their inevitable advances, and for once she was grateful for Emmet's words. It didn't last.

Growing rapidly from a distant buzz to a howling roar, another diesel prop approached the nearest landing strip. Clouds of dust rolled away from the six props twice the height a grown man. Black smoke belched from the engines, which bucked and popped before finally falling silent. Riette had second thoughts. Planes were such a brute-force method of flight compared to balloons and dirigibles.

Soon, though, a line of passengers emerged from the aircraft. Most smiled as they approached; few did when they departed. Perhaps it was all the excitement or fear of getting on the airplane, Riette wasn't certain, but the results were the same.

The first man to pass them was a jolly-looking fellow.

"Fat." Emmet said.

The man turned and mumbled something, looking hurt.

"Come back and fly Midlands Air again," the hawker said to each person as they disembarked.

"Old," Emmet declared of the next woman. Riette nudged him with her elbow. "Big ears," he said to a blushing young man. Riette pinched him. "Scary," he said to a man with wild eyes, and on this Riette had to agree. The man never took his eyes off them after that. He remained near the benches. That he might board the same flight was a frightening thought. Riette counted the minutes, becoming agitated while the flight crew spent more time working on the plane that just landed than the one she'd thought she would depart on. Now she wasn't so sure. Would this plane need to be refueled too? How long would that take? She was considering asking the hawker until Emmet said, "Mean."

A stern-looking woman, gray-black hair pulled back into a severe knot, glared at Emmet. When her cold gaze shifted to Riette, no kindness existed there, only disdain. It stung.

"Perhaps you would like to visit some of the shops while your plane is prepared for departure," the hawker said, her expression openly unfriendly. Two stout men now stood behind her. She and Emmet were no longer welcome to wait there. It was clear. The stern-faced woman looked as if she would say something to Emmet, but her eyes passed over the two guards, and she moved away. Twice she looked over her shoulder.

"How long until takeoff?" Riette asked.

"Oh, it shouldn't be much longer now. We just need to get the plane fueled up. I'm sure you'll have plenty of time to take a walk. Somewhere else." The veneer of her persona had begun to crack.

"Come on," Riette said.

Emmet jumped up, looking happier than he had since reaching the airfield.

Having no desire to walk back toward town, Riette tried to disappear into the crowds maneuvering to and from the airships. Shouts in the far distance gave her a chill. Something had happened, and now someone was desperately searching. They had already come looking for her and Emmet, and she had no idea why, save that she'd always known they would eventually come. Still, it was a shock to find them banging on her door before first light. Having to enact her evacuation plan, she'd felt exonerated for having such a plan in place and at the same time like a complete failure since they would be so easily found. She should have done more. It had never seemed as urgent as their everyday lives. At times it had felt like feeding her own paranoia, but she'd been right all along, and now they would both pay for her halfhearted measures. No curtains awaited her nimble fingers, she had no way to earn more coin, and her survival skills were minimal.

Soon the sights grabbed her attention and were a welcome diversion. A group of workers used their combined weight and a series of pulleys to load cargo onto an airship. Where airplanes were sleek and smooth, dirigibles offered classic beauty reminiscent of seafaring ships. Again, Riette reconsidered her plan. It would be so much nicer to board an airship than to fly, no matter how quickly, to Forest's Edge. She'd already paid for passage on Midlands Air but contemplated her options.

"We'll be boarding for Arden, Jenna Valley, and Riverton in a just a few moments," an older man said. Dressed in a well-pressed black suit with a burgundy vest, lapels, and top hat to match, he grinned from within a neatly trimmed beard. "How can we welcome you today?"

"How much to Riverton?" Riette asked.

"Three coppers," the man said. "Since you're a slight lass. The young fellow rides for free."

"Thank you," she said. The man appeared disappointed she didn't pay right then, but Riette had learned her lesson.

Shouts drew closer. Back in town, three men in long black coats walked toward the airfield. Every step brought them closer. There was nowhere to hide. They were looking for Emmet and anyone else who was different. She couldn't let them find him. Desperate thoughts came to mind, but she drew steady, even breaths as her mother had taught her. That was when she saw Brick. He approached from the west and hadn't seen her yet, but he had seen the Zjhon, who were now close enough to make out rugged black uniforms and solid military boots. These were the Al'Zjhon of which she'd been warned. Her deepest fears had come true and were about to get worse.

Brick was no fool. He knew who had driven Riette to flee. He was a brave and noble man. Marching toward the armed men like a raging volcanic flow, he stopped before them, and his words rose above the din, albeit not clearly enough to be understood. The intent was clear, as was the swift response. No matter how powerful the smith's son might be, he fell after a single blow to the head.

Riette wanted to scream, wanted to run to him and protect him. Always he'd seemed like the strongest person in the whole world, and she'd had him to protect her. She should have let him come. She should have waited for him. Guilt pummeled her and her chin quivered. Emmet grabbed her hand and pulled her away. Since she would have chosen the same direction to flee, she allowed her brother to lead.

"Fly Dragon Airways," a boy a couple of years older than Emmet said. "We can take you anywhere you want to go. No airstrips required."

Only then did Riette see the dragon resting not far away. It was like someone had taken an old horse buggy and strapped it to the back of a rapidly aging reptile. Still, Riette had never seen a real dragon up close before. They had been a rare sight in Sparrowport before the war but even more so during. Towering above the hawker stood a man in a long black coat and top hat. If you didn't look too closely, he wasn't much different from anyone else. His height and alabaster skin marked him as unusual in these parts, but other details nagged at Riette's senses. A seam on the jacket was poorly sewn, and the material was worn clean through in places. The hat, while well made, looked to have lost several battles in its lifetime. He leaned on a cane, the carved snake head in his palm missing one fang. Even while ministering to the dragon, this man was aware of his surroundings. Riette found herself being regarded from beneath a pair of bushy white eyebrows on a face crisscrossed with lines like a dry lakebed.

A sudden wind tore at her belongings, and Riette lost her grip on one of the last things her mother had ever given her. The handwritten note raced along the airfield, driven by unpredictable gusts. "Wait right here," Riette said, but before she ran after the note, she repeated, *"Wait . . . right . . . here."*

Emmet nodded and turned back to watch the dragon.

"Fly Dragon Airways! Because who don't want to fly on a dragon?"

"Does he breathe fire?" Riette heard Emmet ask even as she ran. After a few more darting steps, she reclaimed her mother's note. The Al'Zjhon drew ever closer, and neither the plane nor the airship appeared ready to take off. It made her sick to realize she'd wasted two silvers on a flight she might never take. As ever, she found herself needing to be responsible for both her and Emmet and coming up short.

The tall man was now kneeling before Emmet and handing him a marshmallow on a stick. Riette sucked in a deep breath and pumped her legs. Before she could shout in warning, her little brother stood before the aging but nonetheless formidable beast. Only then did Riette see the dragon's entire face, and it left her speechless. Most of what had once been one side of its face was now gone, in its place weathered copper—deep orange in color but marbled with streaks of green. Within a masterfully forged enclosure, intricate in its detailed re-creation of the creature's wasted face, rested a piercing eye that stared back.

After a deep breath, the dragon regarded Emmet and the marshmallow, rearing up over him. Riette screamed as the dragon struck, snatching the marshmallow from the stick in a single swift motion, leaving the stick and its bearer intact. Emmet never moved an inch.

"You horrible man!" Riette shouted as she got closer. He regarded her with no more expression than a stone. Not taking the time to tell him what she thought, she dragged Emmet away. The tall man watched them go, and Emmet turned to meet his eyes. He pointed back and said, "Magic."

At this, the tall man's face finally showed some reaction, which alarmed Riette even more. Dragging Emmet away, she scanned the remaining ships, looking for any ready to take off, yet all appeared to be somewhere in the process of refueling. The first plane she'd thought she would board was now taking on passengers, one of which was almost certainly Al'Zjhon. Two more continued their search. She'd run out of time.

Others had begun to notice the Zjhon as well. It resulted in a wave of startled exclamations followed by utter silence. All the fighting troops were at the front, and even those on their way were not yet ready for a fight.

"Fly Dragon Airways because we're leaving *right now*."

Riette needed no more urging. What other choice did she have? "How much?"

While fiddling with straps and bits of harness, the tall man shrugged. The young man shrugged as well. He wore a cap like Emmet's and a frilly shirt that in no way went with his overalls. His shoes were mismatched, and something about him was different, but she couldn't figure out what. "Just put your belongings and the kid in the box, strap him in, and climb aboard. Unless you want to ride in the box with the kid."

"No one is riding in a box," Riette announced, but she moved toward the dragon. The Al'Zjhon made their way through the airship passengers. The hawker shrugged and loaded her belongings into the box, which did appear to have seating and a small window. The last bits, those most precious to her, she herself placed in the box after making certain it was secure. The inside was of soft red upholstery and could have seated her and Emmet almost comfortably if not for being in a box on the back of a dragon. The thought gave her chills. The dragon turned to regard her and she reconsidered. At least one did not have to worry about being eaten by an airship.

"My name's Tuck. I'll be your flight attendant," the boy said while securing Riette and Emmet's lap and shoulder straps. Not waiting for him to finish, the dragon stood and turned toward an open landing strip. The carriage bucked and shifted. Tuck wasn't strapped in at all when the dragon started running. After triple-checking the straps and hearing multiple aircraft starting up, Tuck said, "You really should'a put the kid in the box. These straps are made for big people."

"No one is riding in a *box*," Riette said, putting her arm around Emmet and taking up some of the slack in his straps.

Slowly and uncomfortably, the dragon gained speed despite the hitch in its gait. The now constant wheezing didn't sound good either. Riette wished she'd had more time for reconsideration, but life moved at full speed. The airfields ended at sheer cliffs, which was one reason she'd always avoided them. Heights had never been her thing. She was afraid of a steep flight of stairs.

"Is the dragon gonna die?" Emmet asked.

Riette elbowed him in the side. Tuck looked back, eyes wide in shock and incredulity, but he said nothing. The tall man either didn't hear or pretended not to notice.

CHAPTER THREE

Sacrifices are best made by the weak.
—Argus Kind, usurper king of the Zjhon

* * *

Manicured grasses rushed beneath. Issuing a triumphant grunt, the dragon thrust out its wings and somehow caught the wind. With a gut-wrenching upward lurch just before reaching the cliff, they plunged over the edge and toward the rocky shoreline below, lacking the speed most airplanes required for liftoff.

The drop in air temperature was noticeable almost immediately. Riette clutched Emmet to her and gritted her teeth while falling toward the docks. Ships lined the deep inlet, sheltered from storms and forming a prickly fence.

The tall man showed no emotion, and Tuck was almost composed. Emmet appeared to be enjoying himself. Riette screamed.

Well before colliding with any of the ships, the dragon spread its wings wider. Using their speed, the beast aimed for broad, white beaches, where the air grew warmer. Circling the updrafts moved them higher but far too slowly. No sooner had they cleared the cliffs than the first diesel planes raced past them. From an open side door, men in dark coats watched.

One pulled a portable air cannon from within his coat and aimed it at them. It fired with a thump, and a moment later, projectiles struck leather and scale. The dragon grunted but flew on, still climbing upward. The diesel plane gained altitude, turning in a wide sweep. A second plane took off, not showing any signs of Al'Zjhon. A third plane flew in from the south and dusted the airstrip before soaring out over the harbor. This plane was easily identified as a Zjhon aircraft, and it bristled with weaponry. How could they be there? Sparrowport should have been far beyond their range.

Turning in tight circles, the dragon gained what altitude she could before any planes returned. Defenseless against the enemy, their only chance was to hide. But still they spiraled higher.

"What are we doing?" Riette asked. The tall man ignored her. Tuck shrugged. "Does he ever talk?" she asked the boy.

"The cap'n used to talk a lot," Tuck said. "Not much no more. Don't need no words, though. He says what he means just fine. You'll see."

From the wood panel before her came a popping sound followed by fizzing and a dull glow. A sign showing two hands gripping handles was illuminated.

"The cap'n has turned on the 'hold on for dear life' sign," Tuck said.

"You really should'a put the kid in the box. Hold on now. Here we go."

The dragon raced back toward the airstrips with alarming speed. Airplanes approached from two directions. They were doomed. Emmet grinned beside her as if none of this were real, as if they were in one of the stories he liked so much and nothing could actually harm them.

Airships now lumbered into the skies, and balloons drifted on the wind. While racing past the airfield, Riette saw Brick holding his head and boarding a balloon. At least he was alive. Too bad the world had gone mad. She would have liked more time with him.

"What's its name?" Riette asked, trying to calm her nerves.

"*Her* name is Dashiq. And she's a battle dragon."

The captain turned his head and glared at Tuck for an instant. The boy went silent.

A female dragon. Riette never would have guessed. There was nothing feminine about their mount, just a terrifying reptilian predator, and this one near the end of her days.

Just then the Zjhon plane returned, falling in behind. Flitting from side to side, Dashiq did what she could to keep the plane off her tail. Air cannons sounded in rapid succession. Stone shot flew overhead, devastating historic buildings instead of their intended target.

Dipping lower, the dragon raced between buildings, wings trimmed, dodging the falling debris and executing a sharp turn before soaring down a back street. The Zjhon plane roared above, low and slow. Just before the plane passed overhead, the dragon flew straight up, pinning Riette and Emmet back in their seats. Pumping her wings and using claws to run up the side of a tall building, the dragon thrust herself skyward, colliding with the Zjhon plane in midflight. A single bite ruined the plane's tail section, severing structural supports and controls.

It was over in an instant, and they soared over the streets of Sparrowport, unmolested. Anyone who saw Riette and Emmet now would certainly never forget.

A second plane passed overhead. Dashiq broke free of town and raced upward again, this time tracing the contour of a ridgeline where the cold, unpredictable updrafts gave them extra lift. Clouds gathered not far offshore, but getting to them alive might prove impossible. Riette hadn't seen the Zjhon ship go down, and no explosions followed. They would come back.

Leaning out as far as she dared, she watched the balloon carrying Brick blot out the sky behind them. He stood like a man carved from stone, pointing at Dashiq. His lips moved and Riette couldn't imagine what words he spoke. Approaching engines spurred Brick on to motion. Watching and aiming, she could almost see him calculating before he threw what looked like a full picnic basket at the approaching Midlands Air plane, which appeared to be in the hands of the Al'Zjhon. Riette hoped all the innocents aboard the plane survived the day, as Brick's aim was true. Smoke poured from the engine and did not bode well.

"Did she fight in the war? Is that what happened to her?" Riette asked, trying not to think about it but unable to keep from asking. For the first time, the captain responded to one of her questions. He did not answer, but Riette saw a slight movement of his head, a reaction to her question.

Tuck mouthed "battle dragon" and made chomping motions with his hands in front of his face. The captain put a stop to it with a single fist to the leather saddle in which he rode.

Riette was left to wonder how the Zjhon had gotten planes into the air above Sparrowport. Always before, the Zjhon homeland had been far beyond the range of even the largest planes ever built. This changed everything for Midlanders since nowhere would be truly safe.

So far, Argus Kind, the self-made Zjhon king, was only looking for people who were different or unusual, those special or unique in some way. Riette's heart broke for these people, especially knowing her brother was among them. At least twice people had come through Sparrowport looking for outcasts and pariahs, and no one had mentioned Emmet. It was the reason she had stayed. He often made people uncomfortable, but they knew he was just a little boy with developmental issues. They forgave him. The thought brought a tear to Riette's eyes since she hadn't always been able to do the same.

Dashiq soared over a mature forest, where massive trees created an impermeable canopy despite being widely spaced. When a large opening appeared, lake waters reflected the sky, and the dragon dived toward the still, mirrorlike surface. Racing mere hand widths above the stillness created a surreal reflection. Beneath the canopy, gaps between trees did not appear large enough for a dragon to fly through, but Dashiq made it appear easy.

Deep enough within the woodlands so as not to be too close to the lake, the dragon reversed her wing flaps, slowing them before a rocky outcropping. When she landed, Riette saw a waterfall pouring from a cliff twice her height. Moss covered the ground and the lower parts of tree trunks and root systems. Light pierced the canopy, but they would not be easily spotted from above.

The captain was out of his seat, onto the ground, and going over Dashiq before anyone else was unstrapped. From under his seat, he pulled a wooden box filled with implements but went immediately for the fine-tipped pliers.

Three different times, the dragon grunted while the captain administered aid. Tuck guided them down. Riette felt bad stepping on the poor beast, but the young man assured her she would do no harm.

"She's just tired now, miss," he said. "Just needs some rest is all."

"Where are we going?" she asked, not certain she wanted to know the answer.

"Where do you want to go?" Tuck asked.

"Somewhere safe," Riette said without really meaning to. Emmet looked at her with something akin to hope in his eyes, and she snapped back to reality.

"Then that's where we're going," Tuck said.

The captain must have heard the entire conversation but maintained his silence.

"How did you end up here?" Riette asked.

Tuck turned his head sideways and smiled at her. "He caught me picking his pocket. He taught me a lesson . . . and then another lesson. Never really stopped."

"And your parents?"

Shrugging, he looked away. "I vaguely remember having parents."

"My loss is more recent," Riette said.

The boy turned back to her. "Sorry."

She just nodded. Emmet walked to the captain's side and put his hands on Dashiq. Riette feared the man might scold her brother, but he pretended not to notice. It was the closest thing to approval she'd seen from the man.

"Does he treat you well?" Riette asked in a whisper.

"Better than anyone else ever has," Tuck said. "By a mile. We should get something to eat and drink while we've got the chance. When the cap'n wants to leave, we leave."

"How much," Riette asked, growing suspicious.

"How much what?"

"How much is all this going to cost me? What kind of airline doesn't know where it's going or how much it costs to get there?"

"Two coppers each."

"To anywhere?" Riette asked. "What if I wanted to go to the Godfist?"

The captain stopped what he was doing and made a fist. He didn't turn around or make any other gesture, but that was enough to convey his meaning.

"Passengers come first," Tuck said. "Ain't many places we won't go. Ain't much we won't do to ensure your satisfaction."

The captain gave a quick, slight nod before going back to running his hands over Dashiq's scaly armor, Tuck produced pickled eggs and cheese from their stores. Riette wrinkled her nose, but when Tuck went to take the pickled egg away, she grabbed it and bit into it before she changed her mind. It was tart and pungent but not so bad as what she had been expecting. Emmet joined them, seemingly drawn by the smell. He did not hesitate for an instant when Tuck handed him an egg and cheese.

When darkness passed over them a moment later, everyone fell silent.

Above could be heard the creak of line and occasional roar.

"Balloons," Tuck whispered.

"That could be Brick," Riette said, but she, too, whispered, knowing it might not be. When a second balloon floated over, no one spoke.

The captain turned to Tuck and held out one hand, palm up, fingers spaced evenly and pointing up.

Tuck shook his head, and the captain shrugged.

What passed between them Riette could not say, and she didn't like it. The feeling they were hiding something from her persisted, and she kept her guard up.

"We've a long flight coming up," Tuck said. "A real long flight. The dragon would prefer any 'people business' you may have be handled while we're here on the ground. We won't be stopping much."

"You know all that from him holding up his hand?" Riette asked, an edge in her voice.

"I know the place he means. We've gone there before when Dashiq was hurt. It's a long ways away. A week on the wing and no less."

"A week?"

Tuck nodded. "Don't have no choice now. Dashiq needs healing. Dead dragons don't fly."

The captain reacted to the statement but made no other response. His palpable silence irritated Riette. How could anyone keep his mouth shut for so long? And at a time like this.

"Your only other choice is to stay here," Tuck said. "And I wouldn't if I was you." The continued sound of balloons in the area emphasized his words. "You said you wanted to be somewhere safe. This trip will get you part of the way there." The captain gave Tuck a disapproving look. "We leave at dark. You might want to stretch your legs."

Emmet took Tuck's suggestion and walked in a circle around the area. Riette sat nearby on a bed of moss, watching him and considering her options. Planes flew overhead, making her nervous, but she reminded herself that planes flew in and out of Sparrowport every day. It didn't mean they were all looking for them. But the Al'Zjhon *were* looking for Emmet. How they had gotten so far behind the front line was a mystery, but now she knew they could be anywhere. Flying out with Dragon Airways, who definitely had agendas of their own, put her and Emmet in far friendlier hands than those of Argus Kind. His was a twisted and jaded soul who'd seen far too much death. Now he saw little else.

Tuck spoke over his shoulder while sifting through supplies. "I hope you like pickled eggs."

He wasn't making her decision any easier. She saw through his act, though. Sensing a person's inner being was something she had strived to do since Emmet was born. In Tuck, she saw a wounded heart behind a wall of humor and sarcasm. A haunted look came to his eyes far too often. Riette knew that look. At wartime it was far too common. "Would you like a hand?"

The captain tensed. Tuck looked as if he would either laugh or cry. When Tuck laughed, the old man shook his head. After a brief hesitation and with his face flushed deep red, Tuck extended his right arm. The gloved fist appeared no different than the other, except it did not move. After another moment, Tuck removed the prosthetic arm, revealing an arm unlike anything Riette had ever seen. She hadn't been expecting to see any such thing, and she sucked in a deep breath. Tuck pulled away in apparent shame, and the captain turned toward her.

"I'm sorry," Riette said. "I wasn't expecting— I mean— I'm sorry."

"I thought you would understand," Tuck said. "This is how I was born."

"I do understand. Please forgive me. I've reacted horribly and I feel terrible about it. You've been so kind to Emmet." Riette considered what his life must have been like. "People have treated you poorly, haven't they?"

"Not all of 'em."

"Emmet has a habit of bringing it on himself, which I've never understood," Riette said. Her brother cast a quick glance but remained silent. "You did nothing to deserve such treatment."

The captain came dangerously close to laughing. Tuck flushed again.

A shadow raced along the forest floor. Emmet pointed up at the belly of an airship visible through breaks in the canopy. "Mean."

Riette knew better than to disregard his judgments. People weren't generally offended by his statements because they were false. Honesty was not always a welcome virtue.

The shadows grew long, and the light changed hue.

"Time to load up," Tuck said in a low voice. To Riette's surprise, Tuck had adjusted the straps on one side to better fit Emmet, which was a relief. "I didn't figure nobody was gonna ride in no box."

Riette had to laugh, even if his grammar made her twitch. Emmet grinned perhaps a little too broadly.

Before she reached her seat, though, a low, deep rumble approached. Both the captain and Tuck stopped and looked up. An airplane that dwarfed the others flew over, its color deep green and its roar distinctive.

"That's one of ours," Tuck said, while boosting Emmet up behind her. Air cannons sounded next followed by shouts. "The war has come to you."

The vision of buildings exploding in Sparrowport haunted Riette. And somehow her brother had something to do with it. The thought was unfathomable and equally terrifying. Whatever it was he had done, he wasn't going to tell her. She'd always loved him, but misunderstanding had become the understanding between them. When she looked at him, though, she saw her parents, each in his or her own way, a smile, the twinkle in his eye. What never changed was the need to protect him, and that need filled her thoughts. What was she doing? If she left now, what had been her entire life might be destroyed. It hurt to know that was the case no matter what she did. All those she cared about might lose everything as well. It was one thing to leave a life behind and another to abandon it to fate.

Within seconds, the captain and Tuck were aboard and strapped in. Dashiq gave Riette no more time for contemplation. There was no option that would keep her and Emmet safe. Their best chance, in her opinion, was to outrun the danger. She had to hope this dragon had some life left in her. Their departure proved it.

Running with her wings closed, Dashiq charged through the last bit of woods before emerging onto the rock-strewn shoreline. There she extended her wings and glided over still waters, which reflected the battle taking place above. One balloon was on fire, the other completely dark. Using her tail, Dashiq thrashed the image into oblivion and generated forward thrust. With the far trees nearly invisible in the failing light, the dragon soared into the sky, silhouetted by deep purples and oranges. More shouts rang out at the sight of them, and Riette hoped Brick was already back on the ground and safe. The view from above the Midlands shoreline was captivating, and now that the trees were far below, there was much less threat of running into anything. Riette began breathing again.

"Fight," Emmet said, pointing offshore.

Air cannons fired on both sides as an allied plane descended on a fleeing airship. The plane had far greater maneuverability, but the airship carried heavy weaponry capable of destroying the plane with even a single hit. It was a perilous encounter for both sides. Those piloting the plane understood this risk and kept distance between them and the airship. Two-man bow teams nocked thick arrows with strings attached. Unlike any archery taught in the Midlands, these archers aimed far higher, creating an arcing flight.

"Hammer arrows," Tuck said.

The captain nodded.

Dashiq turned farther south, taking advantage of the cover the allied plane provided.

"What do you mean by hammer arrows?" Riette couldn't help but ask, watching the archers reel their shots back in and nock again.

"They got a big, fat, weighted arrowhead. When they shoot 'em up in the air like that, they fall down in a rain of pointy hammers."

The battle above dispersed in the fading light.

"Dragons have their advantages," Tuck said as they soared on the winds, their journey only just begun. "Most of a dragon is better than a whole aircraft any day."

The captain gave Tuck a disapproving look, but the young man never lost his grin.

CHAPTER FOUR

If life hands you lemons, you're less likely to have scurvy.
—Keldon Tallowborn, Al'Drakon

* * *

Hanging from a towering maple, Brick reminded himself never to board a balloon again. Though he remained safely in the basket, he was high off the ground and the basket wasn't going anywhere. His impetuous nature had gotten him into deep trouble again. The thought made his head hurt even worse. The people who did this to him were after Riette and Emmet, which kept him motivated, though he tried not to think of what would happen if they were captured by the Zjhon.

He'd seen them himself; one had elbowed him in the face. No one could deny now the claims that the enemy had been snooping around Sparrowport, looking for people to kidnap—people like Emmet. Those thoughts and the knowledge that he would otherwise starve were all that convinced Brick to climb out of the basket and down a rope that danced in the breeze.

There had been others in the basket with him, but each of them had paid to get on or were part of the crew. All of those people had been wearing parachutes. Having forced his way onto the balloon, Brick was left to go down with her.

Rope climbing was not among his favorite things to do, but strong hands and a muscular upper body made it less difficult. If the rope had been long enough to reach the forest floor, it might have been an easy climb. Instead, Brick found himself swinging with all his might, trying to reach the nearest tree trunk, which was arrow straight and had but one or two branches between him and the ground.

Using all his strength, Brick swung toward the tree trunk. Though he did not get close enough to grab on to it, he did get close enough to push off of it with his legs. This sent him hurtling through the air, and just before he reached the towering maple, the balloon shifted. Leaning sharply to one side, the basket looked as if it might break free from the branches above and tumble to the forest floor below.

When he did hit the tree, he was moving as quickly downward as he was laterally, which made it even more difficult to grip the tree. He needed to slow his downward slide quickly and squeezed the bark to his chest, no matter the pain. This was a life-or-death moment, and he refused to die, refused to let his family down, and refused to let Riette and Emmet down. An image of them flashed across his consciousness along with the pain. The world had fallen into chaos, but he somehow held on.

Using his legs to hug the tree, he let go with one arm. Pain returned when he slid down farther. Crying out, he quickly grabbed the length of rope from his belt and slung it around the tree. He'd cut and knotted the rope for this very purpose. After changing his grip, the rope allowed him to hold his weight with his arms, which let him shuffle his feet downward. At the bottom of his reach, he shifted his weight to his legs and slid the rope farther down the trunk. Getting past the branches proved tricky, but otherwise gravity assisted him and made the descent go quickly.

When he finally reached the forest floor, he collapsed into the leaves, breathing heavily. The next time he saw Riette, they were going to have a long talk about the meaning of the words "wait right here."

The balloon had been over the ocean for much of their trip, and only Brick's experimentation with the weights had allowed him to coax the wounded balloon back over land. At least he hadn't been forced to swim.

It was going to be a long hike back to Sparrowport. Hiking wasn't something he enjoyed doing, and he moved at what might have been considered a reckless pace. Only when a fist of birds flew overhead did Brick stop and look up. Such formations were generally used only for messages of the utmost importance. A moment later, a series of pops sounded just ahead of where he stood. All five birds dropped from the sky; whatever messages they carried would not be delivered.

When someone pushed him aside, Brick almost shouted from fright. A man pulling a log behind him never looked up.

"Grab that other log, will ya?" he said. "We'll have pigeon tonight, so hurry up about it or they'll eat it all while we're out gathering wood."

Over the man's shoulder, Brick spotted a long metal barrel and copper tanks. All the signs were around him, and he'd been blind to them. He'd assumed these woods were unoccupied but had walked right into an enemy encampment. There weren't supposed to be any enemies in this area, but this was war and he'd been careless.

Saying nothing, Brick turned back the way he'd come, dashing through the woods as quickly and silently as possible. He didn't know if the man ever looked back or if anyone gave pursuit. All he could do was run as fast as his body and the terrain would allow and hope he had enough of a head start to keep them behind him.

Foliage flashed by in a blur, some of which demanded a price for passage. Brick did not slow. Even when his sides cramped and his feet throbbed, he ran.

Trees suddenly parted, revealing a large open area. Brick stumbled into the clearing, breathing like a mad bull. It took everything he had to stop before impaling himself on the pitchfork leveled at him. He felt no less careless than when he'd encountered the Zjhon.

"Don't move," the man pointing the pitchfork at him said, constantly shifting his weight and causing the sharp implement to dance in front of him. Brick noticed then that the man was missing a leg from the knee down. Others worked the long grass into piles throughout the field, but Brick could still get away. The more he looked around, though, the less he wanted to run. This was Forest's Edge. He'd found the rear line.

A lanky man arrived moments later. "Who are you?"

Brick was grateful for having had the time to catch his breath. "My name is Brick. I'm from Sparrowport."

"And what has you running through the woods like a night spirit?" the tall man asked, looking down on Brick from what seemed an impossible height.

"The Zjhon attacked Sparrowport."

No one said anything in response.

"They were trying to kidnap my friend, who flew away on a dragon, and I ended up on a balloon that crashed in the woods."

"And why aren't you at the front?" the tall man asked. "You're certainly of fighting age."

"I'm apprenticed to my father, the smith," Brick said, feeling guilty and not for the first time. "I was considered essential for the war effort."

"So those parts that used to come in from Sparrowport were in part your handiwork?"

Brick nodded.

Another man approached. "Let me see your hands," he said.

Brick held out his calloused, gnarled fingers that never quite came clean no matter how he scrubbed.

"He's a smith all right, and he's from Sparrowport. I can see it in his hands and hear it in his accent. I think he's telling the truth, and that means the Zjhon are trying to keep us isolated, which certainly explains why none of our messages have been answered."

"You said your friend escaped on a dragon," the tall, thin man said, a haunted look in his eyes. "Tell me about that."

"The Zjhon were looking for my friend and her little brother, who has always been singled out for being different." This statement brought nods of understanding. This was something they had heard before, given the response. "I tried to stop them . . . but I failed. Before the Zjhon caught up to them, Riette and Emmet climbed into a carriage strapped to the back of a dragon and flew off."

"So it's a girl," the man who'd inspected his hands said. "That explains it. You look a sight, my boy. When I was your age, I felt a lot like you look."

"What else happened?" the tall man asked, his scowl never fading.

"The Zjhon commandeered a passenger plane, and then one of their planes arrived. I boarded the balloon, hoping to run interference for the dragon, which didn't look very healthy to start with. I hit one plane with a . . . projectile, but things went downhill from there. I think I saw one of our planes as well, but it's all kind of a blur from that point on."

Finally the tall man seemed satisfied and extended his hand. The other man retracted the pitchfork.

"I'm sorry for the unfriendly welcome," the tall man said. "These are dangerous times. My name is Tellymore. People call me Telly."

Though the man was no longer unfriendly, a pall of sadness and regret seemed to hang over his every breath.

"Have you seen any dragons?" Brick asked. "Have you heard anything about Riette or Emmet Pickette?" The first question seemed to pain Telly, but he had to press on.

"No," Telly said. "There have been no dragons here in some time. If there had been, I would most certainly know."

"Did you lose your dragon in the war?" Brick asked. Reading people was not normally among his strengths, but this man's every inflection reeked of grief. He nodded in response. "I'm sorry. I have always wanted to do my part to fight the war. I feel guilty that I get to stay behind in the relative safety of Sparrowport while others risk their lives, as surely you have done. I am humbled."

"Don't be sorry or feel guilty," Telly said. "Without the tools and parts you and your father have provided, we would not have lasted this long. Those within the Heights are good at providing big hunks of cast metal, but nobody forges gears of higher quality than Sparrowport.

Brick wiped away a tear.

"Is there another smithy in Sparrowport of which I am unaware?"

"No, sir," Brick said. "Those gears are made by my father and me. Mostly my father, though."

"Then you and your father are to be commended," Telly said. "We've few advantages over the Zjhon; the reliability of our drive trains is among them. Thank you."

Brick nodded, not knowing what else to say.

"If they have aircraft in Sparrowport, then they must have increased fuel capacity, efficiency, or both," Telly said.

"Either that or they found a place to refuel," the man who'd been holding the pitchfork on Brick said.

"They're sure not landing in the jungle," Telly said. "And we'd know if they captured an airport."

"Would we?"

Silence hung for a while. If Forest's Edge were completely cut off from communication, it was possible Dragonport had already fallen to the Zjhon. It would explain their sudden ability to hit Sparrowport from the air.

"Come," Telly said. "You look hungry."

"And thirsty," Brick added.

Telly laughed. "I bet you are."

Among the wounded, Brick was a novelty, a diversion from their mundane existence. He laughed and told tales in between devouring the stew placed in front of him. It felt good to lighten the hearts of those who had sacrificed so much, though Brick couldn't help but feel guilty for any pleasure he took while Riette and Emmet were not safe. And knowing what he knew now, he questioned the safety of everyone he loved. Sparrowport was no longer separate from the war. It was a terrifying thought.

"Most of the troops normally stationed here are out on maneuvers," Telly said. "I'm glad you didn't encounter them on your way here. I don't know if they will seek out these infiltrated areas since these soldiers are supposed to ship out to the front immediately upon completion of their training. We'll likely have to get word to the front in order to see troops deployed. I don't know. It's not my call. I'm just an old man with no dragon."

"And Dragonport?" Brick asked.

"Might have some aircraft left if they're still not under Zjhon control. I'm starting to have my doubts. I think they were counting on this installation providing them with defensive support, and now look at us."

"How difficult is the journey to Dragonport?" Brick asked.

Telly scoffed. "On foot? It's terrible. By plane it's not much better. We used to use pack mules twenty years ago, but the mules have all gone to the front, and the trails haven't been maintained for years. No telling what condition the bridges are in."

Brick weighed his options, all of which were terrifying. To the east lay the swamp, to the west Zjhon outposts of unknown number stood between him and Sparrowport, to the north was a treacherous road to Dragonport, and to the south was nothing but forest and swamp.

"Do you have any reason to believe Dragonport has fallen besides a lack of communication?"

"No," Telly said. "And I pray that I'm wrong."

For most of his life, Brick had rebelled against his father's controlling influence. Now he wished for even the briefest consultation with the man whose opinion he valued more than anyone else's. How could he trust his own judgment in such life-and-death decisions?

Weariness overcame him when the excitement wore off and his belly was full. A bath and a clean bed were provided to him, and he hoped he wouldn't snore. His father always complained about his snoring. With larger issues consuming his thoughts, he drifted off, knowing he would have a difficult choice to make in the morning.

In the distance, he might have heard someone snore.

* * *

"He's going to kill us all," Grunt said.

"Not if we're smart about this," Agger said, already knowing the odds of Grunt's being smart about anything were slim.

"Are you any good at landing these things?" Grunt asked.

"Better than you are. Strap in tight."

No matter how stupid he might seem at times, Grunt cinched his straps tight.

Orange and white cliffs jutted from the ocean, capped with trees and a narrow strip of grassland. Farther north were the main Sparrowport airstrips, but landing a stolen plane there was asking for trouble. Instead, he aimed for a place atop the bluffs, hidden from town by a towering peak.

"Maybe we should just head back to the western fleet and blame Casta for blowing our cover," Grunt suggested.

Agger laughed. "She's his favorite."

"He hates her."

"Exactly," Agger said. "Now shut up and do what I tell you for a change. It'll make it easier on both of us."

"You don't have to be mean about it," Grunt said.

The man was a walking pile driver, and Agger hurt his feelings.

The cliffs drew closer, and all conversation ceased. Neither of them wanted to die. Winds tossed the plane, causing it to pitch and roll. As soon as Agger countered one blasting gust, the wind shifted, growing cold and causing them to drop like a stone.

Grunt started talking again, his words unfit for a pirate's ears. With his feet on the dash and holding the handle above his head, he screamed louder the closer the bluffs drew. Agger was tempted to knock him out just to shut him up, but he'd seen others attempt to do so and fail miserably. Sometimes it was best to learn from the mistakes of others and save yourself the scars. Besides, Grunt really couldn't land this plane in Agger's estimation.

Gripping the controls tightly, Agger flew the stolen passenger plane sideways into the secluded valley, countering heavy crosswinds. When tires touched grass, the aircraft was yanked hard to the right and bounced along a rock-strewn field.

"This was a bad idea," Grunt said as objects streaked past on either side.

Agger did everything he could to slow the plane without flipping it over or onto a wingtip. After a third bounce, the landing gear caught in the turf and brought them to an abrupt halt.

"I can't believe we're alive," Grunt said.

"Thanks for the vote of confidence," Agger replied.

"You're welcome. Now to see if this bird will still fly. That woman is just crazy enough to leave us here."

Agger climbed down and inspected the airplane. Grass and soil clogged the front wheels, but the gear appeared otherwise undamaged. Grunt tried to pull a clump of grass away from the brakes and sucked in a breath when he burned his finger on the shining disks.

There was no hiding the plane. They just had to hope no one would come looking or that Casta Mett kept her word and picked them up an hour after nightfall. Both seemed slim hopes at the moment.

The town of Sparrowport was only a short walk away, which was part of what worried Agger. He'd rather have been forced to climb sheer rock faces than be so easily discovered out in the open. The people on this day, though, had plenty of other things to keep them occupied. Fighting in the street and stolen planes must have caused quite a stir.

Agger led Grunt to a place on the side of the nearby peak where they could watch. Sparrowport swarmed with activity, as he'd expected, and he reconsidered his plan. How were they supposed to kidnap someone from a town on high alert? And in particular, how was he supposed to move anywhere with any stealth having the heavy-footed Grunt right behind him? Agger was fairly certain his shadow's boots were made of concrete.

As darkness fell, the true scale of their challenge became evident. In addition to the streetlights, lanterns could be seen moving up and down the avenues. Even children patrolled the streets, ready to shout at the sight of anything out of place. Agger wondered if Destin Brightwood was among them. All he could do was operate under the assumption that the unpopular boy would remain home. His family's wealth had not been enough to overcome his unusual looks and mannerisms. Finding out such things was what Agger did best. If only he could identify magic or those able to sense it. Like the Pickette boy. He could not be certain, but he assumed that was who had taken the golden knife from right under their noses.

"You really shouldn't have shot that chap, you know," he said to Grunt. "That's probably what got the kid up. He was more than likely standing there when our friend expired." How else could he explain it?

Grunt remained silent. It was probably the wiser strategy, and Agger shut his mouth. Neither had wanted to enter town from the airfields, as most did. Better to scale the walls near the wealthy end of the residential district. Even if the main avenues were heavily patrolled, plenty of side streets and alleys remained in the shadows.

Despite their bickering, Agger and Grunt worked as a team and helped each other down a rock face and over a low wall. When they dropped into a narrow alley, it was like entering a different world. Here every window and gutter could hold eyes, ready to raise the alarm. No matter how skilled, they were immensely outnumbered, even if mostly by children and those too old to fight. Far better to slip in and out unseen.

Moving through darkened alleys, Agger stayed to the center to avoid unseen obstacles. He'd memorized a map of this place and knew where they needed to go. Grunt followed, looking lost and confused. When he tripped over a metal can, it came as little surprise. Agger sighed and drew his blade. No one came.

Grunt giggled.

"Idiot," Agger said. "How did you ever survive the cutting camps?"

"I have skills," Grunt said.

"I would have tossed you out," Agger continued. "It's only by luck that you haven't gotten us killed yet."

"Oh, they tried to cut me three different times."

"And how'd you get past that?"

From the darkness came a dock rat, a dirty blade in hand. Grunt never flinched. Reaching out with viselike fingers, he pinched the man's wrist in a way that made bones pop. Agger was certain the man would be screaming in pain if not for the elbow Grunt drove into his nose.

"I showed them my skills," he said with a grin. "Do you think this kid has magic?" he asked a moment later.

Agger shrugged. "Casta doesn't think so, but we can't trust anything she says. Making us look bad is a hobby of hers."

"Maybe if we find this Emmet Pickette kid, Lord Kind will have less need of Casta Mett."

"And if she finds him first?" Agger asked.

"We're going to need a new kid."

"This kid is weird, and we're not going back empty-handed. Unless you have any better ideas. I suppose we could beat up everyone we see along the way."

Grunt laughed a little too loudly. Agger glared at him. They were nearing the wealthiest district, which was the last place they wanted to draw attention to themselves. These people didn't have to be on guard since they could afford to pay someone else to be on guard for them. As a result, these streets were patrolled more heavily than anywhere else.

"You wait here," Agger whispered to Grunt after a watchman walked past.

Grunt nodded.

Through the night, Agger raced. He'd already identified the door he wanted to target. A metal fence and gate stood in his way. At a full run, he used the metal post holding the gate, since that would be the strongest one, to vault himself over the fence. Landing on soft soles with bent knees, he made only a soft patter.

The lock awaiting him looked far more secure than it actually was. After only a moment of fishing for the center pin, he released the catch. The door slid open, and Agger was halfway inside when the screeching started. With a lump in his throat, he turned to see Grunt open the gate, enter the courtyard, and close the noisy gate behind himself.

"Sorry," he said in a whisper.

Agger was tempted to kill him then and there. Grunt followed him into the house in spite of his insistence otherwise. Why Lord Kind had chosen to handicap Agger in such a way was unfathomable and a waste of his talents. Even in his anger, he knew he would never say those words to his king. He liked his head where it was.

"Stay here," Agger mouthed.

Grunt nodded.

Agger barely resisted the urge to knock the stupid grin from the man's face, but there was entirely too much at risk.

After moving through the pantry and kitchen, Agger climbed the stairs, keeping his weight out close to the edges, where it would be better supported and less likely to cause the stairs to give him away. When he reached the top and turned the corner, the stairs behind him creaked loudly. It was everything he could do not to vent his anger and frustration on Grunt. The man was an incompetent oaf.

In his rage, Agger missed the telltale signs of a loose board in the hallway. When his boots landed on the slight impression in the carpet, it groaned.

"What are you doing out of bed, boy?"

The man's voice sent a sharp chill through Agger. Footsteps behind him indicated Grunt had abandoned stealth. Charging into the room, he said nothing. After a thud and a few grunts, he returned.

Agger just looked at him in pure astonishment.

"It's a good thing I was here," Grunt said. "I probably just saved your life."

No words left Agger's lips. He stood in incredulous silence.

"Come on," Grunt said. "We don't want to just wait around here and gape. Let's get the boy and go."

Someday Agger would find a way to repay Grunt for his help. At that moment, though, he followed the thickheaded man to a closed door two doors down from where the man Agger assumed was the boy's father had been sleeping.

Grunt opened the door with exaggerated slowness but managed to do so quietly. Within, Destin Brightwood slept. Grunt grabbed him and slung him over his shoulder.

"What? Hey?" Destin said.

"Keep your mouth shut, and I won't kill you," Grunt said. "I got the kid. Let's go."

Agger just shook his head. The boy looked at him with terror-filled eyes. Agger just gave him a sad smile back. "I'll try not to kill you either. Just be a good boy, and everything will be fine."

Getting the kid back over the wall and up the rock face proved difficult, but eventually they hauled him up like a sack of potatoes. To his credit, the kid remained silent the entire time. Grunt proved to be excellent motivation.

Moving in the darkness was dangerous and time consuming. Now Agger was grateful for the short distance they needed to cover. He cursed it again when they peeked back into the small valley. At least a dozen lanterns moved in close proximity of the plane they had stolen and left there. So much for their backup plan. She had better not leave them there.

"I'll kill her if she doesn't show," Grunt said as if reading his mind. That alone was a scary thought.

When ropes suddenly appeared in the meadow before them, Agger could hardly believe it. Hovering above them in near silence was an airship, Casta Mett staring down at him.

Grunt shoved the kid up onto a rope. "Climb or die, kid."

Destin climbed. Agger grabbed the rope closest to him and left the ground with familiar reticence. Power and control were no longer his. Now he was simply a passenger. In that moment, the people below spotted the airship and ran toward the ropes. The crew moved with alacrity, and the humming above grew louder. Within moments, they moved out over the cliffs. Agger Dan tried not to look down.

CHAPTER FIVE

Mercy is a sure sign of weakness.
—Casta Mett, Al'Zjhon

* * *

After days in the air, no one smiled much. Places to land were few and tended to be clustered together, which was less useful for Riette's current purposes. Deep, blackish blue waves in every direction became monotonous, making it feel as if they were stuck in one place and would never reach their destination. Riette began to question if any of them even knew where they were going. Only the dragon's innate senses allayed her fears. The dragon read the wind and danced with it. Her flight was graceful and largely uneventful, contrary to how airplane flight was often described. There were indeed advantages to dragons. Tuck pointed and Riette expected to see some tiny rock sticking up out of the waves or a narrow strip of sand. These had been their only refuges during the journey, and Riette hoped never to need them again. Knowing it was inevitable did nothing to quell the knots in her gut. Seeing the faint outline of the largest mountain she'd ever seen left her speechless.

"That's where we're going," Tuck said.

Riette couldn't decide if she was elated or terrified. The end of the journey was most welcome, but she had no idea what awaited her and Emmet. Whatever motives these people had for helping her would soon be known, now that she and Emmet were completely reliant on them for survival. It was a risk she'd known she had been taking, but that didn't reduce her anxiety. She wanted to trust these people who had been so kind to her and had perhaps saved her life, but her propensity for caution would not be overcome, it was what had kept them alive this long.

"Not many folks come here," Tuck said. "We should be safe. Most other places are a long ways off."

That thought alone quelled some of Riette's fears. There had been plenty of opportunity to hurt them, and she did not think these people meant her or Emmet personal harm. Slowly she began to trust. What other choice did she have?

The mountain wasn't the only thing to rise from the depths. A large land mass ran alongside it, a monolithic shelf dropping into deep water. Running through this land mass was a shallow channel, looking like veins of marble in the land, stark white sands standing out amid lush greenery. A ring of pillars taller than any tree Riette had ever seen marked the entrance to the shallows. Twenty-four in all made for an awe-inspiring sight. One stood slightly askew, and signs of cracking were visible. Twisted visages had been carved into the pillars, giving them a much more ominous appearance. Flying low across the waves, Riette could almost feel the dragon's sense of anticipation.

The waters amid the circle of pillars swirled in a permanent but shifting vortex. Smaller funnels broke off from the central maelstrom, each roaring at its own pitch. Not expecting the dragon to fly right into the center, Riette drew a sharp breath. As if passing through an invisible waterfall, the energy changed around them; even the air was cooler. Below, a rotating maelstrom roared with a haunting sucking sound. Its edges not always well defined, the vortex wall danced and moved, but toward the center was a place that clearly stayed dry. There rested an amber statuette, glowing even in the shadow of the water surrounding it. How had it gotten there? Riette asked herself, her curiosity afire.

"Magic," Emmet said. Riette was unable to dispute it. Even the captain nodded in agreement.

"She just wants to bask a bit before dropping us off on land," Tuck said. "This is her favorite part. I think this place helps her somehow."

The dragon's posture and stance made the truth of his words clear. Somehow hovering in the air above the vortex, her eyes closed and muscles relaxed, she looked more comfortable here than any time since they had met. For a brief moment, Riette enjoyed being happy for the dragon. Dashiq sighed and turned on a wingtip toward a scrubby piece of land with a fire pit and campsite in place. The dragon waited impatiently for everyone to unload then stared at the captain for a long moment.

Tuck saw the exchange and immediately began loosening straps and buckles. "Can you help us with this?" Tuck asked. "She needs to heal."

A snide comment about asking passengers to be part of the crew never left her lips. She wanted Dashiq to heal. Emmet started working on some of the lowest buckles without being asked. Tuck nodded and pointed to the next strap the boy should unhook. Riette worried about Emmet getting hurt, but Tuck was so confident, she allowed the risk. She reached up high to grab a strap, and her eyes met the captain's. He watched her every reaction, and she, his. When she glanced at Dashiq and went back to work on the strap, he nodded and did the same. He might have smiled, but Riette's attention was on her struggle with the buckle, which was bound up and holding most of the weight, making it uncomfortable for the dragon, who shifted on her feet. The captain grabbed the harness on both sides and lifted, taking the strain off the strap, which allowed Riette to quickly unbuckle it and move on to the next. Dashiq gave a woof of appreciation.

"Now around back here," Tuck said when the last buckle was released. "We just grab here, lift, and walk." The dragon slipped nimbly from beneath the carriage and immediately flew back to the vortex. "And down," Tuck said.

Though lighter than expected, the carriage was still bulky and awkward, and Riette was happy to lower it to the ground. What worried her was having to put the carriage and saddle back onto Dashiq before they could leave. She tried not to think about it. When a snake slipped into the scraggly weeds surrounding the campsite, watching where she stepped became much more important.

"Don't let none of the snakes around here bite you," Tuck said. "They won't exactly kill you, but you won't live too long neither. And avoid the spiders. And when you go in the water, stay away from eels and deep water. Trust me. Shallow water is bad enough."

Trembling, Riette stood frozen and tried to watch everywhere around her at once.

"Oh, don't worry . . . What was your name again?"

"Riette," she said. "And—"

"And he's Emmet," Tuck said. You've mentioned him a couple times. "It's just that he don't never really talk back to you that way."

"No. He doesn't. Except sometimes. I look into his eyes, and I see him there, trying to tell me something important but he can't. And what he does say doesn't always make sense, or it's poorly timed. I don't know why or how, he just has a knack for saying the exact wrong thing at the exact right time."

"Such a nice kid," Tuck said.

Riette looked to see Emmet stripping down to his long shorts and following the captain, who had done the same. Shaking her head, she was ready to shout for them to stop when Emmet reached out his hand. The tall man stopped, and Emmet's hand disappeared into his oversized grip.

"He'll be fine," Tuck said.

Taking a deep breath and wiping away the tear that slipped from her eye, Riette let Emmet go. She trusted the captain and Tuck and Dashiq. It was not a small moment in her life. Much of what she had loved and trusted had been taken from her, and few had ever managed to penetrate the barriers she erected around herself.

Sitting down next to her, Tuck extended his fully formed hand and took hers. Her first instinct was to pull away, but she didn't want to this time. She didn't want to hide for the rest of her life. She wanted someone to truly know who she was and want her for that, rather than what she chose to show the world.

As night fell, the captain and Emmet returned, soggy and tired but bearing fish, salty fruit, and sparkling leaves.

"Are you hurt at all?" Tuck asked Riette.

"A few scrapes and bruises," she said. "But Emmet might be worse off than I am. I'm supposed to do inspections for cuts and bruises, but I haven't yet. So much has changed, and I just forgot." Familiar guilt returned.

"He already had some saltbark leaf by the looks of him," Tuck said, and the boy grinned back.

The captain stoked the small fire Tuck had built while Tuck offered Riette a single glittering leaf encased in translucent crystals. He held it as if it were a great treasure. "Place this on your tongue, and let the crystals dissolve, then chew the leaf and swallow. It won't hurt you neither way."

Riette decided proper grammar was not always required for communication, though it pained her to do so. The leaf was so beautiful and the presentation so intriguing, Riette accepted it and examined it thoroughly before opening her mouth. Even the smell was magical: sweet, tangy, and salty. Before any of the crystals fell off, she slipped the leaf onto her tongue. The saltiness was almost overwhelming at first, but that soon passed, followed by a light sweetness. In a few moments, only the leaf remained, and she savored its citrus tang.

Resting next to the fire, she and Tuck watched the skies, amazed to see bits of light streaking through them. Everyone had heard of shooting stars, and Riette had even seen one once, but never like this. Every fifth breath brought another streak, all moving in the same direction. Away from the lights of town, the stars were even brighter in the night sky, and that night, with Tuck holding her hand, the stars danced. Riette dreamed of fire in the skies.

* * *

Within the hallowed halls of Ri, the world's first city carved into a mountain, walked a stern-faced woman. Not far away stood a very different kind of hollow mountain. The contrast was an unwelcome reminder of past and, more important, present weaknesses. Without the advantage dragons afforded, the Heights would have fallen long ago. Casta Mett had no love for dragons, but she did appreciate their tactical advantages. The Zjhon were limited to mostly metal, wood, canvas . . . and magic. The last part kept Casta focused. Argus Kind had already assembled the greatest collection of magical artifacts ever known to exist, and sometimes he let her bathe in its power. Other times, he did not. Sent her to find her own replacement, she was allowed naught but the magic she brought into their relationship. Lord Kind said that was itself a kindness since he did not let anyone else retain magic. She was no ordinary soldier. She was Al'Zjhon. She did his bidding, and he needed her to be effective.

Fingering a worn artifact, she once again appreciated the power it granted. Agger, on the other hand, knew nothing of magic. His specialty was tracking people. Her specialty was tracking magic. The two did not always mix well. The boy he and Grunt had taken looked a little odd, with big ears and dark freckles, but not a lick of magic. Identifying other people who can use magic was not among her talents, but she had worked out a simple test using her artifact. When Agger and Grunt presented the boy to Argus, he used a similar test. Holding a sparkling bauble in one hand and Azzakkan's Eye mostly concealed in his other, he watched the boy's eyes. The boy followed the sparkling bauble and never even glanced at the other hand.

"I don't even know why I waste my time," Argus Kind said. "The only thing you two ever brought me was her." He pointed his thumb at Casta. "And my patience with her is wearing thin. Watch her closely. She's withholding information."

Few things were worse than having someone talk about you as if you weren't there, but having the king insinuate she was a traitor put her on more dangerous ground than she had anticipated.

Argus turned and regarded her. "Come on, then. Show me the trinket you've brought me to satisfy my appetite for power."

Again, she was caught off her guard. Fondling the small metal device she'd been holding for that exact purpose, she questioned whether to give it to him or not. He would have her searched, and she had no desire to go through that again. Instead, she essentially admitted her guilt by handing him the mechanical box.

"And let me guess. This won't actually be of any use to me in the war, but it is if great historical value."

It was true. It wasn't her fault not all artifacts were weapons. And magic was magic. The artifact she used to find magic made no distinction based on the purpose of any given artifact, only that it contained a certain amount of power. Such was the mechanical box.

"When the goddess returns to the skies," Casta said. "This machine will tell you how many comets will be in the sky on any given date and the size of the largest."

"I'm certain that will be quite useful in a couple thousand years, but it does me little good. Why did you bring me this?"

"I was drawn to it by the residual power it holds. I thought it would make a good addition to your collection."

"This is war. I need potent magic and a better way of finding it. No more useless trinkets. Bring something or someone useful, or don't come back, any of you."

His words stung. Even though she knew not to expect kindness from him, she had not expected open contempt. Always before she'd held his favor by leading him to fantastic stashes of magical items. Now fewer things remained to be found, and he'd caught on to her turning a single discovery into many smaller ones. Other collections of ancient artifacts were hidden on the Firstland and elsewhere, but Casta Mett had seen how devastating some of those items could be. No matter her ambitions, she did not want anything capable of destroying the world falling into Argus Kind's hands. He was just the kind of egomaniac to destroy the world because he couldn't have everything he wanted.

"Perhaps we should deploy the magic we've already found and put an end to the dragons once and for all," Casta said, despite knowing it was a dangerous subject. It would solve their biggest problem.

Argus Kind looked at her as if she were the greatest fool of all. "We've nearly won the war without using a single magical attack. We've fought fairly, while keeping our greatest weapons in reserve." The madman smiled at her, oozing vileness. "There is only so much magic remaining in this world, you fool. The ancients left us the smallest scraps, and you would have me squander them. When the magic is gone, it's *gone*. Human life is cheap in comparison."

"Should we dispose of the kid, then?" Agger asked, still gripping the frightened boy's shoulder.

"Not yet," Argus said, and he held the boy in his dark, piercing gaze. The boy shrank before him. "What's your name?"

"Destin Brightwood," the boy answered in little more than a whisper.

"I'm going to ask you a simple question. Don't lie to me, now."

Destin shook his head emphatically.

"Who is the strangest kid at school?"

The boy cocked his head in confusion.

"Someone who sees things others don't or hears things others don't or talks about magic?"

"The strangest kid at school is Aric Brilhelm. He eats glue."

The gathered Al'Zjhon withered under the king's gaze. Casta had not overlooked Deacon Rex's absence. She almost missed his greasy smile. Almost.

Argus turned to Agger and nodded but stopped when the child spoke. "The weirdest kid in town don't go to school, though. He got in too much trouble."

"What's his name?" Argus Kind asked, his voice almost laughably sweet. If the boy knew how many deaths this man was responsible for, he might have fainted.

"Emmet Pickette," the boy said. "He lives in Quarter Yard, in the residential district."

Agger and Grunt exchanged a glance, neither smart enough to know they were being read. Casta shook her head, ashamed these men were called Al'Zjhon. It lessened the honor.

"He said there was magic in the old library and got caught snooping around."

These words might as well have been a whistle.

Argus sat rigid in his chair. "You had this boy and lost him, didn't you?"

"We never actually had him, Your Highness," Agger said.

Argus rubbed his temples.

"We did chase after him, but we . . . uh . . . lost him."

Everyone knew better than to mention certain things around Argus Kind, and the man had a keen sense for when someone was intentionally avoiding saying something.

"How did he get away?" Argus asked, his voice deceptively calm.

Casta worried someone might not leave this meeting alive. There was a chance it would be her.

"By dragon," Agger said, keeping his eyes down.

Howling with rage, Argus Kind unstrapped his mighty axe. In a single, fluid motion, he hefted it and hurled it at Agger's head. The man ducked just in time to avoid decapitation; the wooden bench behind him did not fare so well.

"I'm sorry, Your Highness," Agger said. Casta had to admit the man had guts. He pulled the axe free and returned it to his king, handle first.

Argus was silent for a long moment. When he did speak, his voice was like rock on stone. "Casta Mett, you will track down this Emmet Pickette and bring him to me."

Already, plans formed in her mind.

"Agger, you and Grunt go along with her and make sure she doesn't kill the kid. If she kills the kid, I'll kill all three of you. Is that clear?"

Several plans were discarded, and new ones formed in Casta Mett's mind. It was a dangerous game. She had little choice but to play it well. Fortunately for her, she didn't like kids.

When Argus Kind stormed from the hall a moment later, relief washed over all of them.

"I can't believe I'm stuck with you again," Agger said after a deep breath. "I'm a tracker and you're a noisemaker."

"Yeah, but I come in handy at times," Grunt said, his grin never fading. "Remember the time I took that guy's wrist apart using just these two fingers?" He held two thick, meaty fingers in the air and rubbed them together in a way that made a series of pops. Casta had seen him do it, and the sound of it almost made her sick.

"I guess we're following you," Grunt said, looking at Casta.

"I could do without your help," she said.

"That's 'cause you're gonna kill the little bugger rather than allow yourself to be out of a job," Grunt said.

"And a head," Agger said. "Deacon says you are hiding magic from Lord Kind. Can you imagine if someone else shows up and starts pointing out all the things you've been hiding?"

Everything he said was true. Casta Mett considered going after one such object herself at that moment. It would make short work of her colleagues, and would likely be a match for Lord Kind himself, but she was not quite ready for that. "We leave within the hour," she said.

"Where to?" Agger asked. "I'd like to know how to pack."

Grunt giggled.

"A gift from the gods, capable of overcoming the destroyer, shall fall," she said by rote.

"You're going to chase after myths and legends?" Agger asked, appearing truly astonished.

"What will come will come," Casta said. "Those who seek magic, knowingly or subconsciously, will be drawn there, just as I am. We will see what is myth and what is legend."

"What do you want to do with him?" Grunt asked, pointing at the boy who had been trying to become invisible.

"Killing him is too much like work," Agger said. "Let him do it himself." The man turned the boy around and handed him a small knife. "That's all you get. Now run!"

Grunt growled at the boy and snapped like a chained dog.

Casta Mett didn't care. This wasn't the boy she needed dead.

CHAPTER SIX

Welcome to Dragon Airways. Imagine how much better you'll feel without all that baggage.
—Tuck, dragon groom

* * *

Avoiding Agger's jet wash, Casta Mett manipulated the controls gingerly. Every movement, every deviation from course consumed more fuel. No one could say if they would reach the fleet or have to ditch in deep water, far from any chance of rescue. If Admiral Meekam had disobeyed her orders, they were already lost. Given his openly professed opinion of her, this was her riskiest mission yet. All she could do was fly. The decisions were already made, the bones cast; fate would determine the rest.

"If you drop me in that cold water," Grunt said from behind her. "I'll drown you myself."

Casta did not bother to respond. It was not his first threat and wouldn't likely be the last. The fact that he could not swim provided some consolation. She smiled at the thought, but then Agger cut back across her path, and the turbulent air threatened to snuff the engine.

Boil him in oil, Casta thought, turning away from Agger's wash. The man had every advantage and continued to use them against her. He did not have a passenger, so weight was on his side. In these small aircraft, a tiny amount of weight resulted in a significant difference in performance. Casta would have vastly preferred flying alone, but Agger and Grunt were more weight than a single U-jet could bear and still maintain the speed and fuel efficiency required. Casta was not much lighter than Agger, but it was enough to force her hand. She knew they were just afraid she would shoot them down and be finished with them both, once and for all. It might have been tempting.

No matter how much she disliked the other Al'Zjhon, they did fight on the same side of the war, and Argus Kind would be most displeased if two of his hand-picked soldiers . . . disappeared. At that moment, she thought he might lose three at once. No sign of the fleet or land emerged. Not for the first time, Casta tapped the compass to ensure it floated freely and was not stuck.

"You've killed us all," Grunt said before punching the back of her seat.

Casta barely felt it. She had gone into the zone. It was something she'd learned during the cutting camps. When Argus Kind had put out the call for those willing to serve in an elite fighting force, many had answered; few survived. Most were turned away immediately, and others left early on, but

Casta had stayed until the end, defeating her competition by being sharper and more focused than they. There had been better fighters, better strategists, and even those more capable of detecting magic than she—those she'd had to eliminate before anyone else became aware of their abilities. Even her own ability she kept a secret. It was not until Argus Kind himself had threatened to cut her that she revealed her true value. Not only had she completed training beyond the abilities of most men, but she could bring him that which he desired—magic.

Why he wanted it did not matter. He was in power, and that was what he wanted found, even though he'd proven wholly incapable of accessing it. Only items that could be operated by anyone were within his grasp; it was a closely guarded secret but not one that could be hidden from Casta Mett. Knowing this, she did not mind gathering magic for him as much. It coincided with her own desires and allowed her to do so with the full strength and support of the Zjhon nation. And there was no reason she had to give Argus Kind everything she found, so long as she was the only one capable of locating magic.

Argus Kind was not her king, but he was *the* king. Whether he liked to call himself one or not, he became king the moment he killed King Gareth. There were limits to the power of even kings, and asking your executioner to behead his own brother exceeded those limits. Argus Kind had not complained or given any indication he would refuse. It was still unclear whether King Gareth had even known Dogor Kind was related to his executioner. He'd been a good king but perhaps not as aware of the details of his kingdom as he should have been. It cost him his life.

Casta Mett had been there that day. It was the same day that taught her nothing was permanent or sacred, nothing was certain or indestructible. In an instant, the entire world could change, just as it had when Argus Kind turned his axe on the rightful king. No matter how much she and others hated him for that very act, no one could argue that Argus Kind had survived every attempt to remove him from power. The wise accept things they could not change; the ambitious find a way to turn those things to their advantage.

When again Agger seemingly intentionally cut across the air in front of her, Casta's finger drifted to the trigger. It wouldn't take much to bring him down. The U-jet's downfall, besides the weight limits, was its fragility. Future models would surely improve, but these experimental planes were just that. There were reasons Argus Kind had so many trained to fly. Many pilots were lost in battle, but others had been lost in the quest for technological advancement. It had been a costly effort for which Casta was grateful. Without those who had given their lives in the name of progress, she would not have been able to get back to the fleet so quickly—if she made it. Her finger itched on the trigger. It would feel so good to exact vengeance on someone who did his best to complicate her life.

"Do it," Grunt said from behind her. "Do us both a favor."

Grunt was not her friend, nor was he an ally. If she shot Agger down, he would have all the information he needed to have her killed. He was wrong. She'd be doing *him* a favor. Agger continued to move back and forth in front of her, making the urge to shoot almost irresistible. Then, beyond him, the fleet materialized. He was lining himself up to land on the carrier *Terhilian*. That left one other carrier with a clear deck—the carrier *Arghast*— Admiral Meekam's flagship. This ship was farther out, and she cursed Agger for not allowing her and Grunt to land on the closer carrier. He knew she would have burned more fuel because of the extra weight, and he also knew how much Admiral Meekam detested her. Knowing he did it on purpose, she considered shooting him down. It would be a difficult thing to explain away. She could almost feel Grunt gripping the seat behind her. He would probably have been grinning, knowing what Agger had done, but it also put his own life at risk. Agger might not realize just how close he was to losing the only ally he had. Argus frequently paired the two men up due to complementary skill sets. Grunt was not a man she wanted as an enemy.

Looking to her left, Casta pondered the yellow lever, which would blow the hatch. All pilots were required to hand assemble an entire plane before gaining flight clearance, and she knew every inch of this jet. The red handle would eject both seats. She'd hoped never to use either lever, but she also knew she could disconnect the charge beneath her own seat first. If she pulled the red lever without first pulling the yellow, Grunt wouldn't live to tell anyone anything. Slowly she reached down.

"Don't even think about it," Grunt said.

Cold steel on her neck made Casta freeze. "Just getting ready to land this thing," she said. "Agger put us at a disadvantage. We could run out of fuel at any moment. I can feel how light we are."

Grunt said nothing. His gun barrel remained where it was. At such close range, air rifles could be deadly. No matter how large the carriers were, they now seemed small. Twice before on this trip, Casta had landed her U-jet at sea to refuel; both times had been terrifying. Now she was lower on fuel than either time before. She could not afford a single wave off and would get only one chance at this. Towering waves tossed the ships, and a chill wind blew. The landing strip did not simply bob up and down on the waves; it pitched and rolled.

The jet engine's tone changed; fuel was about to run out. Grunt screamed as they dipped lower.

"We might have to ditch," she said through gritted teeth.

Grunt stopped screaming long enough to say, "Don't you dare."

Casta was torn. The pitching deck drew closer, but the U-jet continued to lose altitude. The deck crew waved her off. Too fast. Too low. The crew fled the deck, seeing Casta maintain course. Just before the U-jet struck the deck at an odd angle, Casta pulled back hard on the stick. The nose climbed until she could no longer see the ship at all. She and Grunt stared into the late-afternoon skies until the plane's tail struck the deck, slamming them down with concussive force.

Bouncing and skidding, Casta watched the catch rope approach and slip past without slowing them as it should have. Perhaps the only thing to save them was hitting the deck at an angle and getting turned toward the ship's support structures. Still moving at high speed and her engine fluttering, the U-jet slammed into the aft deckhouse. Fire erupted and Casta struggled to get her belts loosened. Grunt made not a sound behind her. Unbearable heat assaulted Casta. Yanking the yellow lever with one hand to blow the hatch, she unbuckled with the other. She barely heard the charge blow.

Grunt surprised her by making it out of the cockpit first. Grabbing Casta by the shoulder, he pulled her from the wreckage. Perhaps she would have made it out on her own, but she couldn't deny that he'd helped her. She was ashamed to realize she wouldn't have done the same for him.

"That's for keeping us out of the water," Grunt said. "Agger is going to have to eat soft foods for a while when I'm done with him." It was the nicest thing he'd ever said to her.

Firefighters arrived too late. Some fuel did, indeed, remain within the aircraft. When the fire reached the ejection seat charges, they blew, rupturing the fuel tank and creating a second, more powerful explosion that knocked everyone on deck from their feet.

Not long after Casta pulled herself from the deck, Admiral Meekam approached, flanked by two commanders. "What have you got to say for yourself?" he asked, his face mottled red and white.

"That was some landing," Casta said. "It's a shame your men were unable to properly operate a catch rope. Now look what your ship has done to my plane."

Admiral Meekam appeared ready to gut her there and then.

"You're going to get us both killed," Grunt growled in her ear. "I just saved your life. Don't make me regret it."

"The only reason we're here is because of you," Admiral Meekam continued. "And for what? Some flight of fancy?"

Casta remained silent but held the admiral's gaze.

He did not appear impressed. "If you brought us out here for nothing," he said, a dangerous glint in his eye, "I have permission to throw you overboard."

"And if I am right, perhaps I'll throw you overboard, Meekam," she said. It was an ill-advised response, but she tired of his mouth and attitude. "Take advantage of the time to prepare for battle, Admiral. Once I've claimed our prize, we sail for the Midlands."

"We'd already be there by now if not for the likes of you," Admiral Meekam said.

"It's my job to get our king what he desires, Meekam. It's your job to assist me. Be a good boy, and do your job."

Unable to contain his rage, the admiral stormed away, waving his arms and ranting. Sailors scrambled to get out of his way. Both commanders gave her looks of extreme disapproval before following.

"You're not very good at making friends," Grunt said.

Casta Mett ignored him. Grabbing a pair of flags from a stunned sailor, she signaled the closest airship to pick her up. The sooner she was off the carrier *Arghast*, the better.

* * *

Emmet had found paradise—a place where magic always existed. Part of him wished to climb on Dashiq's back and bathe in the energy, but even the waves radiating away from the maelstrom were at times overwhelming, and the dragon needed her own time to heal. Being near the captain made Emmet feel safe, even if he didn't know the man's name. Perhaps it was his age that made him so calm, some wisdom found over the years, but he exuded no anxiety or fear as Riette always did. Somehow that strong confidence rubbed off on Emmet. He found himself doing things he'd never have dreamed of. Just the existence of this place was beyond anything he'd ever imagined. He never wanted to leave.

It occurred to Emmet that the captain's silence also put him at ease. Words antagonized Emmet, never coming at the right time. Yet somehow a gesture or a glance were all the captain needed. A hand on his shoulder was somehow reassuring. A long, calloused finger pointed. Movement finally gave away the snake the captain indicated. The finger shook in warning. If Riette knew . . .

The day before, they had harvested saltbark leaves from the near shore, but the trees were widely spaced, and the captain refused to pick more than a few leaves from each tree. It was smart, Emmet knew, but it made the search more difficult and perilous. Though he could swim on his own, the captain hoisted him up onto his shoulders. When he walked into deeper water, where the current was swift, Emmet was glad for the ride. He felt the inescapable rush pulling at them. Previously invisible rays cast off their camouflage and scurried away from the captain's footsteps. Each one made Emmet hold on tighter until a pair of fingers gently loosened his grip.

The brush was thicker on the far side of the channel, making it easy to travel by water. So close to the confluence, though, the shallow water mixed with deeper, colder water. Farther inland, Emmet had already experienced waters warmer than the baths at Sparrowport. A pair of saltbark trees grew in deep, swift water, jutting out into the flow. Swirling vortices danced in the waters just beyond the stiltlike root systems, which supported the trees and provided hiding places for fish, eels, and snakes. Emmet watched for signs of life in the upper leaves also. As he had before, he sensed a presence within the tree and was overwhelmed by the feeling of being loved and cared for. When he picked the leaves, he knew he did so with permission, which made him feel much better. The leaves weren't for him; they were for the dragon. She needed them.

As if his thoughts were heard, the tree responded by shifting in the breeze and offering up the largest bunch of leaves Emmet had seen in their three days of harvesting. When Emmet handed them to the captain, he stopped and marveled at the bundle before placing them in his basket. A long stretch of knotted scrub dominated the shoreline, and only a single saltbark tree clung to life there. The captain hesitated, perhaps considering whether enduring the cold water and currents was worth it. Emmet silently urged him to go. The tree seemed so lonely.

For whatever reason, the tall man waded into waters almost up to his neck. The shoreline beyond was rocky and nothing grew. This was the last tree in the saltbark grove. The captain couldn't do much but hold on to Emmet and keep the basket dry. Emmet did his best to be quick about harvesting what the tree offered, but the tree wanted him to stay. The dragon needed the leaves the tree offered, but the tree needed him. He could feel it. No words were used, only emotions, which Emmet clearly understood. Placing his hands around the trunk, he let the tree touch him as well. Leaves brushed against his hair, and branches rested on his shoulders.

Emotions rushed in and Emmet did nothing to stop the tears flowing down his face. He would have stayed, could have stayed forever. When the captain used two fingers to break his grip on the tree, he felt anger and resentment, but the man trembled beneath him. He didn't know how much time had passed—time really wasn't his thing—but the skies had grown dark. Any longer and it would be a dangerous walk and swim back to camp.

In spite of all that, Emmet wanted to stay, wanted to help this poor, lonely soul who so selflessly gave. He allowed the captain to pull him away, though, and as his hands left the delicate bark, he felt something in his palm. It was a brown teardrop-shaped seed streaked with white stripes.

"Friend," he said without meaning to.

The captain patted him on the leg and moved toward the center of the channel, but Emmet protested, reaching and pointing to a place along the shoreline between the pair of saltbark trees and the one all on its own. At first the captain resisted and followed his original course, but Emmet squirmed and kicked to convey the urgency. After grabbing Emmet's legs to stop him from kicking, the man turned and moved toward where Emmet pointed. Nothing grew there and the captain was a bit perturbed until

Emmet showed him the seed. The tall man stopped and marveled, questions flowing in silence. But then he seemed to know what he must do. Lifting the boy from his shoulders with one hand, he lowered him into the water. Emmet knew what he had to do as well.

After sucking in a deep breath, he plunged into the cold water headfirst and eyes open. No matter the burn of salty water and the rays that scattered on his approach, Emmet reached into the sandy bottom and burrowed. In the impression he created, he placed the seed before packing the sand back over it. The captain held him by the breeches, ready to pull Emmet up any second, but the boy was not quite finished yet.

Placing both hands over the sand, he sent emotions to the seed, hoping to return the kindness the tree had shown him. Colorful fish in bright yellows and blues gathered around him now, as if drawn by the energy. It felt as if they approved of what he did and would be there to welcome his new friend when the time arrived. The captain's grip grew less tight, as if he somehow understood. Emmet was grateful. No one had ever really understood him before except Mother. She was gone. Eyes and lungs burning, Emmet thrust himself upward. The captain pulled him back up onto his shoulders, and Emmet clung to the man, shivering.

A cool wind cut across the shallows and bit deeply. The captain strode across the channel with speed and purpose. Seeing a large dorsal fin exploring the waters near Dashiq, he moved with all the speed he could muster.

Upon reaching the shore, he thrust Emmet unceremoniously onto the sand, handed him the basket, and pulled himself from the water with a long groan.

"Friend," Emmet said, shivering and pointing. At least this time he'd meant to say it. The captain nodded and guided him back to the fire.

"We were about to come looking for you," Riette said in disapproval. "Here, get warm," she said to Emmet.

He did as he was told, his teeth chattering. The captain also took a moment to warm himself by the fire before taking the leaves to Dashiq. The dragon hadn't moved from where she hovered, and Emmet marveled at her ability to remain there, as if the planet did not covet her as it did everything else. The shark seemed to have moved on, the dragon more than it wanted to tangle with.

When the captain returned from ministering to Dashiq, he came at the closest thing to a run Emmet had seen from the man. He waved his hand side to side at the fire.

"Help me put this out," Tuck said in whisper.

Emmet was already kicking sand and rocks onto the well-established fire and the surrounding coals. Even covered, it would be impossible to hide the smoke and steam rising from it.

"We need to get ready to go," Tuck added. "I'm not sure what he saw, but I know it's not good."

Riette helped Tuck pack their supplies and ready the carriage. Dashiq winged her way to them a moment later, looking half asleep. Emmet wished she could have had more time to heal in the land's energy. He, too, wanted to stay and soak up the magic he'd longed for all his life. A deep sadness filled him upon realizing he might never experience it again. He was not well traveled or well educated, but he'd never heard tell of such a place before. He could only hope other such places existed or that he might find his way back again, but the captain and Tuck wanted nothing more than to leave. It was unfathomable.

Airship engines became audible, and the rest of the world intruded once again. "There!" someone shouted. "I told you I saw something."

Closer the airship came. It was Midlands construction, but that didn't mean it was under friendly control. In times of war, there were often enemies on both sides.

"You need to get out of here!" a man yelled from the airship. Riette appeared crestfallen, as if she'd expected to see Brick, searching for her. Dashiq looked up to the airship and issued a trumpeting call. The Zjhon didn't have dragons. This was something everyone knew. "The Zjhon are coming!"

"How?" Tuck shouted back. It was the obvious question since this place was well beyond the range of most aircraft.

"They've built floating cities," the man cried back. "Huge ships that act as runways. It's insane." The audacity of the plan left the group speechless. "A few of them sank. We picked up some survivors. They say the Zjhon have come here for some event. Something's supposed to happen." Giving truth to the man's words, a Zjhon warplane flew high overhead, most likely scouting the area. "Best of luck to you! We must warn the people. We barely have enough supplies for the trip, but we must tell them what we've seen. May the gods be with us!"

The airship wandered the winds back toward the Midlands, and Emmet wished them good luck. With Zjhon warplanes in the skies, it seemed unlikely. No matter how urgent their departure, there was no rushing the process of harnessing a dragon. Every strap and buckle existed for a reason, and even the order in which they were secured made a difference. Emmet did his best to help but was mostly in the way. The captain appeared to appreciate the effort, though, so the boy did his best to be useful.

Night had not yet fallen, and already streaks of light knifed through the sky. Larger and brighter than any in the previous nights, these were far more personal. Those so far away had been uncaring and aloof. These paid this world a special visit, and their presence would not soon be forgotten. The air sang with their energy and smelled of sulfur.

The last straps were secured and double-checked by lantern light; shadows grew long and deep. Distorted and frightening, voices carried across water and land alike, nebulous and indistinct at first but growing louder all the time. The silhouettes of balloons and airships filled the skies to the east, the sinking sun disappearing beneath the horizon to the west, providing a colorful backdrop behind the mountain.

Emmet followed Riette into the carriage and began strapping himself in. His sister watched with curiosity and concern. He could think of nothing he'd done to annoy her since reaching the shallows. Perhaps that was what concerned her. It was in itself unusual.

Tuck's sucking in a deep breath wasn't the only indication something was wrong. A long peal of thunder lingered in unnatural fashion and grew louder. A bright flash preceded an explosion, and multiple streaks of light bisected the evening sky. The aircraft in the distance were fully visible for a brief moment, the scale of the invasion force overwhelming, especially considering this place was largely uninhabited. Although, they did appear to be correct that something special was happening—something important.

Roaring like an angry dragon, the next bright light was larger and closer than those before. A wave of energy struck the ground, flattening foliage. Emmet worried for the saltbark trees but would perhaps have been better served to worry about his own safety. This streak of light arced low and struck the rocky soil somewhere between them and the mountain in the west. A towering cloud erupted from the impact site. Another struck the shallows an instant later, sending fine mist into the air above.

Lights sprang to life aboard the Zjhon air fleet, bathing the land below in rings of brightness, as if it were high noon but only in certain places. Emmet had never seen lights so bright. The pillars were fully illuminated, and in spite of seeming so permanent, one toppled over as he watched.

Tuck and the captain boarded after final checks, and Dashiq took to the air with greater ease than Emmet had seen from her yet. It made him feel good to know his efforts contributed to healing the dragon who had saved his life and likely would again.

Flying low over scrub-covered foothills, Dashiq took them closer to where the meteorite landed. A single Zjhon warplane flew in low and fired on them as it moved within range. Dashiq was nimble in her evasion. Soon the plane turned off to avoid the dust cloud still hanging in the air. Dirt and pulverized rock rained on them, pelting Emmet's face. Riette covered his nose and mouth with a kerchief, and he was grateful. No matter how much he annoyed her, she loved him—this he always knew.

Still glowing orange within a rapidly darkening outer shell, a melon-sized stone rested at the center of a crater. Pocked and swirled, it looked as if it had been crafted by time itself. It pulled at Emmet and sheared his thoughts, tugging at his perceptions like a deep, black hole. It felt like everything was happening at once. The captain emptied two thick leather bags and put one inside the other. Then he climbed down and used his cane to roll the stone into the bags, which sizzled and smoked in response. Dashiq pushed the captain back toward his seat and grabbed the bags with one claw. It all happened so quickly. Time continued to compress once again, burying Emmet beneath a mountain of information.

Voices cried out, weapons fired, planes flew past. Lights scoured the land. Airships drew closer, some towing two or even three balloons with lights of their own. They had been seen. The Zjhon were coming. Planes were coming. Only then, when the captain took a moment to lay a hand on him before taking his seat, did Emmet realize he had his hands over his ears and was rocking again. Riette whispered to him, telling him everything was going to be all right, but he knew it wouldn't. In the light of multiple airships was a creature not so different from Dashiq but much larger and having no wings.

"Sea serpent," Tuck whispered, his voice trembling. "I knew they could move on land, but I've never seen one come so far inland. He's a big boy."

"Scary," Emmet said before squeezing his eyes closed.

CHAPTER SEVEN

Magic will unite our world or destroy it.
—Argus Kind, usurper king of the Zjhon

* * *

Aboard the airship *Vendetta,* Casta Mett gripped the rails. Lights still streaked through the skies, and no one knew if another meteorite would strike. She'd been right; the ancient texts had been right. This alone exonerated her in her mind, though it wasn't really her opinion that mattered. When the sea serpent appeared, Casta couldn't help but feel the universe was conspiring against her, but this was no time for caution.

"There," Casta shouted, pointing at the cloud of spray glistening in the spotlights. Captain Vaida did not hesitate, knowing this was the reason they had come. Two meteorites had fallen. The one that struck the water would be difficult to find and retrieve; the other would be an easier prize to claim. Part of her wanted to locate it first, but the possibility of two artifacts was more than she could resist. The one on land would wait. Airplanes flew overhead, braving the skies in spite of the fading light and particulate in the air.

As Captain Vaida executed the course correction, Casta saw something that made her blood run cold. Flashing through the spotlights was what could only be a dragon—and not just any dragon but one in particular. Casta Mett hated all dragons, but none did she loathe as much as Dashiq. When her passengers moved through the spotlights, Casta recognized Emmet Pickette and his sister still aboard that ridiculous carriage. Now was the time to kill them all and be done with it. Perhaps victory over one Lord Kind hated so much would take the sting out of losing the boy.

"Change course!" Casta Mett ordered, pointing to where the meteorite had struck solid ground. Other airships were closing on their current position, and she left it to them to retrieve the stone from the water. None of their forces had yet reached the crater site on land. The dust cloud made it difficult for planes and jets to get close.

The airship *Vengeance* was far better designed for this type of mission but lacked the speed of the other craft. It also had a new weapon Casta Mett would love to test on Dashiq: a rotating hammer shot. This ingenious device fired up to a dozen hammer arrows in the time it would take a skilled archer to fire two. There would be no lines attached to these arrows as with traditional hammer arrows, which made it unlikely any arrows fired would ever be retrieved. Judicious use of munitions was called for, and Dashiq was beyond the weapon's range. Grinding her teeth, she watched helplessly while Barabas took the meteorite and Dashiq flew away.

Desperation washed over her. When Argus Kind found out who had beaten them there and claimed his prize, there would be no mercy. Few things enraged Argus Kind more than the mention of the man's name or that of his dragon. Even the Al'Zjhon themselves had been named as a jab at the Drakon and their customs. Argus had done everything within his power to besmirch their reputation and reduce their influence and numbers, and still a single dragon won the day.

Perhaps the planes could have brought the beast down in daylight, but darkness, too, served the dragon. Not for the first time, Casta Mett vowed to wipe all dragons from the planet. They were the one advantage the people of the Heights and Midlands had over the Zjhon, and no matter how much she hated to admit it, they had thwarted her over and over again. Howling with impotent rage, Casta Mett fired hammer arrows into the night, knowing full well none would reach the intended target. This was the last time dragons would beat her, she swore to herself. Knowing Barabas had the boy made everything worse.

Around her, the world continued to change. Columns in the shallows fell, marring what had been a sacred place of power. No matter how much hatred ate at her heart, seeing such a magical and historic place damaged pained her, but it was not her doing. The gods themselves, it seemed, were angry.

A series of flashes from the airship *Dominance* indicated nothing had been found at the underwater impact site. Casta spit on the deck.

"I wouldn't want to be there when Lord Kind finds out about this," Captain Vaida said. "When he hears a single dragon made off with his prize under the nose of an entire fleet, he's not going to be happy." He shook his head.

"We'd best get it back, then, hadn't we?" Casta asked. Vaida was a good man and had done nothing to get in her bad graces, but she would not hesitate to drag him before Argus Kind and let him take the blame.

"What are your orders?" Vaida asked, his flag master ready to convey her will to the rest of the fleet.

"We make for Sparrowport," Casta Mett said. "And we will destroy them. With their airfields in our possession, we'll own both ends of the continent, and we can crush them between us. Even if that were not the case, this is personal."

Someday soon the boy and his sister would return home. They always go home.

* * *

A lonely island with a few scrubby trees felt like paradise to Riette after days in the air. Emmet played in shallow puddles where fish and crabs gathered. Tuck and the captain tended to Dashiq and themselves, which left her to walk the beach alone. Just the act of moving felt glorious, even knowing it would be too brief. She'd seen the Zjhon fleet by way of their lights. The naval fleet dwarfed even the air fleet, and it was obvious this was far more than an exploratory force searching for magic. This was an invasion.

Riette kicked a rock, suspecting they weren't going back to warn the people of Sparrowport or the Midlands. Dashiq knew where she was going and could have easily followed the same path back to Sparrowport, but Riette did not recall seeing this island on the way to the shallows. She also thought their course was taking them much farther east. The captain now kept the strange stone that had fallen from the sky close to him. Putting it near Emmet had caused her brother great stress, and the captain kindly hid it away.

"Magic eater," was all Emmet had said in regard to the stone. How magic could be bad, Riette did not know, but she had stopped automatically disregarding Emmet's words. Often his words were proven correct, even if ill timed.

"Time to go," Tuck said.

Riette sighed and helped Emmet up to his seat. Tuck had her brother strapped in and double-checked before she could get her own straps secured, and she had two fully functional hands. It made her feel clumsy. Tuck checked her straps and patted the captain on the shoulder. She didn't see the captain give the dragon any input, but Dashiq stood and ran along the rocky sands a moment later.

Once back in the air and settled, Riette could no longer hold her tongue. "Where are we going?"

Tuck looked back with guilty surprise; perhaps he hadn't been expecting her to figure it out so soon.

"We're not going back to Sparrowport, are we?"

Tuck's look of guilt grew more distinct. "No."

"Why not?"

"Wouldn't do no good," Tuck said. "Would've been a waste of time."

"A waste of time?"

Tuck looked as if he might crawl up Dashiq's neck to get away from Riette. "What would they have done if we warned them?"

Riette hadn't been expecting that question. "Prepare . . . and send word for help."

"And I bet they've been preparing since we left. Seems to me a Zjhon warplane had been spotted over Sparrowport and even knocked in a couple buildings if I recall. They know."

"But—"

"And we can get the word for help out quicker than they can by going straight to the source."

"We're going to the front?" Riette asked. Her heart fluttered from fear and anticipation. So often she'd dreamed about going to the front and bringing her father home, but it was a most perilous journey. "You think that's safe?"

"Ain't no such thing as 'safe' at the moment," Tuck said, and the captain nodded. "We have something that could help win the war. If you can't be safe, might as well fight."

"What exactly is it that you have?" Riette asked, her voice low and cold.

"Not sure yet," Tuck admitted without looking at her. "But we know the Zjhon really wanted it."

The captain held up his hand, calling for silence, and Dashiq took them into the clouds. Aircraft patrolled the area, and all discussion ceased, but that didn't stop Riette's mind from conjuring one scene after another where all of them died. Having days on end to think about it didn't help. When the coastline finally did come into view, Riette wondered if she knew her geography. What she saw resembled the western boundary of the Jaga swamps: Forest's Edge. The town itself was farther north, but they were technically still in the Midlands. Tuck worked on a written message while they flew. He stuffed a rolled parchment inside a red kerchief filled with dried beans.

Men worked the forests below, and soldiers trained in newly cleared fields. Beyond lay airstrips not much older. Seeing shorter runways than in Sparrowport, Riette was now glad she hadn't taken the diesel plane she'd purchased tickets for. The landings must be terrifying. Even riding atop a dragon, Riette had reservations about coming down amid so many trees.

A dozen or so small farms occupied the few clearings visible in the north. What had once been the most remote farmsteads in the Midlands now supported a burgeoning new hardwood industry and the military's rear post. Most of the aircraft resting alongside the airstrips wore military colors. Signs of those wounded in the war were present to the keen eye, especially as they drew closer to what was easily identified as a medical facility.

Cries of "Dragon!" aroused the community. Even those with wounds freshly bandaged came to windows and doorways to see the dragon land. They were disappointed. Rather than land, Dashiq flew low enough that Tuck was able to toss down the message without its exploding on impact. Confusion and dismay followed.

A gangly man loped onto the field, waving his arms and shouting. Looking extremely disappointed when they soared past, he ran out to retrieve the kerchief of beans. After a brief review, he took the message to where troops practiced.

Within a short time, forces marched west. Riette sat back as they flew east, knowing at least someone would help protect her homeland. The captain had heard her complaint and offered a compromise. By notifying the rear guard directly, he saved time she would have wasted. It gave her some small comfort.

Dashiq kept to the edges of the jungle, flying along the shoreline. When they did reach the grasslands west of the swamp, Riette was grateful. The thought of being anywhere near the jungle terrified her. Better to face the Zjhon than to be eaten by any number of creatures both large and small.

"Last time we were here, the fighting was concentrated in the south," Tuck said under Riette's worried gaze. "We're hoping to come in behind it. Don't worry. This ain't our first go-round. The cap'n knows his business."

* * *

A metal hand on her leg woke Riette from a deep sleep with a start. Tuck holding a finger over his mouth was the first thing her blurry eyes saw. Knowing something was wrong, she woke Emmet and urged him to remain silent. She might have been better off to leave him sleeping, but she knew how he reacted when awoken by something that frightened him. This was no time for uncontrolled shouting.

The sun was just clearing the horizon, and most of what Riette saw were foggy shadows, but when the shapes grew more distinct, it was apparent what those shadows represented. Hundreds of airships, balloons, and other aircraft gathered. Two ship-borne airstrips longer than any others they'd seen looked wide and smooth enough to safely land even the largest aircraft. Twelve engine diesel props dwarfed smaller planes, but the much smaller U-shaped crafts caught Riette's attention. She'd heard rumors of pulse jets in development, and seeing them in Zjhon hands did not bode well for the future. The allies fell further behind every day.

Beyond the airfields, orderly rows of tents formed small, identical cities. It was efficient, calculated, and frightening. The enemy had but to bide their time and build up an overwhelming force. When she thought back to the floating cities, she realized how close they already were to achieving that goal. It was hopeless.

Crosswinds pushed them deeper inland and caused the carriage to strain against the harness. Carried by the wind, the noise caused a nervous soldier to look up. His voice carried back, shouting in alarm. Dashiq flew with all haste. It wouldn't be fast enough. The air was clear, the faint covering of fog remaining below quickly burning off. The great hollowed mountains of the Heights, visible in the distance ahead, teased of safety just beyond reach.

The captain pulled a string, and the "hold on for dear life" sign fizzed to life.

Riette would have laughed, but aircraft firing behind them made it clear the Zjhon were coming. Only the morning dampness worked in their favor. Even with a target in the air, Zjhon pilots knew better than to fly with cold piston engines. There was one noise, though, that rose in pitch and sounded like an approaching hurricane. Streaking across the sky came a U-shaped plane with backswept triangular wings, the oscillating roar awkward and harsh until it found harmonic resonance. Suddenly in perfect synchronization, the jet engine sang a pure note, its exhaust fumes fading into a shimmering clear wash. No matter how deadly, one had to admire the technical achievement.

At that moment, though, that very innovation was coming right at them. The pilot was willing to give his or her life to take down the dragon, but Dashiq was no easy target.

"I hope they like pickled eggs!" Tuck said, cradling an almost empty jar. Though he was upside down when the jet passed, Tuck made a perfect throw and landed an egg on the jet engine's intake. The jet lost its resonance and for a moment sounded as if it might stall, but then it cleared up and once again found its rhythm.

Three times more jets harried them, doing their best to slow the dragon down. A formation of planes came from behind, and Dashiq did everything possible to maintain speed and still avoid the jets. They had come to expect the jets not to have weapons, but the next carried rapid-fire air cannons delivering a steady torrent of scatter shot. The sickening sound of the shot hitting Dashiq's wing was followed by a slow downward spiral.

Thinking to take advantage of the wounded dragon, the jet circled back for another pass. Again weapons fired but the dragon was more nimble than the pilot had been expecting. With a single rake of her claw, Dashiq crushed the engine's intake. Soundlessly the jet dropped from the sky. The others turned back toward the airstrips, from which a massive flight of diesel props approached.

CHAPTER EIGHT

The best use of power is to gain more power.
—Deacon Rex, Al'Zjhon

* * *

"Buckle up, Buttercup. It's about to get bumpy," Tuck said.

Scatter shot struck the carriage. Riette hadn't been hit. She checked on Emmet, who appeared to be fine. It was too close. The firing from behind was not continuous; planes had to jockey to get into position, and Dashiq took advantage. The first hollow mountain approached fast, a huge flight deck cleared and ready for them. The dragon lined up for the landing and made a perfect target. Most of the planes veered off but two persisted. Scatter shot rained down on them. Riette was struck in the arm, and Tuck cried out. At least it hadn't been stone shot. While the scatter shot affected a wider area, it penetrated with far less force. Nonetheless, stinging welts grew on Riette's arm.

Another round of scatter shot struck Dashiq in the right side of her head, where copper met flesh. The dragon had been lined up perfectly with the landing strip, but now she dropped sharply. Another flight deck appeared below the first. This one was fully occupied, and people ran in every direction. Some tried to save the aircraft moored there, while others leaped out of Dashiq's path. An instant before her face would have struck the stone, her head flew back and her wings flapped. She did crash into a mid-sized four-engine prop plane but did only minor damage. Afterward, no one knew what to do, looking at Dashiq as if she were a ghost.

Most kept their distance. The captain nodded to the man who was about as welcoming as a cold blade.

"So what's all this, then, DeGuiere?" the hard-edged soldier asked.

DeGuiere? Riette silently asked.

"We brought you something the Zjhon want badly," Tuck said, already sounding defensive. Riette didn't like the way this was going, but there was little she could do about anything at that moment. She and Emmet were just along for the ride and did their best to remain invisible.

"Do you need a child to speak for you now?" This brought laughter from a group of men watching from nearby and making no effort to conceal their appraisals.

Tuck opened his mouth. The captain, as Riette continued to think of him, silenced Tuck with a hand on the shoulder. Looking incensed, the young man pleaded with his eyes to be allowed his say. The captain pointed back to Dashiq. With obvious reluctance and a steady glare at the gathered men, Tuck made his way back to the dragon. This brought a roar of laughter that made Tuck blush furiously. Riette wanted to smack them on his behalf. Emmet, at least, was silent. Ever since arriving, the boy had been engrossed in their surroundings.

Everyone's attention turned back to the captain. "I can speak for myself," he said in a voice like tumbling granite. His words were not slurred; they were malformed, slow and drawn out, the right side of his face drooping. "What the boy said is true. The Zjhon wanted this." He held up the sky stone.

Laughter again filled the flight deck. Riette joined Tuck in staring the rude men down. Emmet examined the chamber walls, thinking only the gods knew what. The man talking with the captain turned around to face the rude men. Now some snickered.

"Scowl all you want, Gerrig. He ain't welcome here after what he did. I'd be within my rights to kill him here and now."

"You'll have to go through me," Gerrig replied, turning his back on the men, who made a show of being afraid. "What is this . . . rock?"

"It fell from the sky in a ball of light and struck the land a mighty blow," the captain said, his speech coming to him a little faster the more he spoke. "The Zjhon were there with a naval fleet and more than fifty aircraft . . . waiting for this. We got there first and stole it out from under them."

"Where did this happen?" Gerrig asked, suspicious.

"The shallows." This statement brought scoffing and accusations from the assembled group, which was now growing larger.

"Zjhon aircraft can't reach the shallows," Gerrig said.

"They can now," the captain said.

"That would mean the Midlands would also be within their range . . . and our flanks . . . our entire supply chain."

There was no more laughter.

"Come with me," Gerrig said.

"Yes, sir, Commander Gerrig, sir," the captain said, but then he glanced back at Dashiq.

Tuck had already begun attending to the dragon's wounds, which appeared to be minor but numerous. Riette had seen him give the dragon their entire saltbark leaf supply, and she hoped it would be enough to keep her alive. Being left to these people's mercy was not something she wanted to consider.

The captain waved for them to join him. Dragon grooms had shown up to assist in Dashiq's care, and Tuck had returned to staring down the soldiers, who continued to laugh at him.

Gerrig saw it as well. "Come on, then. Dashiq will be well cared for."

Visibly hesitant to leave the dragon behind, Tuck took a moment to talk with the much older grooms about Dashiq's care. These people nodded silently and listened, but the gathered soldiers now laughed at the dragon grooms.

"You will show some respect, Duggan," Gerrig said to the man leading the group.

"Send them back up to their own level, and they'll get plenty of respect. Down here, we respect loyalty and steel."

Massive workbenches holding partially assembled engines gave Riette an idea of what he was talking about. Taking Emmet's hand, she practically dragged him to where the captain waited. He said nothing.

"A doddering old fool riding a crippled dragon with a crew of simpletons!" Duggan said, barking a laugh.

Emmet heard the man and shrank against Riette in fear.

Tuck also heard. As they passed before the group, enduring their leering grins, Tuck turned and took three steps, which put him right in front of Duggan. The man was easily three times his size, yet Tuck stared at him as if he were the one looking down. "Ignorant fools should not speak of matters that do not concern them."

"Be careful, now," an ugly man said from behind Duggan. "You might hurt his feelings."

"I've wrestled dragons," Tuck said before Gerrig could reach him. "I ain't afraid of you." This brought the most raucous round of laughter yet. Men goaded Duggan for allowing a child to scold him. "You see that kid over there you frightened?"

Everyone listening looked at Emmet. Riette quailed under the scrutiny and squeezed her brother's hand more tightly. Emmet looked back with a complete lack of fear; in fact, he smiled.

Tuck wasted no more time. Using his strength and body weight to his advantage, he placed a well-executed kick on the side of Duggan's knee. There was a sharp crack followed by a shrill cry. The man swiped at Tuck as he fell, but the boy deftly stepped out of his reach. "That's for him," he said, pointing to Emmet.

"The gods sometimes mete out their judgment with swiftness," Gerrig said. "These people are in my custody. Any assault on them will be considered an affront to my family. Have I made myself clear?"

The gathered men mumbled and dispersed. Duggan got to his feet but walked with a pronounced limp.

"You are not to touch another person without my leave," Gerrig said to Tuck.

"Yes, sir."

"But I thank you for doing what you did," Gerrig said. "I appreciate the laugh. But I'm afraid there won't be much more of that."

Silence hung over the upper deck, which remained empty. Gerrig said nothing as they crossed the barren expanse, persistent wind rattling dragon harness all that broke the stillness. The captain walked with his cane, and Gerrig had to visibly slow himself to not outpace the group. He said no more until they reached a series of halls leading into a part of the Heights occupied by only humans.

"I wish you luck, my old friend," he said to the captain. "There won't be much I can do for you from here."

"You've already done enough."

Riette still had not gotten used to the sound of his voice. It was deeper and raspier than she had imagined. Since only half of his face cooperated with his speech, she guessed he had suffered a stroke. It would explain why he had spoken so freely when first meeting Tuck but had then stopped. Riette had known folks who never recovered from such ailments.

Guards watched in silent curiosity, but no one stopped them until they reached a set of ornate doors with handles shaped like battle axes. Riette could not hear exactly what was said to the guards, but Gerrig appeared confident. One slipped inside, preventing them from seeing anything or hearing what took place within. When he returned, he whispered to Gerrig before both doors were pulled open.

"Commander Gerrig," a stern voice said from within.

On trembling knees, Riette entered the war room. Dominating the chamber was a table with a scale model of the known world built into it. Wooden seas bordered land masses and provided flat surfaces, few of which were free of papers, figurines, and what looked like toy ships and aircraft. Amazing detail was visible in the masterfully crafted representation of their world. Places Riette had never known existed were shown. She could barely take her eyes away from it. When she did, familiar fear returned.

The man standing on the far side of the table dominated the room with his presence and made the soldiers below look nonthreatening. Other people in military garb continued as if no one had entered the room, but the big man glared with eyes afire. "I allowed you to leave this place once," he said. "You're a fool to return. What do you want, Barabas DeGuiere?"

The disdain in his voice was clear, and even Riette recognized the absence of any military title; she also made note of his first name: Barabas. It was an uncommon name, save in the mythologies. To be named after such a great figure must be difficult; so much to live up to.

The captain showed no sign of taking offense. "I serve as I've always served, General Katch, sir."

To his credit, this man did not laugh at the captain's infirmities. "Do you mock me?"

"No, sir. I'm not the man I once was." It was clear the general had no love for Barabas, but his eyes softened a fraction. Riette could not imagine what it must have felt like to make such an admission. "I came because the news won't wait. The Zjhon have outflanked you."

Several people in the room scoffed at the notion, but General Katch stared and waited.

"They've sailed an armada equipped with their own air support and the ability to launch aircraft at sea." His words came a little faster the more he spoke, but it was embarrassing for him when he had to wipe away the moisture at one side of his mouth.

"You've seen this yourself?" the general asked.

No one else in the room spoke. Barabas now had their full attention. "Aye. In the shallows."

General Katch scribbled a note and, with a whispered command, handed it to a young woman standing nearby. She dashed away.

Tuck stepped forward, his eyes downcast. "May I speak, sir? It is difficult for him." The captain's head lowered a bit at these words, but he did not argue. General Katch gave the boy a curt nod. "The Zjhon converged on the shallows because they knew something was going to happen. They were waiting for that." He pointed to the sky stone. "We just happened to be close by when it struck, and we beat them to it."

"What are its properties?" asked an older man with wild, curly hair.

"We don't know," Tuck admitted. "But we know the Zjhon wanted it badly."

A low murmur ran through those assembled, and the man approached with a sense of reverence. Barabas did not hesitate to turn over the sky stone, something of which Riette questioned the wisdom. A little leverage could not have hurt their chances of leaving this place alive. She was beginning to doubt his sanity for bringing them there in the first place. He'd nearly gotten them killed to take them someplace they were demonstrably unwelcome.

General Katch let out a deep sigh. "If I find out your words are false, your lives are forfeit." Riette wanted to smack the general but did her best to remain silent and invisible. "If they are true, which I suspect they are, then you've done us a great service, even if it is already too late."

Barabas looked up, deep concern in his eyes. "How bad is it?"

"Every day, they get stronger and we get weaker. Every time the Drakon deploy, fewer return, and we are still playing catch-up with regards to aircraft development and construction," General Katch replied. "That can only go on for so long before we're overrun. Based on your words, that will be soon. If we send our air strength to the west, then the Heights will surely fall. If we lose the Midlands, then we lose our supply chain. Either way, we lose."

"Then don't do neither of those things," Tuck said, and all eyes turned on him. To his credit, he did not flinch under scrutiny. "Send everything you got in a single strike."

This proposal was met with an angry backlash from almost all those gathered since it would doom both the Heights and the Midlands. Tuck had expressed what they already knew but did not want to admit. The Zjhon had already won.

General Katch held up his hand, and the room fell silent. "Tell me, boy. Why?"

"If they've sailed two fleets, how much strength could they have held in reserve?" The general nodded and allowed Tuck to go on. "They're counting on catching you by surprise." The captain put his hand on Tuck's shoulder, a clear sign of his support. Tuck spoke with bolstered confidence. "If you launch your offensive so the eastern fleet can see, they'll surely pursue you, knowing their homeland defenses are weak."

"Assuming they truly are weak," General Katch interjected, but he still looked to Tuck to see what the boy would say.

"I guess you're just going to have to decide which way you want to die," Tuck said.

Riette held her breath, fearing her friend had gone too far. She had no time to wonder at the thought of actually having a friend.

With a barking laugh, General Katch turned to the captain. "You've taught the boy well."

"He's wrong," the captain said. Surprise and hurt showed on Tuck's visage, but the older man squeezed his shoulder. "Their defenses will be considerable. I agree with his suggestion nonetheless. Better to die taking the fight to Argus Kind than through attrition."

"I don't like you," General Katch said. "And I don't like what you did, but you are correct in this."

Barabas nodded but before he could say another word, shouting erupted in the halls. "No weapons in the war room," a guard shouted from outside just before the chamber door burst open.

The man who entered was among the least friendly looking people Riette had ever seen and she trembled. Beside her, Tuck must have sensed her distress, for he took her hand in his and gave it a gentle squeeze. The gesture brought feelings she did not understand, but she forced them down.

"What is *he* doing here?" the warrior's question was an accusation toward everyone gathered, and few met his eyes. Tuck was among those few, which incensed the man even further.

"Barabas has brought dire news, Al'Drakon," General Katch said, "and an object sought by the Zjhon, though it is of unknown utility."

"And you bring the traitor here, so he can see our plans and report our weaknesses back to the enemy?"

"No matter what you think of Barabas," General Katch said, "no one has offered proof he serves anyone but his own people."

"He used the last of our magic to save himself and a dragon who has lived beyond her years," Al'Drakon said. "That is proof enough. He took from us the only chance we had of defeating Argus Kind."

Barabas stood tall and did not flinch under the accusations.

"You know that's not true," General Katch said. "Had he allowed Dashiq to die, the Zjhon would have captured the magic anyway. Better to have the power used to save one of our own than to fall into the enemy's hands along with all the rest."

"One of our own," Al'Drakon spit. "You're a fool who cannot see when he's been betrayed."

"Al'Drakon is a position of great honor that affords you complete power over the Drakon, but it does not grant you the right to insubordination. You've come armed into a sacred space. This is forbidden. Do not make me judge you as harshly as you judge him. The purity and sanctity of this chamber have been maintained through ritual and honor for a thousand years, and today you mar that record. Do not force me to have you removed."

The tension in the room held most in silent rigidity, but Tuck glared at the man in open contempt.

Al'Drakon cleared his battle axe from its mighty sheath. "Who would you have remove me? I risk my life and that of the Drakon every time I leave to defend this place, and you side with a traitor!"

"I side with no one but my own counsel," General Katch said, not backing down from the open aggression. His eyes showed no fear. "I've no more love for Barabas DeGuiere than you, but we do not always get to choose our allies. The news he brings is dire and his counsel sound. A wise man would at least hear his words."

Al'Drakon allowed his axe to rest once again in its sheath, still in violation of protocol. Crossing his arms over his chest, he silently dared anyone to challenge him.

"The Zjhon have built floating airfields and have outflanked us," General Katch said.

"And you've seen this yourself?" Al'Drakon asked with clear contempt.

"No," General Katch admitted. "This news is too recent to have been verified, but aircraft are being readied as we speak. In the meantime, we would be wise to consider the counsel afforded us and make our own decisions."

"What, then, does the traitor advise?" Al'Drakon asked, now glaring directly at Barabas, who did not meet the warrior's eyes.

"He and his companions have advised us to take the fight to Argus Kind."

"And leave the homeland undefended? Ha!" Al'Drakon barked a harsh laugh. "Why not just surrender?"

"What would you do?" Tuck asked. All eyes turned on him, and none were friendly. "Keep doing what you've been doing? Have you driven the Zjhon back? No! And yet you ignore folks wiser than you."

"Be quiet, boy," Barabas said, pulling Tuck back from the table. The young man looked ready to leap across the war models and fight Al'Drakon himself. His hand, still gripping Riette's, trembled with rage but did not pull away, as if he took strength from her.

"Ah, the traitor speaks!" Al'Drakon said, and the captain finally met his eyes. "It seems the last of our magic was not enough to preserve your pretty mouth. Pity. Are there any other precious resources we might squander to preserve your useless hide, Al'Drakon?"

"I relinquished my right to that title," Barabas said. "But I did not give up my right to serve my homeland and her people. Think of me what you wish, but accept the truth. We are already defeated. If we take the fight to the Firstland, at least we can inflict some pain on them before we are too weak to do anything more than die."

"By the sound of your speech," Al'Drakon said. "You'll be the first among us to die. Not soon enough for me."

No matter how much the warrior goaded him, Barabas remained calm and humble. This fueled the warrior's anger. When a dozen guards entered the room and surrounded Al'Drakon, the font of his rage would no longer be contained. He brought his axe to bear, making Riette fear he would slaughter them all. Instead, he hurled it at the ancient wooden doors. The mighty weapon cleaved the mural carved there, causing irreparable damage to the masterful artwork. "Take it," he said. "I do not need it. My bare hands are all I need to wring the necks of fools, or do you think to deprive me of those as well? Come. Take them if you dare. For all your foolish protocol and ritual, you cannot change the fact that we are all weapons— some far more effective than others."

Slowly and without turning their backs on him, the guards retreated. One man grabbed the axe handle and worked it free of the door. A moment later they left the room and closed the damaged doors behind themselves. Emmet fidgeted beside Riette and let go of her hand to pull at loose threads in the hem of his jacket.

"Stop that," Riette scolded, but her attention was soon drawn away.

"I won't claim to understand all the rituals and protocols, Al'Drakon," General Katch said. "The ancients left us more riddles than answers, but our fathers taught us the things they did for a reason. And their fathers before that. I'll not abandon their teachings because you find them inconvenient. If we must perish, then let us do so with our heads high and our honor intact."

More dragon riders slipped into the room, gathering behind their leader. At least none appeared to be armed, but the tension in the room grew. Even General Katch looked nervous.

"And why are there children in the war room?" Al'Drakon asked. "Does that not fly in the face of your teachings?"

"I brought them here," Commander Gerrig said. "Not all those in the Heights act with integrity these days, and I was left to fear for their safety. They arrived with Barabas DeGuiere and are under my protection."

Al'Drakon spit on the floor. "You choose the companions of a traitor over your own people."

"If you call him a traitor again," Tuck said through gritted teeth, "you'll have to deal with me."

This brought laughter from many in the room. Some laughed at Tuck, but others laughed at the much larger warrior. Both flushed deep red.

"I said be quiet, boy," Barabas growled.

"Speak to me in that manner again, and there'll be no one who can save you," Al'Drakon said.

"You might frighten some folks," Tuck said, his hand clenching tightly around Riette's, the captain's hand seemingly the only thing holding him back, "but I ain't one of those people. If you want my respect, stop acting like a spoiled child."

"Silence!" General Katch said. "One more word out of either of you, and you'll speak next from the dungeons. Have I made myself clear?"

Al'Drakon ignored the general and continued to glare at Tuck and Barabas. Tuck, though, turned to General Katch and inclined his head in a sign of acquiescence and respect.

"Barabas DeGuiere has brought us intelligence . . . which will be verified," the general said, stifling any more words from Al'Drakon. "And he's brought us an artifact that may yet be of use to us even if we do not yet fully understand it. He's kept this object from the Zjhon and turned it over to us. That is an honorable act. Once we've verified the intelligence, he and his companions will be free to go. Until then, he's to be confined to dignitary quarters along with his companions. They are to be treated as honored guests and will be guarded at all times so they do not have to worry about anyone bearing them ill will. If there's nothing else, you may all leave. *Now*."

No one moved. Barabas appeared to be fighting some inner battle. "There is one more thing," he said before the guards could lead them away.

General Katch held up his fist in silent command.

Tuck squeezed Riette's hand and looked to her with regret in his eyes. Never had she been so terrified and confused. All the times she'd questioned the captain's intentions came back in a rush. Never had he asked for payment or explained why he'd taken her and Emmet away from Sparrowport. Her guts twisted.

"The boy is special."

Cold fear was like a knife in Riette's gut. She pulled away from Tuck in anger.

"Don't," Tuck said but he never got the chance to say more.

"I brought him here because I believe he can sense magic."

Everyone began to talk at once. Anger, resentment, and incredulity filled the room. Riette turned to Tuck with hatred in her eyes, no matter his pained expression. He had betrayed her. They both had betrayed her. "You monster!" she screamed at Barabas. He accepted the accusation and remained silent. "How are you any better than the Zjhon? You wanted the same thing they did. At least they were honest about their intentions. You lied to me!"

"Once a traitor, always a traitor," Al'Drakon said.

In the commotion, Riette lost track of Emmet, and she searched for him frantically, despite knowing there was nothing she could do to save him now. Deep within the Heights, there was no chance of escape. Barabas DeGuiere had doomed them as surely as if he had taken them directly to Argus Kind. Still, she could not help but try to protect her brother. At that moment, the rest of those assembled realized the boy had disappeared. Riette hoped he did possess some magic that would allow him to escape even if she could not.

Then she saw him, though, crawling on all fours beneath the table, making his way to the back of the chamber, where a pair of sconces flanked what looked like a shrine of some sort. Knowing others would follow her gaze, she pretended to search the rest of the chamber for him, all the while trying to analyze the shrine's every detail. Dark gray liquid filled glass containers on a slab of alabaster. Within black stone was a subtle inset, barely visible but distinct in its form. When Emmet emerged from under the table, he held in his hand something like a golden dagger, equally distinct in its form—the inverse of the cavity he moved toward.

Unable to fathom how her brother had come by such an item or what he intended to do next, Riette watched in silent horror. Then she remembered the footprints in the hallway. The room exploded with activity when others followed her now static stare and saw the boy approaching what appeared to be a sacred place. With quickness she hadn't known he possessed, Emmet reached up and placed the golden dagger into the orifice in which it fit so perfectly.

A dagger it was not; what Emmet held was a key.

CHAPTER NINE

Dragon Airways. Stay clear of the pointy bits.
—Tuck, dragon groom

* * *

Time slowed. Emmet moved beneath the enormous table, making his way toward what looked like a shrine. It called to him, just as the dagger had but far more loudly. The rest of the world faded away. Only the key and the altar existed. He understood now. Everything became clear. The other people in the room moved in slow motion, and Emmet took his chance. All his life he'd yearned for magic, and finally it was before him in all its glory. A foot of rock stood in the way, but he had the key. Though it possessed magic of its own, the key was but a gateway to the real thing.

Not hesitating, Emmet placed the golden artifact within the impression that had waited a thousand years to receive it. The fit was close and clean. Torches, their flames dancing slowly, illuminated gray liquid in an intricate glass vessel on one side of the altar and clear liquid on the other. Those apparatuses fed long necks embedded in stone.

The key seated fully. A bright flash and a loud pop made Emmet cover his eyes. Pungent smoke drifted in tendrils above the altar. The liquids drained from the glassworks into the rock wall, the gray liquid forming a sparkling vortex, as if the liquid were somehow metallic. Nothing happened at first, but then a low grinding sound that Emmet could feel in the soles of his feet emanated from stone. It grew louder over time, and finally the granite altar moved. The thick slab retracted into the wall with agonizing slowness. Inside, a glistening object shone. Before anyone else could get close enough to see, Emmet slipped his hand inside, grabbed the gleaming object, and stashed it in his coat.

Inexorably the altar slid open, and soon the men reached him, pulling him back until time compressed once again. Everything happened at once, and Emmet curled into a ball, waiting for it to pass.

* * *

Riette watched in horror as Emmet triggered some kind of reaction at the altar. He'd been right all along. She had doubted him but he'd known. Each realization made Riette feel worse. Her brother had gifts, and she had purposefully overlooked them. Now she saw him through new eyes, even while trying to figure out how to save him. Slipping under the table, she followed the same path he'd taken and grabbed him by the jacket while the rest of the people in the room focused on the altar. He did not resist; instead, he followed her back to where they had been standing.

Feeling impotent and afraid, all Riette could think of to do was stand still and pretend nothing had happened. It was a stupid plan, which made her furious with herself. Tears would not be contained, making her even angrier.

"I'm sorry," Tuck said.

Riette glared at him, filled with rage. He recoiled. She was proud of herself for not speaking. Had she done so, someone would surely have noticed how extensive her vocabulary was. Instead, the altar's contents entranced them. Riette couldn't see from where she stood, and her imagination reeled with possibilities. General Katch had one of his men retrieve an item from within the altar, and everyone held their breath when he reached inside, hoping the tales of treasure guarded with traps were not true in this case.

Perhaps the key had disarmed any traps or none had ever existed, but the man pulled his hand free to a chorus of relief. A small wooden box covered in gold filigree rested in his palm, and at the general's nod, he opened the serpent-shaped clasp. Riette stood on her toes, trying to get a look at what was inside, but her view was blocked. Eventually she was able to glimpse a pair of clear gemstones. One was clear, at least. The other was streaked with white.

"Cache stones," Al'Drakon said with a hint of reverence. He did not admit Barabas had brought something of real value, but he did take a long look at Emmet. It made Riette shiver. So many emotions and so much stress ran through her, she thought she might crack.

This was not the first time she and Emmet had faced death, and she squeezed his hand in reassurance. He had a glazed look in his eyes, and she wasn't certain he could hear her at the moment, but she knew he was in there. He'd always been there. It had been impossible for Riette to understand why he did some of the things he did. His actions and words had made her life difficult at times, and she had resented that, but now she felt a great deal more. It went so much deeper. He was her brother, and she needed to help him. All his ramblings about magic had been real. Finally she knew what she had to do. Her purpose was clear. She would find a way to get him whatever magic he needed.

"Now let us go," she said loudly and in her firmest tone. "My brother has given you a tremendous gift, and now all we ask is that you *let us go*."

"You'll be on a flight once the fog lifts in the morning," General Katch said, and no one dared say otherwise. "Take them to guest suites, and see to their needs," the general said to his guards, and the men led Riette, Emmet, Tuck, and Barabas from the room. Every turn made Riette feel more like she was trapped, as if she were being taken deeper into a stone prison.

Guards stood watch at each junction. Sneaking out of the hold would be impossible. Even if it were possible, they wouldn't be able to just board a dragon or plane and fly away. Never had she felt so confined and powerless. Emmet, on the other hand, was unafraid. She took strength from his walking calmly beside her, as if taking a stroll through the park.

When the guards stopped before ornate double doors, Riette felt a little safer given the luxury of the accommodations. Steaming baths had already been drawn in stone basins fed by channels cut through solid rock. The place was a marvel, and not all of it was hard and cold. The carpets here were plush and soft. Sleeping pillows of such size and depth Riette had never seen before and the sheets adorning them called to her. Toward the back of the hall was a private chamber, complete with baths and pillow beds . . . and a door. Riette wasted no time claiming the room for her and Emmet, and to her surprise, no one argued.

Not long after she settled into a bath, a knock came at the door. "Some refreshment for the lady and her brother."

Hearing a female voice, Riette allowed the woman to enter. She was so glad she did. The woman had a kind look about her, and she carried a tray laden with the most delightful-looking morsels. Without saying a word, she put down the tray, bowed her head, and left. Riette and Emmet shared the feast until only a few crumbs remained on the tray. Riette didn't know the name of the tangy sparkling drink, but she couldn't get enough. When that, too, was gone, she could no longer keep her eyes open. The rush of the day's events had passed, and now she felt drained. The pillows embraced her like a long-lost friend, and Riette slept.

* * *

"Do not scold me," General Katch said.

Al'Drakon stared back, implacable. "Then do not do so to me. We've both done what we thought was right." Silence was agreement enough. "I don't like Barabas DeGuiere, but he may have at last done his duty. While it does not forgive his past crimes, I must acknowledge what he's done."

"It's not enough," the general said. "Even if we send our full strength, that little bit of magic will not be enough to conquer someone who's been stockpiling artifacts for years."

"Stockpiling," Al'Drakon said. "All that magic in one place. All we would need is a trigger . . . and to know where exactly the stockpiles are."

"You can't think to take the child into battle!"

"The kid dies either way. My way is just faster," Al'Drakon said. "You think me harsh and crass, but which is better, to leave the boy to starve or to give him a chance at being the greatest hero his people have ever known?"

General Katch rubbed his temples. His life had been reduced to impossible choices. Almost every path led to utter chaos and destruction. No one would win this war. Argus Kind failed to see he was destroying the things he coveted. By conquering the Heights and the Midlands and even all the Jaga, for what the swamp was worth, he rendered it a shell of its former self. Such a waste.

The Midlands were indefensible from naval air strikes. It was a painful truth that gave the general shivers. Never had he thought Zjhon aircraft capable of reaching the Mids, let alone being able to refuel and return. Once they took over the western airfields, only the Heights would remain free, and they were already prisoners within the hollowed mountains.

"What other choice do we have?" asked Al'Drakon.

"I don't like it," the general reiterated.

"I don't like any of this, but if there's even a fraction of a chance we can win this war, then I'm acting on it."

"I won't stand in your way," the general said with a deep sigh.

"That's all the help I need."

"I know," General Katch said. He watched the dragon rider go with deep resignation and overwhelming regret. He was a better man than this. They were better people. But desperate people did things of which they would never have dreamed themselves capable.

Even if the man were correct and succeeded in his audacious plan, it would hardly secure victory. The Zjhon had used very little magic in the war—a war they were clearly winning. If the Drakon failed to destroy all the magic, would the executioner-made-king lash out with every weapon remaining to him? It was a frightening thought. Without the Drakon, the Heights would fall more quickly. After that, not much mattered.

With few choices remaining, General Katch grimly orchestrated final defenses.

* * *

Shadows stirred in the darkness, silent but undeniable. Emmet watched a muscular man approach from the direction of what had previously appeared to be solid stone, but the illusion had been destroyed. Riette snored loudly from nearby, masking any noises Al'Drakon might have made. She was so peaceful in that moment, and Emmet was happy for her. This was how he wanted to remember her.

Knowing what was coming, he hoped life for her would be easier without him, even though he knew it wasn't true. To make a sound was to wake Riette and most likely result in her death; she would never let him go without a fight, even one she knew she couldn't win. Emmet could not have that on his conscience. Riette meant everything to him. She'd done for him things no one else would have or could have done. She had endured more than any one person should ever have to.

Dressed in full battle gear, Al'Drakon smiled at Emmet. Somehow they had an understanding. Emmet would help them save the world, and they would be nice to his sister. It was enough. Emmet put on his boots and gathered his things in silence.

The warrior's expression showed both respect and surprise. In the end, he held out his oversized, calloused hand. Emmet took it and quietly walked alongside him. A final glance back to Riette left him with a quivering lip and tears in his eyes. The dragon rider let go of his hand and patted him on the back.

Now that the decision was made and their escape nearly complete, Emmet wanted to get on with it. He understood what they needed of him. He was the child who could sense magic. They wanted him to find magic. It was the one thing he did well.

Most conversations held in his presence operated under the assumption that he did not listen, pay attention, or understand, but he heard everything—experienced everything. Sometimes it was too much, and he wished to forget, but he could not. The bright side was that he was almost always underestimated, and he knew how to use that to his advantage—sometimes. In this case, the fate of everything he knew rested on him and the Drakon. The thought made him feel small and woefully insufficient. To ride with the legendary dragon fighting force was something of which most kids in the Midlands dreamed, but now Emmet Pickette was afraid.

The tunnel ended in a place like nothing he had ever seen. A giant cave opened into the night sky. Stalactites hung down from high above. The cavern floor was mostly smooth except for occasional stalagmite clusters polished into swirling spirals. From one wall, moss crept, slowly taking over. Covered in green, a face carved into the stone spewed clear water from its mouth. A pool formed below, ringed with equally moss-covered stones.

If not for other amazing sights, Emmet might have strayed—the urge to explore was strong. The dragons awaiting them resembled Dashiq except they were bigger and less friendly. They wore saddles similar to what Barabas and Tuck rode in, but there was no buggy strapped to the dragon behind those saddles. Emmet was a little disappointed. These dragons carried a cargo of compressed air and munitions. Emmet presumed there were snacks hidden in there somewhere. He had a few strips of dried meat and some hard cheese but little else. He'd be of little use to these men dead, and he assumed the problem would solve itself.

"Dragon!" Emmet said loudly, his voice echoing through the cavern. By the time Emmet experienced the thought, he knew what Al'Drakon would say.

"Be quiet," the warrior whispered in a growl.

After being strapped in, Emmet didn't have to wait long. The dragon took three steps before launching into the darkness. Fires dotted the landscape below, showing just how close the enemy had come. The large dragon turned away from the lights and soared through darkness like a shadow on the wind.

"What's his name?" Emmet asked while chewing on goodies he'd found in his saddlebags.

"Berigor."

* * *

For the first time in a long time, Riette awoke feeling refreshed. Part of her felt the urge to wake up and mind her responsibilities, but she was so comfortable. The pillow bed promised to cradle her for hours to come. The silence coaxed her back to the place between sleeping and dreaming. Whispers and the smell of food tickled her senses, but still she slept. When finally she did wake, the meal had gone cold. Riette's brain was finding it difficult to keep up. Ravenous, she consumed the food before realizing Emmet's bed was empty. For half a second, she thought he might have wandered off, but then she remembered where she was. All the comfort was gone like being dunked in cold water.

"Barabas!" she shouted. "He's gone! You monster, he's gone!"

Tuck arrived a moment later, his face a mask of shock and horror.

When Barabas came into the room, Riette threw the food tray at him. He was no more or less happy than usual. "Hush," he said. "We've got to go after your brother."

"What do you mean, 'go after'?"

"Emmet has left for the Firstland with Al'Drakon," Barabas said.

Tuck remained speechless, looking shocked.

"How could you let him go?"

"I did not know," Barabas said.

"Liar!"

The man nodded and accepted the accusation. "I'm going to find your brother. Do you want to come?"

How could she trust him? Why would she trust him? Because he was the only friend she had. Because no one else here had reason to do anything for her, let alone try to rescue her brother. Whether his words were true or not, Riette reasoned she had no other choice but to accept his help. In the end, if she had to choose based on trust, it would be an easy decision.

When Commander Gerrig arrived, Riette wordlessly turned her anger on him.

"I am very sorry about your brother," he said. "I did not know."

It was a common refrain, and she trusted him no more than she trusted Barabas. She no longer identified Barabas as "the captain." Now she knew who he was deep down: Barabas DeGuiere—traitor.

Commander Gerrig walked to the sleeping chamber she had shared with Emmet, the one she'd chosen because it had seemed like the safest choice. In the back wall, he slid open a secret entrance. The stone was real, but clever engineering allowed it to move as if floating.

Anger and resentment flooded Riette's being. This was how Emmet had been taken from her, but then she also realized her brother must have gone either willingly or by extreme measures. He had not tried to wake her, and she had to cope with not knowing what really happened. Somehow she knew he had gone of his own accord, a brave and noble fool. Feeling like a complete dolt, she followed Barabas through the same halls Emmet had used during his escape, feeling betrayed, abused, and unloved. A hand landed on her shoulder.

"I'm sorry," Tuck said.

"Get your hands off me, and don't ever touch me again," Riette said. She did not realize the extra insult until after she'd said the words and she continued. "You knew. You *knew*. You are not my friend."

The words took their toll. Tuck backed away, giving Riette at least some of the space she desired. He deserved it—every word—yet she felt bad for hurting his feelings. What madness had she contracted to be so conflicted about a single person? He was cruel and unforgivably dishonest, yet he had saved her life. He'd been nicer to her than even Brick had ever been. The thought made her shed a tear on her friend's behalf, no matter what had become of him. The way she had left wasn't something of which she was proud.

When they reached a natural orifice in the mountainside, dawn's first blush colored the horizon. A cool breeze whispered of spring, and the world below was blanketed in fog, some of which glowed from within or was burned away completely by massive fires.

"If you fly into the rising sun, you'll have the best chance of avoiding pursuit," Commander Gerrig said, "from either side of the war. No guarantees, though."

His words were chilling. Barabas was so unpopular, he was unwelcome everywhere. In some ways, she pitied the man. It didn't take long to get everyone strapped in, and Commander Gerrig wasted no time in going back the way he'd come. Dashiq did not bother to run; instead, she simply fell from the Heights. Riding the currents above the tree line, she made the act of departing quietly all but impossible. Gritting her teeth was the only way Riette kept from screaming, and she just managed, though her jaws ached. Flying into the sunrise was unpleasant. Crouching low, Riette hid from the intense light.

Few words were said for the rest of the day. Riette did her best to sort through a barrage of feelings. Through that reckoning, no one emerged unscathed, her outlook gloomy. When a stark white line of rock, looking lifeless and sun bleached, appeared in the waters ahead, Riette could think of few less appealing places to take a walk. Even with that in mind, the thought of stretching her aching legs and back was still attractive.

As they drew closer, a few signs of life were apparent. The land had strange trees with domes of hearty leaves atop a myriad of arrow-straight branches sprouting from equally straight trunks. Each one bore scars, though—some fresh, some old. Claw marks raked the white bark, fresh red sap flowing from the more recent wounds. Once they had disembarked, Dashiq went straight to the trees. She was the only one Riette trusted. A dragon could not know the crimes of men, and she had always done her best to keep Riette and Emmet safe. But now Emmet was gone. It was a circular thought pattern, one that brought anger and guilt. She was supposed to have protected her brother, and others had betrayed them both. Trying to chase the thoughts away, she took a much-needed walk.

"Dragon's blood trees," Tuck said from nearby.

"Oh," Riette said, not meeting his gaze.

"The dragons like the sap and use their claws to mark their territory."

"Mm-hmm," Riette said, not looking at him.

"Aw, come on," Tuck said. "You know you're interested. You're just pretending not to be because you're mad at me."

"Mm-hmm."

"Well, I never meant you no harm, and I might've saved your life a time or two, so I think you should forgive me."

"Mm-hmm."

"I didn't know this thing with Emmet would happen," Tuck said with what appeared to be sincerity. "The cap'n didn't neither."

"He doesn't seem to have many friends, this captain of yours," Riette said, not caring if he heard her or not. "Do you ever wonder why that is? Perhaps it's because he's a bumbling idiot."

"Just because he talks funny don't mean he's stupid," Tuck said. "Just like your brother ain't as stupid as you think."

"Don't you use my brother against me!"

"Sorry," Tuck said.

"You say that a lot, you know. Ever wonder why that is?" Tuck did not meet her eyes. "It's because you're a jerk."

"I deserved that one," Tuck said.

"And a lot more."

"And a lot more," he conceded with a sigh. "I didn't mean nothing."

"Anything."

"What?"

"You didn't mean *anything*," she said, no longer able to resist.

Tuck just shrugged and handed her a cask of wine, which did not hurt his chances for forgiveness. "Don't worry. The gods are with us."

"They are?" Riette asked. "I sure haven't seen them around."

"Ah, but you've seen magic," Tuck said. "And magic is of the gods." He held his hands in the air in a dramatic gesture.

"I've seen tricks and chemistry but not so much magic."

"You sure about that?" Tuck asked, looking sideways at Dashiq. The copper bridgework reconstructing her face was scratched and dented but nonetheless magical. The glass eye remained intact, though it lacked the life seen in her remaining eye. The old dragon chewed the red, sappy wood with one side of her mouth, which was clearly not the natural order, but she managed to squeeze out some of the desired nutrients and medicinal properties Tuck droned on and on about.

Barabas signaled them to load up, already knowing Al'Drakon and the others had stopped there. Fresh claw marks on almost every tree were both evidence of their passing and a not-so-subtle message to Barabas—or perhaps more accurately, Dashiq. The dragon took it upon herself to leave a response. Riette could not imagine how the other dragons would interpret it or even how they felt about Dashiq at all. Were politics and rivalry purely human? Riette suspected not.

"I'm still angry with you," Riette said to Barabas before climbing back aboard. He nodded in acceptance and said nothing while helping her up. Tuck followed and made certain her straps were tight. It was among the reasons Riette couldn't doubt his sincerity in wanting to protect her, but she didn't always trust what he thought was right for her, and that was the rub. It continued to chafe as the journey wore on, always one step behind the Drakon—and her brother.

CHAPTER TEN

I do not loath magic. I detest power in the hands of others.
—Argus Kind, usurper king of the Zjhon

* * *

Deacon Rex would complain about his circumstances, but at least he was alone. Casta Mett and the others could tear each other to pieces for all he cared, so long as they left him out of it. Already he'd planted carefully crafted doubts in the king's mind with regard to each of his esteemed colleagues. Casta Mett was hiding things and was fool enough to think no one would notice. He didn't have to be able to sense magic to know when someone was hiding something. It was a skill he'd relied on his entire life. Argus Kind had unlocked what magic Deacon Rex possessed, and he would be forever grateful.

He had been successful in the past, but nothing to match being Al'Zjhon. The ability to access magic coupled with an ample supply of something normally so rare, Deacon Rex was a formidable man. The skills developed by thieves and assassins largely overlapped, and those same skills applied to treasure hunting. Deacon Rex had never been one to specialize. Look at how well that was working out for Casta Mett.

Moving through the jungle was not something at which he was practiced or skilled, however. At least for the moment he could simply row his way toward the west, following narrow channels meandering through lush, green swamp.

Knowing what created the channels made Deacon nervous. If he went into the water with a swamp pig, he wasn't likely to come back out. The huge creatures appeared lazy and slow when wallowing in mud but were far faster than they appeared. Thus far, Deacon had not seen a single one. The evidence didn't lie. They had been here.

Worse was yet to come. He'd flown over the swamp and was aware of what he was doing. Not for the first time, he cursed himself for a fool. He'd chosen the most difficult mission of all just to get away from a woman. Perhaps she had won after all.

A deep squealing erupted from the water ahead. Deacon Rex watched the swamp pig emerge from the depths right in front of him. Using his oar to slow his lightweight canoe, he prayed he would see the back end of a swamp pig and not the front. The creatures were known to charge anything that challenged them. His luck held but would be tested again soon. Already foulness filled the air. Even if the vegetation here had not yet succumbed to the creeping wrongness dominating the swamp, it would soon. It was inevitable.

It took a brave fool to seek magic within the swamp, but he would not be alone. The people of the Heights and Midlands knew they were doomed. Why not risk a few lives to see what twisted magic rules the swamp? Deacon hoped to get there first. It was unlikely he'd be able to retrieve an object powerful enough to corrupt a third of a continent, but if he found something, he would return with larger numbers.

Within the rotting swamp, Deacon was drawn ever on. The place called to him in a way no other magic ever had. Argus Kind had unlocked his magic by allowing him to touch an object of immense power, Azzakkan's Eye, but never had Deacon sensed power over a distance. This place reeked of twisted, corrupted magic that seeped into his bones until he thought the stench might never come out. Deeper he went, driven now by the need to see the power calling him. His innate ability to squeeze through tight places served him well.

Days and nights passed, but he could not say how many. The swamp had become a part of him, and he, a part of the swamp. It leached into him and might never let him leave. Only the magic he carried kept him from falling into the abyss. While the quagmire tugged at his sanity, he rubbed his thumbs over pure, unadulterated power—a gift from Argus Kind. Most of the time, he kept it hidden; it drew the shadows.

After what felt like weeks traveling on foot, Deacon Rex found himself staring into a dark green meadow, sharp-tipped saw grass promising a toll of blood. Beyond, though, waited a low but sprawling outcropping of black crystal. It looked like one giant crystal with just the very tip showing. It was not just something he surmised. Power reached deep into the land. It pulled on him so strongly, he worried his eyes might be sucked from his head. Whispers of madness spoke of twisted sentience. Tearing himself away, he realized this was far beyond anything he'd ever imagined. Above the stone, wild dragons flew in lazy circles. No wonder no one else had harnessed this magic. One might as well lasso the sun. Now he understood why no domestic dragon would dare come anywhere near.

Deacon Rex was going to need a better plan—a much better plan.

Leaving proved far more difficult than getting in. He'd been drawn by magic, almost as if in a trance. Moving away from that same magic, every step was a struggle. The swamp turned on him—not that it had ever been friendly. Now, though, safe, dry passage was twice as difficult to find. Having been graced with a colorful vocabulary, he honed his cursing skills. Deep into a particularly salty tirade, he suddenly froze, uttering not a single additional word. Before him, golden eyes with pupils like oblong slits watched through the vines and focused on him.

Reaching for his bag, Deacon Rex hoped Argus Kind's gift would be enough.

* * *

The Firstland rose up from the sea like a lingering cloud bank that later solidified into dry land. Berigor flew along a narrow valley lined with giant carvings of male warriors. A pair of statues protruded from the valley walls and crossed swords over the river, each with an arm in the water. Swirling eddies surrounded the massive statues, and Emmet was glad they weren't on a seafaring vessel. When the dragon flew beneath the crossed swords, one of which had long since lost its tip, Emmet held his breath, fearing he would be dashed upon the ancient carvings.

No one made a sound. Al'Drakon rode before him, fiercely concentrating on the way ahead, planning their every move. Alongside them flew Ariodarch, Tarin and Dosser on his back. The other dragon was smaller than Berigor and bore deep scars. These were battle dragons, Emmet reminded himself. He hoped never to witness dragons fighting. Flying to war upon one made that unlikely. Still, if this were to work, it would be a surprise attack. Everyone on this mission was there for a reason. Al'Drakon would have come alone, but Tarin and Dosser had insisted he would be unable to subdue all the guards and protect Emmet at the same time. Thus it had been decided.

Emmet understood enough to be afraid. They were flying into enemy territory, searching for the largest collection of magic items known to exist in the world. The thrill of getting to locate that much magic made Emmet giddy, and he had difficulty spending more than a moment considering the rest of the situation. Already the magic called to him. Time skipped a beat, and he hoped it would not compress. This was no time for an episode.

When the tip of a hollowed-out mountain became visible, both dragons dipped low and landed along a rocky shoreline. Too much daylight remained. Al'Drakon dismounted, reached up to grab Emmet, and helped him down. Nightfall approached but the outline of the mountain was still visible. Al'Drakon led Emmet farther along the valley floor until much more of the mountain could be seen. For Emmet, nothing else existed. The place radiated magic on a gigantic scale, and he was overcome. For so much of his life, he had sought out any morsel of magic. He would have been so happy with some little sliver of energy, some mere spark, and here was a conflagration like a land-bound star.

"Do you see it?" Al'Drakon asked in a whisper.

Emmet almost laughed but instead nodded and pointed.

Al'Drakon used a stick to draw the mountain with its many entranceways and zigzagging stairways. Emmet pointed to one doorway in particular, fourth down and third in from the west. Others also shone, but none so brightly as that one. Emmet held his hands out wide. Pointing to the other doorways, he held his hands closer together to indicate less bright. They would have stayed longer, but aircraft overhead sent them scrambling for cover. There was no way to know if they had been seen. All they could do was hope for the best, which was unnerving. It made the wait for the dead of the night even more painful. When at last the rest of the world slept, Al'Drakon roused Emmet and asked him if he was ready. Emmet nodded. He'd always been ready for this.

Berigor moved with quiet strength, allowing Al'Drakon and Emmet to mount. Creaking leather and the wind catching the dragon's wings were the only evidence of their passing. Ariodarch flew in Berigor's shadow, low and silent. When the valley opened and the entire hollow mountain became visible, the scale of what they were taking on was apparent. An even larger mountain loomed in the background but was not their destination. Moonlight left the mountains in stark relief, the ramparts and stairs on the nearest shining blue. Unlike the Heights, this mountain appeared to have been hollowed out by man, either that or much smaller dragons. Even if it had once been inhabited by dragons, none remained. Argus Kind hated dragons.

Berigor used their speed to scale the mountain, hugging close to one of the stairways. Ariodarch mirrored this approach on the neighboring stair. When they reached the fourth entrance down and third in from the west, both dragons landed atop the stairs, doing their best to remain silent, though it sounded like a great echoing commotion to Emmet. No matter how excited he was about the magic flowing from the doorway, the sense of danger was inescapable. Al'Drakon dismounted and helped Emmet down, this time placing the boy directly beside him. Tarin and Dosser slid down from Ariodarch, flanking Al'Drakon and Emmet. The dragons regained the skies with barely a sound.

Along with the magic overwhelming Emmet's other senses, lanterns glowed brightly within. Guards flanked two doorways.

Using blunt, thrown weapons, Tarin and Dosser both cast two attacks at once. All but one guard were struck unconscious by the initial attacks, and he soon joined the others. These guards had been half asleep; no one had yet raised an alarm. Deeper into the mountain they went, following Emmet's direction. Al'Drakon did not argue or hesitate; he simply moved forward with an outrageous sense of confidence.

Could nothing stop this man?

Another pair of guards was subdued without incident. Emmet was amazed how easy it was to penetrate the Zjhon defenses until he stepped into the magic room. "Wow," he said. *"Magic."* When the thought hit him an instant later, Emmet could not believe any words had left his lips at such a crucial time. Four guards appeared from within a museum of magical artifacts. Glassy orbs and staves immediately caught Emmet's attention, but there were also bowlike weapons and behind them a gleaming saddle that looked the right size to fit Dashiq. Al'Drakon intercepted one guard who moved to yank on a rope hanging from the ceiling. Tarin launched more blunt weapons, but these people were more alert and prepared for a fight. At the same time, two men closed on Dosser and another grabbed Al'Drakon from behind.

Emmet meant these people no harm, and he cringed at the thought of hurting even those who fought against the Drakon. When the alarm sounded, it was clear at least some of those who'd been subdued were now coming to. Al'Drakon had the wooden box in his hands, but the stones were still inside. He should have taken them out sooner. Emmet, on the other hand, stroked a clear stone. Though rough cut, its surface was smooth as silk. No one had seen him take it from the cache in the Heights. The memory was almost enough to make him smile if not for also being sad. He missed Riette.

In spite of all that, he chose to focus on the positive. Never before had he known such power and magic, and he was giddy with it. Rubbing the cool stone with his thumb, he leaned into time. It stretched. As if by his command, the world slowed around him. The harder he tried, the more slowly it moved. It gave him time to think, time to move, time to act. For so much of his life, time had been his enemy, and now for once he possessed the ability to use it as a tool. He understood why Argus Kind hoarded the magic. Who would not desire such a wondrous collection? His methods for acquiring many pieces could be called into question, but that seemed far away at the moment.

Even with time slowed, Emmet felt the magic intensely. The thought of destroying it all made him sick, but some part of him understood why. Seeing Al'Drakon about to go down under two guards and bright lights now shining into the room, Emmet hurried. Magic flowing into his body from the stone. He continued stretching time while orchestrating their escape. Flinging glass spheres into the air was just the first part of his attack. A stave knocked over here and a bowlike weapon fired there, a kick to the knee one long instant, a shove the next. Sirens wailed and the keep awoke. Emmet looked back at the Drakon, who fought in slow motion. For an instant he wished he could move them through time with him, but then he considered the consequences of inflicting others with his condition. He wouldn't wish it on anyone. Even with all this magic, he was still out of synchronization with the rest of the world. And now he was destroying it all, knowing he might never again get the opportunity to unlock the mystery of his craving for magic. Already he knew he would not be satisfied. All the power in the world was useless absent the knowledge of what to do with it. That thought brought him to tears.

The Drakon finally turned the corner, and Emmet did everything he could to disrupt those rushing into the main hall in various states of undress. Racing to each searchlight, Emmet aimed them strategically, blinding the Zjhon. More lights combed the skies outside, crisscrossing and searching. Emmet thought he saw a shadow move through the searchlights. Heavy weapons fired. He could only hope the dragons would survive and return in time.

The first flash did not seem real, but the following thump set Emmet's teeth on edge. The chain reaction he had started now cascaded. Al'Drakon and his men did not move quickly enough. Emmet looked down at his palm, at the now milky stone streaked with white. He understood what it meant, but no time remained. The irony was not lost on him.

Using every bit of magic at his disposal, Emmet drew the Drakon to him, not physically but vibrationally—just a little tug then a push. With that, the men sped through time, wise enough to take advantage of the situation and not question it. Perhaps they had experienced something similar in battle, but Emmet doubted it had ever been this extreme. Even for him, this stretched time to its limits—or *his* limits, as the case may be.

When they reached the ledge, the dragons weren't there. Time had run out. Multiple air cannons turned toward Emmet and company, ready to blast them into the air. Emmet jumped.

Berigor and Ariodarch fought to get closer but were taking fire. It was already too late. Time retracted with sudden ferocity and he fell. The rough-cut magic stone he held grew hot, chalky, and rough while he slowed his fall with magic. After a final crack, the stone shattered and was sucked away by the wind, broken down into naught but white dust.

* * *

Soaring low over the valley floor, twisting and turning amid structures both natural and man made, Dashiq flew. Lights flooded the night skies. A pair of dragons took heavy fire, able to dodge most but not all of it. This was among the oldest cities in the world, and it was defended by the latest technology, which prevented the dragons from getting close to the city of Ri. Though their planes remained grounded, balloons and airships also made their way into the sky. Riette held on tightly.

Flapping her wings and using every muscle to propel them forward, Dashiq gave an effort born of desperation. A cry escaped the dragon when a bright light flashed above, making the searchlights seem like mere candles.

A wave of energy raced toward them, the world shimmering and shifting beneath it. Into the night flew three figures. When the shock wave hit, Dashiq somehow used the energy to send them skyward in a rush of rumbling wind. Screaming filled the air and was overshadowed by an even brighter flash. Drowning out all other sound, the mountain split and shifted. It did not come tumbling down, but the stairways and facades were irreparably damaged. The interior spaces couldn't have fared much better.

The screams grew louder in the wake of the second blast. Emmet's ended abruptly when he struck the back of the seat. It took a moment for him and Riette to recover enough and think to get him strapped in. Al'Drakon struck the carriage before Emmet was secure. Bits of wood and fabric broke off, torn away by the racing wind. Another man fell past them while Dashiq continued to climb. Though he missed the carriage completely, a muted thud sounded a moment later accompanied by a loud grunt.

Racing past the openings in the mountain, they made a difficult target for the remaining defenses. Airships filled the skies but did not fire toward the mountain. When Dashiq cleared the peak and tried to escape, they would be subject to overwhelming fire. The dragon must have known this, for she executed a sharp turn.

Riette was unsure how she could have known, but Dashiq turned right in front of a man who could be none other than Argus Kind. In one hand he held an object that glowed like fire even to Riette's vision. She couldn't imagine what it must look like to Emmet. It was still so hard to believe he possessed such a skill, yet clearly he did.

"Kill them all!" the enormous, muscle-bound man shouted before leveling a bowlike weapon at them. A burst of fire raced toward the carriage. From within his pack, Al'Drakon removed the pocked sky stone. His instincts proved invaluable. The fiery column bent and changed direction enough to strike the stone instead of Emmet. Though it glowed within his grasp, the strange object absorbed the attack.

"You will pay for this! Your people will pay for this!" Argus Kind's words came out strangled and ever higher in pitch. There was something in his reaction that went beyond the fury over being attacked. Was it recognition?

He was correct, though, about a price to be paid. Trying to do too many things at once, Al'Drakon failed to maintain a tight enough grip on the sky stone. The force of the attack sent it tumbling from his hands. So much had gone into keeping the object out of Argus Kind's possession, Riette watched it fall with deep regret.

Dashiq soared back down into the valley, over the shops and homes those above would be loath to destroy. Fighting still took place on the mountain, and Riette guessed the remaining Drakon were keeping the airships occupied.

Al'Drakon finally managed to get himself strapped in, and he held on to Emmet in a great bear hug. Looking back, where once the rear of the carriage had been, she saw only Dashiq's tail, Tarin wrapped around it, holding on for his life.

"This carriage is terrible," Al'Drakon said. "Give me a saddle any day."

"It beats riding in the box," Riette said with a shrug.

When the sea came back into view, the sun had just peeked above the horizon. Soon airplanes would take to the skies, and the open air would be far too dangerous.

Emmet pointed to the tallest peaks, "Magic."

Even atop a dragon, it was a near impossible place to go. He might as well have pointed at the moon. Few other choices remained. They could hide in the jungle, but those places were themselves dangerous and easily scoured from airship and balloon. Only a crazy person would try to fly through the peaks Emmet had indicated. Yet that was where Dashiq headed.

Riette had begun to wonder just how much control Barabas had over their destination. It seemed more like the dragon decided where she wanted to go and Barabas pretended it was his decision. Either way, Riette was powerless. Her pulse quickened with each breath. As they rose higher, the battle above the mountain fortress became visible once again. Lights still illuminated the fading darkness, but diesel engines were audible in the distance.

Two airships collided and took out a balloon, all of which caught fire and crashed into the valley below. When a dragon appeared from beneath and leaped free of the wreckage just before it struck the cold stone, it was clear what had caused the crash. Dragons, too, fell. Few remained. Still Dashiq climbed.

When the first diesel props knifed through the air, casting throaty echoes into the canyons, the dragons dispersed. Riette couldn't say if anyone had seen the lone dragon flying into the peaks, but the height was now dizzying.

"It's too much," Al'Drakon said.

Barabas held up his hand in a fist. "My dragon. My rules."

Al'Drakon said no more. He, especially, understood the life-or-death nature of their situation. The dragon pushed herself to her very limits, and everyone knew there was a chance she might push too hard or too far. Their lives depended on the strength and valor of a retired battle dragon, and she showed there was life in her yet.

Grunting with effort, Dashiq cleared a ring of jagged stone peaks to reveal a stunning view. The valley below was shallow, a mere impression amid the towering peaks, but here were ancient ruins constructed in similar ways to the columns in the shallows. Translucent green stone pillars glowed in the growing daylight. Cavelike entranceways surrounded the inner sanctum, rounded and smoothed from perhaps ages of use. A black stone larger than an airship dominated the center of the sanctum. Like an extension of the mountain itself, it issued a deep current of energy that gushed from the heart of the land like a mystical font. Even the grasses that grew around the mighty stone were short and neat, forming clean lines and edges. Regardless of how strange the place might be, it radiated a welcoming aura.

Dashiq turned three lazy circles over the black stone before coming to hover over it, suspended by tricks in the air currents and perhaps magic. It seemed strange to Riette to know mystical energies were real. Always she had rejected the notion such objects of power truly existed or might somehow help her brother. The last part came with a sting of guilt. She had not paid enough attention to his words. Because he had difficulty communicating, she had disregarded the only communication he'd been able to manage. It shamed her.

Now, though, she understood, and there wasn't much she wouldn't do to help her brother find whatever it was he needed. Even with the challenges he faced, her brother had done amazing things. How could she not try to have just as much impact on her world? Even so, Emmet and Al'Drakon's effort had not been enough. Clearly Argus Kind wasn't killed in the attack. Much of his magical arsenal had been destroyed, but Riette knew almost no magic had been used in the conquest of the Heights and the Midlands. Now Argus Kind would be furious, and there were bound to be consequences.

Barabas disembarked first and helped Tuck down. Even they were awestruck. Al'Drakon went next, carrying Emmet with him. Riette almost resented the act, but her brother was perfectly at home with the warrior. Other than kidnapping him and carrying him into the most dangerous situation possible, it appeared the man had taken good care of her brother. Riette truly did not know what to think, so she climbed down without a word and took in the marvels surrounding her. The sense of history this place exuded was undeniable, and the land's power was so intense, even she felt it.

"I owe you a great debt," Al'Drakon said to Barabas.

"You owe me nothing."

"You owe *me* something," Riette said, and she approached Al'Drakon filled with righteous rage. "How *dare* you kidnap my brother and take him to war." Using her index finger, she poked him in the chest to make sure he understood just how angry she was.

"Your brother is a hero," he said.

"Well, good for him!" Riette said. "And I was left to think him dead. What gives you the right to do such a thing?"

Al'Drakon stared at her for a moment before responding. "Is a Zjhon fleet truly within striking distance of the Midlands?"

"Yes."

"Then your brother is already lost," Al'Drakon said.

Barabas grunted but said nothing.

"We did not win the war today. All we did was take away our enemy's favorite toy. We made him angry and he will lash out with all his remaining power, which is considerable. The Midlands will fall first, which will starve those in the Heights. It is inevitable."

"Then you risked all that for nothing?"

Barabas grunted again, perhaps even laughed. It was difficult to tell.

"A quick death is far better than to wait in fear and suffering," Al'Drakon said.

"Then it is a false victory," Riette said.

Barabas clapped for a moment. "The girl amuses me," he said. "A battle was won today, but we came here to finish the war."

"It's not your decision," Al'Drakon said. "You've done well and may truly have saved us all, but I do not follow you."

"Why do you hate him so much?" Riette asked, her index finger ready to poke.

The dragon rider gave her an unfriendly glare.

"It's because the captain ain't one of them," Tuck said.

Al'Drakon harrumphed.

"The captain, or should I say Barabas DeGuiere, Al'Drakon, the chosen of Dashiq, is an islander." Both men seemed uncomfortable, but Tuck continued his scolding. "And then when he and Dashiq were wounded not so far from here, they had a choice between death and using the last magic they possessed—the last known magic anyone other than Argus Kind possessed."

"Would they have died without using the magic?" Riette asked.

Neither man moved or spoke.

"The captain might have lived but not Dashiq. He'd likely have been captured or killed soon after," Tuck replied.

"He could have died with honor," Al'Drakon insisted.

"Maybe that's what he's doing now," Tuck said, his own emotions causing him to speak louder and higher in pitch. "He is not required to die on *your* preferred time line. And if he hadn't used the magic, Argus Kind would have it . . . and Dashiq would be dead . . . and so would you . . . and your friend Tarin over there too."

Silence hung for some time. Al'Drakon looked as if there were a war taking place inside him, but eventually he nodded. "I . . . was . . . wrong."

Never had Riette heard a more pained admission. Up until that moment, the man had clung to old hatred no matter the truth before him. It was easier to hate than forgive. He had taken over the position Barabas had once held, giving him plenty of opportunity to find fault with his predecessor—an outsider.

Riette was beginning to understand. "How did an islander become Al'Drakon?"

Both men looked at her as if to tell her she was nosy, but Tuck answered anyway. "Dashiq chose him. Al'Drakon is the person bonded to Al'Drak. If Al'Drakon is killed and Al'Drak remains alive, the dragon may choose. It can stay and select a new rider, or it can go and a new Al'Drak will emerge. Berigor was a clear choice for succession even then. But Dashiq decided to do things differently and flew off to the islands to find a gangly old man." This time it was Al'Drakon who laughed. "She brought him back to the Heights, kicking and screaming, hanging upside down from her claws. Then she deposited him on the airstrip and dared anyone to touch him. It must have been difficult to have Berigor assume the role of Al'Drak while Dashiq had been gone, only to have it taken away."

"I am sorry about that," Barabas said.

"It certainly wasn't your fault," Al'Drakon said and laughed. "You did come in upside down, as I recall. You may have taught this boy too well, you know."

At this, Barabas laughed and nodded. "It was not an easy time for any of us. I still don't know why she chose me."

The dragon eased over to him and nudged him with her jaw.

"She thinks you're cute," Tuck said.

The sound of diesel engines echoing in the valleys reminded of the danger. Though it seemed unlikely any aircraft would venture this high into the mountains, Barabas waved for them to inspect the cave entrances. Carrying the remaining lantern from the carriage, he selected one and walked in. Each was large enough to admit a full-sized dragon with room to spare, and Riette wondered just how large the dragons must have been to create such enormous structures. Even within, the walls were smooth and relatively free of dust and debris. A constant breeze moving through the cavern might have something to do with it.

"The Drakon will hide in the jungle until nightfall. After that, they'll fall back to the dragon's blood trees, and then back to the Heights to mount a final stand."

"And you want us to take you to the jungle?" Tuck asked.

"I don't know," the man admitted.

"That's the smartest thing I've ever heard you say," Barabas said.

"If you stay here," Tuck said. "You can help us finish what you started and take down Argus Kind. But your dragon might leave without you, and the Drakon might think you're dead and replace you. I'm betting that would suck."

Barabas gave Tuck a look that said he might have gone too far, but Al'Drakon just nodded. The sound of aircraft grew louder and louder until it was overwhelming. Riette reached the cavern entrance first, half expecting to see cannons aimed at her. Instead, she saw nothing. The peaks around them blocked much of the view, and Riette moved toward a low point.

Al'Drakon gave her a boost, and she climbed atop the mighty stone outcropping. From there she could see hundreds of aircraft launching at once. Row upon row of dirigibles, each heavy with its payload, just barely kept their cargo above the waves. Below most hung six-engine diesel props—bombers—suspended by heavy cables. Others carried entire squadrons of U-jets. The horror of what she saw temporarily overcame her fear of heights, though she stayed far from the edge.

Reaching down, Riette grudgingly helped Al'Drakon up. Barabas gave Tuck a boost. When she turned back again, the scale of the drop fully registered. It was as if she stood on the top of the world, which was now small and pointy. One false move, one misstep, and she would die a horrible death.

"There's nothing I can do," Al'Drakon admitted. "The Zjhon have supply lines and technology well beyond our reach. Once that many bombers and fighters are in range, they can take the airfields, if they haven't already. The Zjhon will control the skies and everything below."

"They might've left most folks alone, you know," Tuck said to Al'Drakon. "Sure, they would have taken out those in power, but what good is a nation of dead people? Better to keep them alive and paying taxes. But now you've gone and made the madman angry. Logic no longer applies."

"Thanks," Al'Drakon said.

"You're welcome," Tuck said. "What are you going to do about it?"

"I cannot stop them even with Berigor. I should have stolen more magic, something to use against them."

"Did you get anything?"

"There was no time. All I have are these." He pulled a small wooden box from his pocket and opened it. Inside rested two stones, one clear and one cloudy. "They won't be enough to turn the tide."

"But they may help us," Tuck said.

Al'Drakon nodded.

"Tonight we finish what we started," Tuck said.

Barabas inclined his head.

Al'Drakon bowed his head in acceptance. Was that a tear she saw falling from his chin?

"Anyone hear buzzing?" Tuck asked.

With the sounds of the air fleet diminishing, Riette did hear a more localized noise. Turning back from the dizzying view, she saw hornets the size of hummingbirds, and they didn't look happy.

CHAPTER ELEVEN

Winning by force is more costly than victory achieved through diplomacy and skill.
—Barabas DeGuiere, dragon rider

* * *

Getting away from the hornets unscathed had Riette's heart beating fast. Taking in her surroundings with greater care, she recognized a number of melon-sized paper nests. Hornets of such size would surely pack a powerful sting.

"We must warn the Heights!" Al'Drakon said while pulling at his beard.

"It won't do no good," Tuck said without humor. "They already know we're at war and that we've already lost."

Al'Drakon shook his head, refusing to believe the truth. "There must be a way to stop this madness!"

"Perhaps," Barabas said. "But we've a better chance of finding a way here. At the least, we should cut the head from the snake and remove Argus Kind from this world. Those who survive will at least thank us for that."

It was the most Riette had ever heard Barabas say, and his speech was marginally improved after recent use. If only he would speak more often, the effects might prove less debilitating. She didn't want to admit it might not get better but did anyway. Delusions had not served her; better to understand reality and act accordingly than to survive on unrealistic hopes. There was a place in her life for hope, but that place was small and thin at the moment.

"How do we attack a man who must now be on full alert?" Al'Drakon asked. "Only a fool would be complacent now."

"Maybe," Tarin said, joining them. "But you can only watch so many things at once. Especially if you just sent the bulk of your forces overseas."

"He won't have sent all the aircraft," Tuck added. "Open air in daylight will be a nightmare."

"With all the lights, nighttime won't be much better," Al'Drakon said.

"We should search the other caverns to see if there is anything that might be of use," Tarin added.

Barabas waved for them to go while he made his way back over to Dashiq. She floated above the black stone. He placed his hands on her side and closed his eyes. Riette wasn't certain what impact the act had, whether some energy passed between them or if he somehow healed the dragon with his own intentions, but she relaxed even further. Her chin turned slightly upward, and her hooded eyes fluttered.

Tuck inspected the carriage and clucked his tongue. Al'Drakon and

Tarin disappeared into one of the caverns. Emmet had moved alongside Barabas and laid his own hands on the dragon. Dashiq grew still and Riette didn't want to break the magical silence.

An occasional hornet flew past where she rested, and other insects crawled about. When air cannons erupted, no one was expecting it. They were yanked from their meditations and explorations. Tuck was the first to reach where Riette now stood. After giving him a boost to a spot away from any hornet nests, Riette had to wait in suspense.

"Oh no," Tuck said. "Berigor."

Al'Drakon heard his dragon's name and scrambled to reach the overlook. Riette extended her hand. Tarin grunted loudly while letting his leader climb on him. When he reached the top, Al'Drakon gasped but said nothing, which made Riette even more worried. Pulse jets now entered the valleys, their distinctive thumping sound resonating. More weapons fire followed. Jet engines passed overhead, and their roar grew softer. A moment later, Tuck and Al'Drakon dived from the overlook back into the valley. Claws scrabbled at the stone before digging deep. Berigor pulled himself over the promontory, and everyone within the small valley retreated. Berigor crashed into the space they had just vacated and let out a pitiful moan.

It did not require any knowledge of dragons or animals in general to know Berigor was severely wounded. No matter how nimble in the air, the valiant beast had taken repeated hits from heavy weapons. That kind of fire would have annihilated any man-made aircraft. For the moment, he remained alive. Al'Drakon ran back to his dragon, openly weeping. "You giant fool," he said. "You weren't supposed to come back for me. You were supposed to be marking dragon's blood trees right now."

He did not say the dragon would also have had an entire air fleet bearing down on him. Grief was more powerful than logic; his friend was dying. Riette had only come to see it during this journey. These people did not simply ride dragons; they were family to the creatures. There was love and respect between them and undying loyalty. It broke Riette's heart to watch someone lose the individual who meant the most to him; whether it be dragon or human, the feelings couldn't be all that different.

"I was wrong," Al'Drakon cried. "I'm sorry. I take it all back. I'm so sorry."

Barabas DeGuiere stood then. No more did he represent a traitor in Riette's mind. He was a complex and deeply private man, but she had come to see a hero's soul beneath his brusque personality. When he placed his hands on Al'Drakon's shoulders, the man sobbed. Riette didn't know what he said, but there seemed to come an agreement between them.

Dashiq glided to where Berigor lay. Slipping behind the larger dragon, she eased under his wing then under his torso. With a mighty grunt, she helped take the dragon's weight, and he moved slowly but steadily toward the ring of crystals. The closer they moved, the more powerful the updraft became. Soon the dragon supported his own weight with his outstretched wings, and Dashiq slipped out from under him.

Al'Drakon removed the small wooden box from his pocket and handed it to Barabas with tentative awe, a spark of hope visible in his eyes. Riette hoped Barabas truly did possess the magic to heal the noble beast. From within the compartments on Dashiq's saddle, Barabas withdrew two cloth-wrapped bundles. The first contained copper rods. The other he placed to one side, unopened.

Never had Riette truly seen magic in action, and she was fascinated. Barabas handed one of the stones from within the box to Emmet with some whispered words Riette could not hear. She supposed if he went to the trouble of whispering, the words weren't meant for her, but she hated not knowing.

After going over the dragon thoroughly, Barabas identified his most grievous wounds. On the dragon's side, he directed Al'Drakon to place his hands, close his eyes, and concentrate on sending healing energy to his loyal friend and companion. Barabas and Emmet focused their energy on the side of Berigor's face. Like Dashiq, Berigor had taken a hit where he was most vulnerable. The plates covering his torso distributed impacts over a much larger area, but a dragon's head and face were far more delicate.

Yellow and blue light leaked through Emmet's fingers, making Riette shade her eyes. If not for seeing it herself, she would never have believed. Even Barabas appeared surprised, watching how Emmet worked the copper with his hands and energy alone. Metal flowed like syrup, yet her brother was not burned. It took Barabas three tries to achieve the same effect, but soon they applied the metal directly to the dragon's wounded face, filling the gaps and fusing the remaining structure together. Where his eye had been, Barabas fashioned a socket. Precision and detail flowed from the man's mind, and Riette was impressed with his vision and craftsmanship. This was surely an uncommon skill.

Emmet focused on the teeth, bridging a gap in the jawline, he formed new teeth to match those remaining on the opposite side of Berigor's jaw, paying close attention to how the teeth interlocked with those in the bottom jaw. Over time, the dragon's face took shape once again. The metal glowed as if freshly polished. Dashiq's metalwork was pocked and aged in comparison.

After examining the stones he and Emmet held, Barabas nodded and moved to where Al'Drakon stood, eyes closed and meditating with all his might. Barabas spoke softly and the fierce warrior walked to Berigor's head. When he saw the metalwork, he wept once again. Riette suspected it was something few people ever witnessed. It reminded her even hardened soldiers were human. Her father had never been a fighting man before the war came; he and those like him were different. Riette had always hated those who started the wars and so callously sent regular people to their deaths. Now she had come to see some of the truth, and she wasn't certain how much more truth she wanted.

Barabas opened the bundle he'd set aside and pulled out three glass orbs. None were the size of a real dragon's eye, but they represented something important to a dragon: symmetry. "Azzakkan's Eye they're not," Barabas said. "But you may take the one you think best suits him."

Al'Drakon selected a glass sphere wordlessly and approached Berigor; the eye he'd selected closely matched the green flecks in the dragon's remaining eye. After laying one hand on Berigor's neck, he reached up and pressed in on the metal rim surrounding the empty eye socket. The segmented ring rotated outward, making the opening just a fraction larger. After placing the glass sphere into the socket and releasing it, the segmented ring retracted and held the sphere firmly in place. Somehow the eye followed him as he moved away.

"You have been too kind to me and to Berigor," Al'Drakon said, going to his knee. "I relinquish my title to you, Barabas DeGuiere. I am but Keldon Tallowborn."

"No," Barabas said. Keldon looked up at him. "I'm retired."

"You have an interesting way of spending your retirement," Al'Drakon Keldon Tallowborn said. "If we survive the next couple days, I might just join you."

"You might not have no choice," Tuck said. "If your brothers think you're dead, then surely you'll be replaced." The young man pretended no one glared at him.

"Do you think he'll live?" Al'Drakon asked, looking in that moment like a vulnerable little boy.

"For a time," Barabas said.

"It takes extra effort to keep them charged with energy," Tuck said.

Barabas nodded.

"Best not to travel too far from places like this," Tuck continued. "If you must, look for saltbark trees."

"Only ever found those in the shallows, and they don't produce leaves every year. A fickle hope."

"It's all we've got," Tuck said. "The dragon's blood trees help as well but are less potent. If you have magic . . ."

Emmet held out the two stones he carried. One was now completely opaque white, while on the other, a few clear streaks remained. Precious little magic. Reluctantly Emmet handed them back to Keldon, who placed them in the wooden box.

Needing rest, Riette moved just far enough into one of the caverns to be in the darkness. There, she propped herself up against the cold stone wall. Emmet followed and leaned up against her. Together they slept.

* * *

Riette woke with a start, thinking she heard a far-off boom, like thunder except it didn't come again. When she reached for him, Emmet was gone. In a panic, she rubbed her eyes and tried to find her brother. Stumbling back into the light, which was now fading to deep shades of purple, she found the carriage tossed to one side. Dashiq hovered over the black stone wearing only her war saddle, which had two seats.

"You weren't going to tell me, were you?" Riette asked, incensed. "You were just going to fly off with Tuck and leave us here?" The look on Tuck's face spoke for him. Emmet had his jacket buttoned and stood ready to mount. "Oh, no. Not again you're not. How could you think this in any way acceptable? How are you any better than—" She looked around. Berigor was gone. Al'Drakon and Tarin were gone. Barabas shrugged under her questioning gaze.

"They'll come back for us," Tuck said, not daring to meet Riette's glare.

"You knew they were going to leave without telling me," she said.

He averted his eyes.

Even though she knew he was torn between what Barabas wanted him to do and what she thought was only right, she fumed. Stealing her brother and using him like some tool of war certainly was not right. The more she thought about it, the angrier she became. When she approached Dashiq, Tuck moved out of her way. It was the smartest thing she'd seen him do in a while.

Emmet looked down from the saddle. "Don't be sad," he said.

Riette stopped in her tracks. He was at peace. He was not afraid or even under duress. He was in that seat because he wanted to go. Who was she to make him stay? A fine job she'd done of keeping him safe. Already he'd proven himself in battle, which boggled Riette's mind, and she did not forget what was at stake. Everything she loved and knew would likely be destroyed in the looming invasion. It was a matter of time before the fleets converged. Riette felt utterly useless. She was just excess weight and had to be cast off. Tuck might know exactly how she felt, but she was angry and afforded him no empathy. Too many times he'd lied to her. Even if he'd thought those lies were in her best interest, it did not excuse the deceptions. Relationships were built on trust, and she could no longer trust his words.

"I'll come back and get you," Emmet said when Barabas strapped himself in. In that moment he resembled a normal boy, one who loved his sister and was going to defend her. He locked eyes with her, and she heard his voice in her mind say the words, "I love you." Expressing emotion had never been among Emmet's strong points. The rarity of those words, even if only heard in her mind, meant more to Riette than anything else. In spite of all her mistakes, all her resentments and bad judgments, he still loved her.

"There will come a time when you'll have to choose between me and him," Riette said to Tuck, locking eyes with him. "I suspect I know what you will decide."

Tuck grew smaller. "I'm sorry," he said before walking over to Dashiq and double-checking the straps.

His shoulders shaking brought no joy, satisfaction, or absolution. There was only pain and guilt. No matter how hard she tried, she wasn't finished being angry yet.

Just as the stars began to shine, Dashiq used the air currents to spiral upward over the green crystal columns. Barely a sound was made when she tucked her wings and disappeared from view. No matter how hard she tried, Riette could not find them again. They might as well have ceased to exist, and the thought nearly crushed her. Tuck offered his hand when she climbed down, and she accepted it, trying to be a bigger person. Even so, she did not smile or thank him.

"Did you see what they did to Berigor?" Tuck asked when the silence had hung too long.

Riette nodded.

"I mean, I knew the cap'n saved Dashiq, but I could never picture exactly what it was he'd done. Now I'm even more amazed the old bird still flies."

"What happened with Al'Drakon and Tarin?"

"Don't know," Tuck said. "I fell asleep and when I woke up, the cap'n was tearing the carriage off in a rage. Was it the explosion that woke you?"

Riette nodded again.

"It was out to sea," he said, pointing beyond the city. "No idea what or why."

Riette took his hand once again, also grabbing his false hand. "Will you make me a promise?"

Tuck looked as if he were trapped in front of a stampeding bull. "I . . . uh . . . maybe?"

"Do you think I am capable of handling the truth?"

Tuck nodded.

"Do you think I deserve to know the truth?"

Tuck nodded again.

"Then will you promise not to lie to me ever again?"

"I promise," Tuck said.

"Good. Now how do you feel?"

"I'm not so sure they're gonna come back for us."

It was not how Riette had expected the conversation to go.

* * *

Shadows moved through Windhold, but few were there to see. Far larger than the hollowed mountain of Ri, this hold had been carved out by dragons, and by the looks of it, big ones. Here the Zjhon had an amazing facility for storing, testing, constructing, and deploying aircraft. Steady winds consistently blew in the same direction, which made perhaps everything but landing ideal. Berigor had no trouble clinging to the mountainside. Allowing them to climb across his tail to gain entrance to the hold, he never made a sound. The repairs to his face must have given the beast newfound strength, even as they made him look like a living work of art.

Two guards moved through the assembled aircraft, the lanterns they carried making them easy to spot. While he mourned the loss of Dosser, Al'Drakon Keldon Tallowborn was fortunate to have Tarin at his side. He was part of this mission for numerous reasons, his understanding of aircraft engineering chief among them. At each jet, he loosened four connections. For prop planes, of which few remained, it took only a moment for Tarin to score two rubber lines, leaving them intact but dramatically weakened.

The process took time, and Keldon wanted nothing more than to be done with it and get rid of the cargo he carried. One wrong move, and they would both be history. Getting to the antiair guns was the riskiest but perhaps the most important part of their mission.

Only a single aircraft remained, bathed in moonlight, closer to the entrance than others, and Keldon considered leaving that one alone. Tarin moved before he could give the order. Keeping to the shadows, Keldon could only watch in silence as the guards converged on where Tarin worked. Holding his breath, Keldon prepared to attack. Tarin was no fool, though. By the time lantern light reached where he'd been working, he'd faded back into the shadows.

To get to the guns, the two Drakon would have no choice but to leave the relative safety of the shadows. This part required patience, which had not always been Keldon's strong suit. Again, the guards converged not far away. Had they been paying attention to the aircraft, they might have seen two men who were really too big to be playing hide-and-seek.

Tarin shifted and his leather boot creaked. Suddenly both guards were alert, and still Keldon had to wait. He did not want them to raise the alarm. Better to let them get as close as possible then deal with them quickly and silently. Before the guards got near enough, a bright orange flash out to sea lit up everything, followed by a reassuring boom. It was at least in some ways reassuring. He'd recognized the clay fire bombs immediately upon finding them in the caves. Such marvels were well described in the histories, even if lost to modern times. Berigor dropping one in the sea proved the weapons were still viable no matter their age. It also provided a distraction. Both guards ran to the edge of the wind channel and looked out at a sparkling orange plume with a roiling cap that jutted up from the sea. Nothing else was visible, and they argued over what it might be.

Knowing how devastating the weapons were, Tarin handled the ceramic spheres he carried with exaggerated care. While it might have saved their lives, it also took longer. Tarin was still exposed when both guards turned, without warning, in response to angry shouts at the other end of the wind channel. The explosion had everyone on edge. If only Berigor had waited just a little longer.

Standing stock still, Tarin let the guards walk past then dropped down to hide beside Keldon. One man looked back a moment later and hesitated, but the shouting grew louder, so he turned away. Tarin and Keldon crawled to the entrance, climbed outside, and clung to the mountainside, hoping their ride would get there soon. One mountain down, one to go.

* * *

Emmet shivered as Dashiq plummeted into the deepening darkness. There would be no surprise this time. The Zjhon would have been on their guard even if not for explosions off the coast. Barabas did not claim to know what was going on, but Emmet suspected Keldon had something to do with it. It wasn't much of a plan, but they had no better options than to barge in and try to steal Argus Kind's magic. If not for Emmet's ability, none of this would be possible. He felt both pride and an overwhelming sense of responsibility. There was fear as well. He understood the danger they faced and the reasons it was still worth the risk. An attack so early in the night might not be what the Zjhon were expecting, but they were on full alert when Dashiq brought them into view. Dozens of lights converged on them with blinding heat. Shouts rose up when the dragon crested the nearest peak.

The next moment changed everything. The response from every gunner was the same; every one had Dashiq in his sights, and they all fired almost in unison. Emmet closed his eyes as the first cannon exploded in a ball of fire and sparks. A moment later, he opened his eyes again, amazed by the rolling explosion. Normally the air cannons had a specific, recognizable sound. This was a fiery inferno turning long gun barrels into twisted heaps of metal. Aircraft launched from Windhold, not far away, which did not bode well. While he and Barabas might get in, getting out could be tricky.

The planes would have to fly at night, which was difficult enough. Still, the first pulse jet rounded the corner and thumped toward them and into the spotlights. The U-shaped jets had been retrofitted to carry their own lighting systems, blinding Emmet as they approached. The pilot got off three shots before the plane started emitting white smoke. In the span of a few breaths, the U-jet spiraled into the valley below. Other planes did not make it that far. Sudden movements while dodging crashing planes initiated other failures until aircraft rained from the sky.

"That crazy fool," Barabas said with a note of what might have been pride.

Smiling, Emmet pointed toward the brightest magic. Barabas guided Dashiq using his knees, and she landed on the ledge, allowing Barabas and Emmet to dismount within the entrance. The remains of two large guns flanked the halls. In spite of the Drakon's efforts, a diesel plane rumbled through the valley and opened fire on Dashiq. The dragon pressed deeper into the hall to escape the attack.

Emmet pointed to the back of the chamber and to the right. "Magic."

Laughter echoed through the cavern. It was a deep, angry laugh that twisted Emmet's guts. From the darkness emerged a man more frightening than any of Emmet's nightmares. He wore black armor and carried a six-foot-tall axe. It was the headsman's axe, the very one he'd used to kill the previous ruler and thus become king. He wore no helm, and the glint in his eye reeked of pure evil. This was a man who cared for none but himself. Except perhaps the Al'Zjhon. Barabas had warned of this elite fighting force, but Emmet already knew them; they had hunted him before.

"Mean," he said, pointing to the woman who walked alongside Argus Kind. Her form-fitting leathers appeared to allow a wide array of movement. If Argus Kind was a battle axe, this woman was a surgical blade. There were others: the man who could contort his body to fit into small spaces and the man who watched from the shadows. Every instinct told Emmet to run, but he extended his hand to Barabas, and the big man lowered his.

Again Argus Kind laughed. "I knew you would come back, Barabas. I should have killed you more thoroughly the first time. Now I know better." He hefted his axe, making his intentions undeniably clear. "And you brought the boy. I have to thank you for that. He'll be among my most prized possessions."

Hearing himself referred to as a possession made Emmet shiver. Riette would not like that. The thought of her made him want to cry, but he remained strong. Barabas needed him. Dashiq would not fit any farther into the hall, and she turned around to face the incoming airplane. Without ever firing another shot, the plane sputtered and spiraled out of control, Keldon's sabotage perhaps late but nonetheless successful. The man wasn't so bad as people made him out to be. Emmet saw the good in almost everyone, but that was why Argus Kind and the Al'Zjhon frightened him so much; he found no good left in them. Something had hurt them all so badly and for so long, they no longer wanted to do good or be good. Destruction was as gratifying for them as creativity was for most.

In Argus Kind's hand was the source of all the magic Emmet had sensed: a glassy orb of some sort, he could not tell exactly what type. "It must have been difficult, watching your dragon slowly die. You should have let it be quick and spared the poor beast. Look at what she has become. If only she'd had this." He turned the glassy sphere to reveal the most realistic-looking artificial dragon eye Emmet had seen. Every other one he'd seen was carried by Barabas, but they did not compare to this one. The detail, the life, and the magic within this eye were far beyond any other.

Emmet realized then just how much magic Argus Kind had needed to gather to throw him off the track of the most powerful magic. No wonder he had allowed so much to be stored in one place and left at risk. It had simply been bait meant to keep anyone from taking the real prize.

"Azzakkan's Eye," Argus Kind said. "I suspect you've thought about this a time or two while she fades away—the one object that might not only heal your dragon but might actually make her better. We all know the stories, of course, but I know more. Only I took the time to trace all the legends back and had the guts to retrieve physical evidence that proves the stories were real and true. If all you're going to do is sniff at the dirt, you don't deserve the power."

"There is power enough to share with the world and do what's right," Barabas said. This brought new laughter from Argus Kind and the Al'Zjhon. "There has never been need for war."

Though it looked as if he might say something more, that was when Dashiq struck. Like a snake, her tail shot out and smacked Argus Kind across the wrist, hard enough to send Azzakkan's Eye flying and Argus Kind reeling in pain. Emmet stretched time, knowing he could not do it for long. He made it only halfway to the still airborne sphere when time began to compress again. Panting hard, Emmet tripped. For a moment, time remained stretched, and he reached out his gloved hand, grasping for a chance at salvation. Just as his fingers closed over the glassy sphere, a sleek black boot stepped on his wrist. Emmet screamed.

CHAPTER TWELVE

Peace is an illusion. The wise prepare for war.
—Agger Dan, Al'Zjhon

* * *

"Now!" Barabas shouted.

Using his free hand, Emmet pulled the cloth over his face. Soft bundles struck cold stone. For a moment, there was silence, but then an angry buzzing filled the hall, followed by screams. No amount of bravery or training can overcome pain and primal fear. Emmet curled himself into a ball and hoped the hornets would leave him alone. The Al'Zjhon were far from defenseless and, after the initial shock, covered their exposed flesh. From within their robes, they armed air rifles. Compressed air tanks hissed. Pellets stung Emmet's legs, his thick leggings and boots preventing more serious injury.

Chaos ensued. With the mean woman still standing on his wrist, Emmet sneaked a glance back at Barabas. He fought to reach him. The woman fired relentlessly, and the closer he got, the more pain showed on his face. The smaller air-powered weapons were less potent than their larger brethren but inflicted damage nonetheless. A hit in the right place could result in blindness or death.

Emmet did not want to see his friend hurt, especially not while trying to save him. When the mean woman shifted her weight, he took full advantage. So engrossed with inflicting pain on Barabas, she was unprepared when Emmet yanked his hand free, spun, and kicked her in the knee. The woman's leather garments were thick and well padded. His kick did little damage, but it did distract her long enough for Barabas to scoop a hornet nest still stuck in its burlap sack, and he threw it at the woman. It struck her full in the face. Emmet scrambled away. Her screams retreated toward the back of the hall.

Time had fully compressed, and the other Al'Zjhon advanced, doing their best to ignore the swarming hornets. A heavy weight struck Emmet from behind, sending him sprawling. Somehow he managed to hold on to Azzakkan's Eye, but it cost him. He'd fallen too close to one of the nests and could no longer avoid being stung. Already his face swelled and the vision in his left eye grew dark. His screams added to those of the mean woman and others. Dashiq roared behind him, her breath sending the paper hornet nests tumbling toward the back of the hall. Rough hands grabbed him. Only the sight of alabaster skin kept him from putting up a fight. More weapons fire ensued, and Barabas grunted with each hit. Twice he stumbled and Emmet feared they would both end up in a heap, but somehow the man reached Dashiq and tossed the boy into the saddle.

There was no time for securing straps, and Emmet held on tightly when Barabas gained his seat. Dashiq turned and launched herself back into the sky. Still holding the glassy sphere in one hand, Emmet gripped the saddle with his other. Dizziness threatened to overwhelm him, hornet venom coursing through his veins. The pounding in his head grew louder, accompanied by flapping wings and heavy weapons discharging.

Argus Kind's troops had successfully replaced some of the damaged air cannons. The world jerked sideways and Dashiq let out a moaning woof as heavy stone shot struck her in the thorax. For a time they tumbled, the ground rushing up to meet them. With a wheezing moan, Dashiq found strength she had somehow held in reserve and skimmed low over the city. Catapults, air cannons, and bows fired, creating an echoing chorus. An arrow sank into Emmet's boot, the tip digging into his flesh, but he could not remove it. The erratic flight gave him no chance to stash the glossy sphere in his pocket, and he was too busy holding on to do anything else. Only straps kept Barabas in the saddle, and Dashiq wobbled in the air. Was it worth it? Emmet wondered.

Only when open seas rushed beneath them did Emmet stash Azzakkan's Eye within his coat and secure two straps. Though far from safe, it was better than nothing. Barabas did the same, though he favored his right arm. No one left Ri unharmed, but he could still feel the power emanating from the ancient artifact.

Dashiq circled back, presumably headed for Riette and Tuck. A distressing sight waited. Battle balloons filled the skies, bristling with weapons visible beneath the raging fires keeping them airborne. Airships crept around nearby peaks, though none were high enough to reach the secluded valley with the green obelisks.

Struggling to gain altitude, Dashiq didn't look as if she would be able to return there either. Despite being out of range, those aboard the balloons opened fire. Though it inflicted no damage, the act made it clear there would be a price for regaining the shoreline. Dashiq used the only advantage she had left at that moment and dived closer to the waters below. With nothing to illuminate them, the balloons ceased fire. Searchlights scanned the water, looking for them, but the dragon showed her skill by staying ahead of the piercing light beams. Twice lights passed over them; twice Dashiq altered their course.

The far side of the island nation was more lightly defended, and the dragon used the opportunity to gain altitude. No thermals waited to lift them higher as the ground below them cooled in the night air, and Dashiq had to work for every bit. Emmet remembered once asking if the dragon was going to die. Now he understood it was inevitable. No matter what

Barabas held in reserve to care for his dragon, he would only be delaying the loss of his beloved friend. Tears flowed from Emmet's eyes in spite of one's being swollen shut.

When the peaks they sought came back into view, it took Emmet a moment to recognize them. His blurry vision did not help, and the different angle made him question his own judgment, but there was no doubt that was where Dashiq was headed. What troubled Emmet most was how much higher they had to climb before reaching the valley where his sister and Tuck waited. His concern increased when an airship emerged from behind the peaks. Soaring higher than they, the airship glowed like a beacon in the night. Searchlights scoured the landscape, looking for Dashiq and her passengers, but the captain of this airship had something else in mind. How they knew where to look was unknown to Emmet, but the cold feeling in his gut grew while the dirigible moved ever higher.

Gusting winds tossed Dashiq about. The airship above was subject to the same and perhaps worse. Unpredictable crosswinds were difficult enough to deal with, but swirling eddies created by the peaks, which disrupted the prevailing winds, were treacherous and unpredictable. Unlike whirlpools in the seas, these were invisible. Emmet and Barabas watched, horrified to see the airship moving ever closer to the valley. Armed men climbed down a rope ladder that twisted perilously in the winds. No matter how much he wanted these people to fail in their mission, their bravery was undeniable. Perhaps the consequences of failure were worse than death. It was possible, he knew, and he tried not to think about the fate awaiting Riette and Tuck if they were captured.

Higher the airship drifted, trying desperately to avoid the jagged peaks, but the winds proved too much. Twice the men on the ladder were dashed against the rocks. One let go of the violently swinging ropes and clung to a rocky promontory, but within moments, he lost his grip and disappeared into the night, his screams growing faint then ending with chilling suddenness. Though he hated to see anyone die, this gave Emmet some hope his sister might yet be saved. Balloons joined the airship in its quest, their fires burning brightly, trying to overcome the churning air and gain the necessary altitude. Horizontal thrusters gave these balloons far more directional control, but they also added weight. It was a difficult balance to manage.

If not for the unspoken need for stealth, Emmet would have cried out. He watched in terrified silence while more men descended rope ladders now dancing above the mystical valley. Two men made the jump before a downdraft sent the rest crashing to the sacred stone, their fate perhaps more kind than those remaining aboard. No matter how the captain tried, his orders audible across the distance, the airship remained out of control.

Drifting higher, the dirigible sought to escape, but the valley had remained long undiscovered for good reasons. With a single gust, wind sent the airship crashing into the jagged peaks. Flames leaped higher when the canvas skin ruptured. A tearing sound was followed by snapping timbers. The ship began crashing into the valley itself, but the winds were not done with her yet. Even while the crew fought to gain control of the mortally wounded airship, the captain shouting for them to land in the valley, the flaming ship was thrust outward. After a final collision with the mountainside, it plummeted to the distant valley floor.

With only battle balloons remaining in the night skies, Dashiq circled closer, trying to gain altitude and avoid the spotlights at the same time. It was no use. The wounded and weary dragon was unable to climb high enough. Bright lights blinded Emmet; they had been spotted. Shouts rose up from the balloons, and soon the sound of weapons filled the valley, echoing like rolling thunder.

Only the unpredictable air currents kept the dragon and her passengers safe. Unable to reach the valley by flight, Dashiq did the only other thing she could; she flew straight toward dark stone. Ferocious air currents swirled along the rock face, slamming them into the peaks with gut-wrenching force.

Refusing to give up, Dashiq dug her claws into the rock face and even used her tail for stability while she climbed one agonizing step after another. Again lights pooled on them, and the battle balloons fired. Lacking a stable firing platform, the shots mostly missed their marks, but a few came too close for Emmet's comfort. One struck the stone directly above them, rock fragments raining down like a storm of knives. Dashiq screamed in pain or perhaps just in refusal to die, Emmet was unsure. It was the weight that saved them. Battle balloons could carry only so much ammunition, and most dropped back toward the valley floor, presumably to reload.

Taking advantage of the respite, Dashiq climbed with all her strength, groaning and whimpering. It pained Emmet to hear her in such distress, and he rubbed her neck in encouragement. Moments later, they crested the rocky peaks in much the same way Berigor had, and the dragon tumbled into the valley. Not far away, Riette and Tuck stood side by side, each holding a round object in their hands. Two of the Zjhon who had dropped into the valley from the airship faced them. Another watched Dashiq approach. After picking herself up, the dragon walked with a pronounced limp.

"Stay back!" Riette screamed, but the Zjhon took another step closer. It was their last. Tuck and Riette each threw a clay sphere, and twin explosions rocked the small valley. The concussive force nearly sent Emmet tumbling from the saddle. The remaining Zjhon soldier looked around, realizing he was lost.

"Hold," Barabas said to the man in the most intimidating voice Emmet had ever heard, his slur barely audible. Dashiq continued forward, glaring at the man who cowered before her. "It seems you've a decision to make. You can die right now, or you can talk. Choose."

The man hesitated.

"Choose now or I'll choose for you."

Dashiq swung her head in his direction again, and the man fell trembling to the ground. "I surrender," he said. "I'll talk." He then threw his weapons at Tuck's feet.

Barabas ignored the man after that. His concern for Dashiq was palpable. The carriage rested nearby, partially repaired, but it would do none of them any good if the dragon died. Emmet, too, placed his hands on the noble dragon's side, and she trembled beneath his touch. Hovering over the black stone amid crystalline pillars, she looked almost well, but he could sense she was not.

"You want to live?" Tuck asked the Zjhon soldier.

The man just nodded.

"Then help us with the carriage. It's badly damaged and we were only expecting two passengers. If you want off this rock, I suggest you do your best. Otherwise you might end up splattered on them rocks way down there. I'd bet a fall from this height would be a bad way to go."

Barabas put a hand on Emmet's shoulder, breaking his trance. The man held out his calloused palm. The look on his face spoke of a request rather than a demand.

Pulling the glassy sphere from his coat, Emmet felt warmth emanating from it. It pulsed in harmony with his breathing but he knew it had life of its own and had merely synchronized with him. Having sought magic for so long and lacked synchronicity his entire life, Emmet did not immediately relinquish the ancient artifact. Legends of the first dragon rider and her dragon were known to everyone, though. The Eye would far better serve Dashiq.

His skin felt cold and somehow incomplete when he dropped the sphere into Barabas's palm. The man's reaction made it clear he felt it too. Most people would feel nothing. He and Barabas were different, which frightened people. It had taken seeing the problem from the outside for him to understand his own life. So many times he'd thought people mean, rude, and inconsiderate—and perhaps they were—but now he understood most were just afraid, or at the very least uncomfortable. In Barabas, he'd found understanding and hope. Things could get better. This he poured into his physical bond with the dragon. He, too, had been injured in the fight, and the hornet stings throbbed. Even in her wounded state, Dashiq sent him energy as well; he'd never experienced anything like it.

He felt Riette's hands going over him in much the same way Barabas treated Dashiq. "I'm sorry," she said. "I never should have let you go, and now look at you. I wasn't sure you'd make it back at all." The catch in her voice conveyed her emotions more than the words.

"I'm all right," Emmet said. Riette sobbed in response. He grabbed her wrists and gently placed her hands on the dragon. "She needs us."

Not opening his eyes, Emmet allowed his other senses to expand into the area around them. Much in the same way he sensed magic, he could sense life; deep down, he knew the two were the same. While life sometimes felt cold and mundane, existence itself was magical. Too few recognized the mystical world around them, only seeing the pain and suffering. He gently included Riette within his energy field, and she stopped crying.

Tuck and the Zjhon soldier worked on the carriage, but Emmet barely noticed. The sensation emanating from Azzakkan's Eye drowned out just about everything else. It moved away from him as Barabas approached Dashiq's face, and he could feel its influence fading the farther away it got. A soft click was followed by a moan Emmet felt through his fingertips. An instant later, warmth once again flowed into his hands, just as when he'd held Azzakkan's Eye. The physical bond had been reestablished with the dragon, who acted as a conductor. The stone was at home in her artificial eye socket, and the dragon reveled in the magic pulsing through her. Barabas had modeled the eye socket using detailed descriptions of the ancient artifact, hoping someday he would find the magic needed to make Dashiq whole. He had expected too much.

So tightly connected to the dragon and the power flowing through them both, Emmet experienced Dashiq's pain. Even possessing one of the greatest and most complex magics ever known, the dragon could not defeat death. Determined to do everything he could for her, Emmet drew deeply. Never would he have imagined such glory. From the black stone beneath him, he felt the land's energy flowing upward and through him, infusing him with its majesty. The green crystals resonated in harmony with the land itself and played a majestic tune inaudible to most but like a sweet lullaby to Emmet. Empowered, he reached through Dashiq, allowing her to become an extension of himself. Drawing from Azzakkan's Eye, he now understood its true purpose. This magic joined dragon and human into one. Such intelligence and compassion overwhelmed Emmet, and he felt shock from Dashiq, too, as if she'd never imagined such nimble thoughts.

Though he could have marveled at their connection for days, Emmet now felt the dragon's pain as his own. Beside him, Barabas drew a sharp breath. Through the bond, Emmet knew the man had just laid hands on her side once again. He, too, would feel the magic and the pain—and the connection. Emmet was grateful for the help; already he felt drained.

"What are you doing?" Riette asked. "What's happening?"

Doing his best to ignore his sister and everything else, Emmet concentrated on the pain, allowing himself to feel all of it: the broken ribs, puncture wounds, and more on top of already arthritic joints. Even Riette wept from the agony. How could they ask Dashiq to go on? It was too much for any living creature to endure, especially one so well loved and who'd done everything within her power to protect them. Emmet had known the dragon for a short time but had already grown attached. Now, through the magically enhanced bond, he learned she had fought for all of mankind, acting as a protector he'd just never known he possessed. No longer able to feel his own body, Emmet soothed and mended, using what was now Dashiq's Eye to focus and channel the energy flowing from the land and crystals and filling the air. It was glorious and torturous all at once.

"Emmet!" Riette shouted, though she sounded far away.

He hadn't meant to stop; he wasn't done yet. The dragon still had pain. No matter his desires, he found himself faceup on the black stone, a painful lump forming on the back of his head.

"Are you all right? Are you hurt?"

Her words drifted past him but didn't sink in. Only when Dashiq nudged him with her maw did he become truly conscious again. Even in her weakened state, she somehow found the energy to send him healing. It did not take away his wounds, but he felt them less acutely and his vision gradually returned. The worry on Riette's face made him feel terrible. So many times he'd seen that look, and he hated being such a source of stress in her life. Someday he would find a way to change that.

"I'm fine."

"No, you're not!" Riette said, and she carried him to a place where soft grasses grew. He felt cold and disconnected, but he appreciated the effort nonetheless. The grasses cradled him, and the cold helped ease his pain. The touch of her fingers brought the sense he was loved, and that helped more than anything else.

* * *

Barabas walked to Riette's side. "How is he?"

"He's weakened and injured thanks to you."

"He fought honorably and may have saved us all. I did my best to protect him."

"It wasn't good enough," Riette said, aware she was being unreasonable. Somehow knowing was not enough to change it. "What's next? Have him fight Argus Kind himself?"

"He came close already," Barabas said.

The Zjhon soldier's eyes went wide at this statement, and the man seemed to shrink in on himself.

Riette could find no words.

"Your brother is braver and stronger than you believe. Size and age are not limits on the power of one's spirit."

"Surely you've figured that much out," Tuck said from behind her. When Riette spun on him, he recoiled.

"Next," Barabas said, ignoring the exchange, "we need to get the carriage back on Dashiq and get away from here. They'll be back. With a few modifications to one of their airships, they'll be able to get here more safely. I want to be gone within the hour."

"She needs longer," Emmet said.

"No, I don't," Riette argued.

"He's talking about Dashiq," Barabas said. "And he's right but we don't have any more time. We've reduced their capabilities, but they still have greater resources than we do. We need food and safe haven if such a thing still exists." The Zjhon soldier remained silent. Barabas turned on him. "How many more aircraft do you have?"

"Many," the man said, but whatever defiance remained in him drained away under the combined gazes of those assembled. "Have you seen the fleet at the Heights?"

"Many times," Barabas growled.

"That is but a quarter of our strength. Three fleets have sailed. The last is divided up into a dozen pods kept at a safe distance."

Barabas nodded. The man's words explained how more and more aircraft kept arriving. "Get the carriage loaded," he said. "It's time to go."

Everyone worked together to get the bulky carriage onto Dashiq's back. The dragon had to land to allow it, and already she appeared less comfortable. Riette felt terrible inflicting pain on the old dragon while struggling to help secure the cumbersome carriage, which was even more unwieldy due to the damage and hasty repairs. With the cinching of each strap, Dashiq groaned, and Emmet moved to put his hands on her again.

Riette grabbed her brother by the shoulders. "Not yet," she said. "You need your strength as well." For once, her brother obeyed in silence, and Riette was thankful. Her heart already ached with worry. The swelling in his face had gone down some, but still he looked like a different person, which freaked her out. Soon, though, they were boarding.

No longer did Riette feel like a mere passenger fleeing the Al'Zjhon. Now she felt like a true combatant in the war. Emmet's contribution was greater than hers, but she, too, had faced death and had killed. It was not something she could think about without tears gathering in her eyes, but she refused to cry, refused to show any sign of weakness. Emmet needed her; she was all he had. Part of her knew the statement wasn't true; Tuck, Barabas, and Dashiq had become like family to Emmet in many ways. Riette had tried to keep her distance, especially knowing they hadn't always acted in her and her brother's best interest, but they had also saved his and her lives multiple times. Like family, she didn't agree with everything they did, nor did she always like them, but they had thus far proven loyal. Also like family, she was pretty well stuck with them, at least for a time.

Once she and Emmet were strapped in, Tuck and Barabas climbed to their saddles. Before they were secured, Dashiq disconnected herself from the land once again. The remaining Zjhon soldier looked up with fearful eyes.

"You've two choices," Barabas said. "You can stay here and hope your brethren are kind enough to come back for you, or we can take you down. Which will it be?"

The man stood speechless for a few moments, considering his words.

"You have three seconds."

"Take me."

The man had no chance to say more before Dashiq snatched him up in her claws. His screams echoed within the valley but ended in a strangled cry. Three times the dragon circled the rising winds emanating from the secluded valley before she cleared the peaks and flew to the far side of the Firstland, where the land was wild and unruly. Here no structures or other signs of human settlement existed.

Soaring low over a black beach, Dashiq released the Zjhon soldier and sent him tumbling along the sands. Perhaps it was a cruel fate, but at least this way the man had a chance at survival. There were no guarantees the rest of them would fare any better. Still, it made Riette cringe when towering creatures emerged from the forest, possibly drawn by human scent. The last she saw the soldier, he was running along the shoreline. In spite of his being her enemy, she wished him well.

Dashiq turned out to sea, and Riette prepared herself for a long journey. There simply was no way to cover vast distances quickly. Barabas had not said where they were headed, most likely due to the presence of the Zjhon soldier.

"Where are we going?" Riette asked.

"Home," Barabas said.

It was enough.

Beside her, though, Emmet stirred. Turning to look back at the largest of the hollowed mountains on the Firstland, he pointed. "Magic."

"We have what we came for." No matter what Barabas said, though, Dashiq turned toward where Emmet pointed.

At first, Riette thought Barabas might protest, but he remained silent, presumably trusting his dragon's instincts. She was still trying to figure out how they communicated and which of them was truly in control. The more she observed, the more she thought it was the dragon. Their current circumstances served to strengthen that belief.

People shouted from within the fabled halls of Windhold, and Riette began to wonder if the dragon simply wished for a quicker end. They were flying into enemy territory in the full light of day. Already heavy weapons fired on them in spite of their being well out of range. Still following Emmet's direction, Dashiq moved higher. Riette looked down her brother's arm to the exact spot where he pointed. Near the peak, far from the mighty wind channels in the heart of the mountain, a dark entrance became visible. No people or aircraft could be seen, and the channel did not go all the way through the mountain as the larger, lower channels did.

All the hair on Riette's neck stood as they closed in. Despite her condition, Dashiq executed a landing so soft and controlled, it felt as if they were still flying. Darkness awaited them, yet Emmet still pointed.

Barabas lit a lantern and left the saddle as quickly as his body would allow. "We don't have long. They will come."

Emmet climbed down before Riette could get herself unstrapped, and she hurried to join them before the precious light moved too far away. Within a few breaths, she raced after them. It didn't take long for her to catch up. Both had stopped and stood in silent disbelief. Before them, on an ancient stone pedestal, was a saddle not unlike the one Dashiq currently wore, save it was studded with clear gemstones that sparkled despite what might have been thousands of years of disuse and neglect. By her guess, the Zjhon had not discovered this place. Layers of dust on the floor gave evidence it had long been undisturbed. How the saddle remained so clean was a mystery, but she had her guesses.

No one spoke. Dashiq moved to where they stood and lowered herself. Barabas unstrapped his saddle but appeared uncertain. Based on the wear, she guessed his saddle was very old, perhaps the only one he'd ever used. The one awaiting them appeared far older, and Riette hoped none of it had rotted over the eons.

With practiced movements, Tuck and Barabas removed the saddle, able to leave the carriage strapped in place. The new saddle was perhaps a bit too large for Dashiq, but Barabas used an awl from his bags to make new holes farther up the straps before buckling them. Soon he climbed up and strapped himself in to the sparkling saddle. Riette took her seat once again, and even she felt the power coursing through the dragon. Perhaps Emmet had saved them all—again.

CHAPTER THIRTEEN

When flying with dragons, sometimes the best one can hope for is a well-executed dangle.
—Tuck, dragon groom

* * *

With her hair tied up in the tightest bun possible, Riette let the wind hold her in place. Never had Dashiq flown so fast, nor had any dragon in a thousand years. Having the tales she'd grown up on suddenly become reality, heroic figures now flesh and blood, made Riette question everything. Nothing was as it had been in Sparrowport, but not everything was bad. No matter how difficult and terrifying things had been, she knew Emmet better now than she had her entire life. She was proud of him and understood his behavior so much better. The more magic he came into contact with, the less frequent his outbursts and episodes became.

No matter how fast they flew, nothing could make such a journey short.

"And for today's inflight meal, we have smoked fish strips and pickled eggs," Tuck said.

Riette wrinkled her nose. It felt like forever since she'd eaten anything other than smoked fish and pickled eggs.

"And whatever you do," Tuck continued, "don't ask for salt."

Diving low, Dashiq extended her claws forward and dragged them through the water, sending thick spray over her passengers. Barabas shook his head. It didn't take long for them to dry, and they ate in silence, having long since run out of things to talk about. When Dashiq roared, even Barabas jumped. Moments later, a form was visible in the air before them. His movements erratic and his flight path too low for comfort, Berigor carried two passengers. No matter how she'd felt about Keldon Tallowborn in the past, Riette was happy to see the men alive, grateful for what they had done to help Barabas, Dashiq, and Emmet. If not for their bravery and ingenuity, Riette would likely have had to watch her companions die. She'd seen the battle from above; Dashiq would not have been able to dodge such overwhelming fire. Based on Berigor's flight, he had not come away unscathed.

"We were going to come back for you," Keldon said after the initial shock of seeing Dashiq approaching at such high speed and wearing a glittering saddle, "but he's hurt bad."

"You did plenty," Barabas said. He would have gone on, but the dragons interrupted with a conversation of their own. Riette had no idea what their roars conveyed until Berigor moved over top of them. Dashiq slowed, matching his speed. Lower the larger dragon came, claws extended. Riette trusted Dashiq implicitly, and she didn't think Berigor would intentionally hurt them, but he was an enormous creature who was visibly injured; one mistake could be deadly. A moment later, his claws closed around the root of Dashiq's tail.

Firmly connected together, the two dragons wobbled in the air, dangerously close to the waves below. Riette nearly screamed when Berigor's torso came close to crushing them all. As Dashiq pushed them higher, the larger dragon exerted tremendous downward force. Soon, though, the majestic creatures found synchronicity. Trimming his wings, Berigor moved into a more aerodynamically sound position, and the air around them became less turbulent. Gradually their speed increased, but never did they quite reach the speed Dashiq could attain alone.

Whatever comfort level Riette had developed with regard to flying adragonback, nothing had prepared her for this. Emmet appeared unconcerned, but at least Tuck had the sense to look worried.

"What are we going to do?" Riette asked, unable to endure the silence any longer.

Tuck shrugged. "The war ain't over yet, but at least the war ain't over yet." He had a way of saying things that made no sense yet made perfect sense. "The gods have been watching over us thus far. I just hope they haven't grown tired of us."

"The gods?" Riette asked. "With all the terrible things that have happened, you really think the gods are watching over us?"

"Perhaps they are having a good laugh at our expense," Tuck admitted. "I like to think there might be someone on my side, and maybe every once in a while, they might nudge things in my favor."

"And what if you're wrong?" Riette asked.

He shrugged. "What's the use of being right if it don't make you feel no better?"

Resisting the urge to correct his grammar, Riette responded, "What's the use of feeling better if you're wrong?"

"I suppose it's all in how you look at it," Tuck said.

Barabas nodded and Riette let the conversation drop. All she really wanted was to be back on dry land, able to walk and stretch. She worried her bum would be completely flat when the trip was finally over. Seeing the dragon's blood trees come into view was among the happiest moments of her life. They had at least made it this far. She was not home yet, but she was one step closer. Part of her wondered if any home remained for her, but just being back in the land of her birth would be reassuring. Not until she'd had to leave had she realized how comforting familiar surroundings could be. Another part of her wanted to see the faces of people she cared about. The thoughts brought tears. The wind sent them streaming back along her cheeks, and she rubbed her eyes. Dashiq made the final approach. With a roar, Berigor released his grip on Dashiq and soared away from her, his wings popping and cracking as he extended them after so much time mostly retracted.

Moments after Dashiq alighted on the rocky, shell-filled shoreline, Berigor landed not far away, groaning on impact. Everyone dismounted with haste and remove the saddles. Keldon and Tarin attended to Berigor. Riette helped Emmet down and assisted in unstrapping the carriage. Their makeshift repairs had made it more difficult to remove and apparently far less comfortable for the dragon. Once they had the carriage lowered to the rocks, Dashiq moved to Berigor, her glittering saddle still firmly secured. The two dragons had a low conversation of rumbling, whines, and woofing grunts.

"You should have told me what you were doing," Barabas said to Keldon. For a moment the two men just stood and stared at one another. "But I also appreciate what you did. Your sacrifice was great."

"You would not have agreed to the plan," Keldon said. "I knew we could do it but didn't have the time to explain it to you, so we left while you all slept. It was clear you needed the rest before you would be fit for battle. I took a calculated risk."

Barabas nodded his head and said no more. Reaching for the pocket of his long coat, he found it torn, the contents lost to the wind. He sighed.

"Let me have your coat," Riette said.

Barabas gave her a confused look.

"Just take it off, and let me have it."

The tall man nodded and did as she instructed. From within her bags, still stowed away in the carriage, she retrieved her sewing kit. It had been so long since she'd sewn, the needle felt strange in her hands. Even with a thimble, her fingertips were soft and tender in comparison to when she had worked as a seamstress on a daily basis. It did not take long, though, before she found a rhythm that soothed her senses and brought a familiar calm. It was as if her mother were there with her. Stitches became difficult to see through her tears, and when she wiped them away, she did a double take. What was that sticking out of the water?

"Look out!" she shouted.

Emmet hit her then, knocking her sideways and causing her to fall on the stones, skinning her palms. The coat, needle, and thread flew to one side. An instant later, heavy shot struck the place where she'd been standing a moment before. A shower of hot rock and shells erupted, stinging anyone close. More cannon barrels were visible when Riette looked back to the water. Scrambling to get herself and Emmet to safety, Riette realized there was no safe place to hide. The island was smooth and worn. The dragon's blood trees, all that protruded above the surrounding stone, were too far away to be much use at that moment.

Her brother's coat collar in her hand, she ran for the trees. Berigor roared and thrust himself between the air cannons and the six people on the shoreline. Those lurking below the waves were relentless, and the dragon cried out. Dashiq, though, took to the air. Never had Riette seen such an angry creature. Light flared around the metal structure embedded in the right side of her face and the glittering saddle, which was currently empty. Azzakkan's Eye blazed. Electric plasma erupted from Dashiq's open jaws. Like a tornado of fire laced with lightning, the torrent blasted back the shallow waters and exposed three oblong ships somehow operating while fully submerged. Riette couldn't imagine how terrifying it must be onboard such a vessel and counted her blessings she was a dragon rider. She'd never thought of it that way until then, but the benefits were obvious when your mode of transportation can also act on its own to protect you.

In that moment, Riette was exceedingly thankful for dragons. No more shots were fired, and what remained of the underwater craft disappeared back under the waves. Cannon barrels still protruded from the water but now rested at odd angles, the ships listing and turning in the surf.

"There will be more!" Barabas barked.

No one needed to be told what to do next. Wiping blood from a cut not far from her eye, Riette considered herself lucky. Once again her brother had saved her life. She had underestimated him, indeed. It made her swell with pride and guilt at the same time, though she'd begun to forgive herself for being wrong for so many years. She'd done her best and would do better going forward. Nothing was more important at that instant than getting the carriage strapped back on. It seemed foolish now to have taken it off; even knowing Barabas had wanted to inspect Dashiq for wounds. They were at war, and they had been careless; a price would be paid.

Al'Drakon and Tarin ran toward their saddle, but Berigor removed that option. Swooping across the shoreline, the dragon grabbed one man in each claw and flapped his mighty wings, no matter how much it must hurt. Lacking Azzakkan's Eye and the stone-encrusted saddle, he flew away looking no better than when they had first encountered him.

"To the Heights!" Keldon shouted while dangling from Berigor's claws.

"We'll meet you there!" Barabas bellowed.

* * *

Smoke on the air was the first sign they had reached the war zone. Cloudy skies made for unpleasant flying and low visibility. In spite of that, wreckage that was scattered across the waves was unmistakable. Here and there masts protruded from the water, and in some cases, large sections of dirigible remained afloat. Some wreckage was still occupied by airmen clinging to it in hopes of being rescued. Cries for help were replaced with warning shouts. Dashiq ignored them.

There had been no sign of Berigor for days, and now Riette suspected she knew why. The larger dragon was headed for the Heights. Dashiq had taken them farther south to where the fleet gathered. The hum of engines announced airships ahead, and they were on full alert. Urgent orders being issued made it clear they knew Dashiq and her passengers were coming. The dragon exerted power with grace and ease, flying with a level of confidence and speed that put even airplanes to shame. Fire and lightning danced along the copperwork reconstruction of her face, and Riette braced herself, habitually double-checking Emmet's straps to make certain he was secure.

Chaos erupted when Dashiq burst from the clouds above the main Zjhon fleet. Airships crowded the skies, many of which still bearing the planes they had transported across the vast seas. Riette thought for an instant they might not be too late, that there might be a way to save her homeland yet, but then planes streamed from the naval fleet and dropped from the airships carrying them. The air became the most dangerous place on the planet. While the cannons below were no doubt loaded with heavy shot, they did not dare fire into the air above them, knowing they would take out their own ships and aircraft as well. Small shot, however, was a much better risk, and U-jets screamed through the air, casting streams of scatter shot before them.

Dashiq navigated the wind, guided by a symphony she alone heard. With subtle movements, she dodged fire and aircraft alike, all the while placing herself in such a way that any fire directed at her and her passengers was also aimed at another jet or airship. Many pilots realized this too late when the dragon darted out of their path, revealing one of their own now in the line of fire.

Dancing through the air fleet, Dashiq used the planes against the naval fleet, causing them to collide with one another and damage the ships below. Some, though, she simply grabbed out of the air with her jaws and whipped her neck to send them hurtling toward her target. Those above and below the carnage saw what was happening and abandoned caution. Heavy weaponry opened fire; no one was safe or immune.

Completely changing her tactics, Dashiq dropped low and raced along the waves, forcing all the guns to follow. It took a few moments for the lumbering guns to move into place and commence firing again. It was a foolish thing to do, but panic had set in. Dashiq was no normal dragon. Lightning danced over her entire body now, and Riette gasped when she realized it pulsed over herself and Emmet as well. There was no pain; she felt invigorated by the energy. It flowed from the saddle and around them all. Riette noticed the stones decorating the saddle no longer shone as brightly and slick as they once had. She didn't know how much power the saddle possessed, but there appeared to be limits.

At the sound of air cannons firing, Dashiq soared straight upward, large stone shot narrowly missing her exposed breast. Some had expected this move and left their cannons aimed skyward, but the dragon had effectively divided their fire and made evasion more manageable. From the high-pitched shouts below, it was clear her tactic had been effective in getting the Zjhon to attack themselves. The air fleet moved north, toward the Heights, their bomber fleet mostly intact. Dashiq pursued and only then released the pent-up energy pulsing around them. Riette felt it rush out of her along with her breath. Emmet appeared ready to pass out, even Barabas swayed in his saddle. Wood canvas and even metal burned at the touch of dragon fire. Within minutes, the entire fleet of airships lit the clouds before crashing into the sea.

Airplanes zipped past, firing rounds that made the air sing of death. Only the dragon's evasive maneuvers kept them alive. It was a tenuous existence, and Riette continued to lament her lack of control over the events that ruled her life. Holding on with all her strength, she was powerless and small up against forces that would tear her world asunder. Diesel planes now approached, outfitted with the largest firing tubes yet. Smoke poured from them, and rockets took flight. Zipping through the air across an erratic flight path, these missiles followed the dragon's movements, and even more concerning were the explosions when they got close. With her ears ringing and the ends of her hair singed, Riette knew it would take but a single direct hit from one of those weapons to knock them from the sky.

Dashiq lashed out, filling the air with dragon fire, and Riette sensed the strain it put on dragon and saddle alike. Aircraft dropped from the skies like a deadly rain, and most of those loaded with rockets exploded before hitting the water. Within minutes, much of the eastern Zjhon fleet had been destroyed.

Not looking back, the dragon flew north. A portion of the air fleet had escaped to assault the Heights, and there was little chance Dashiq would make it to the mountains in time to prevent major damage and casualties. But she was in a perfect position to make sure those aircraft had nothing to come back to.

"They are beaten!" Riette shouted. "We should finish them off!"

Barabas shook his head. "We've only so much magic. The Heights can hold against the likes of them. We must save our strength for what's to come. This is far from over."

Riette crossed her arms over her chest but considered his words.

Farther inland, the weather cleared and the Heights were visible in the distance, along with the aircraft circling the mighty peaks. Darting between those shadowy silhouettes were dragons.

"We have to save them!" Riette shouted involuntarily.

"The Heights will hold," Barabas said.

Dashiq continued to fly north and west.

"There's no one at all defending Sparrowport. We can fly around the swamp to the north and stop at Dragonport."

No one flew straight over the twisted Jaga swamp. It was said wild dragons ruled those skies. Such were the stories told to children in Sparrowport to keep them from wandering too far, but Riette had never seen a wild dragon. Riding a dragon made her second-guess that preconception. All dragons had seemed like mythical creatures, just stories and legends, until she had seen them herself and they became real. The thought gave her chills and made her wonder how many of the dangers from fireside tales were also real.

Dashiq, unlike any other dragon, gleamed in the afternoon skies. Her copperwork facial reconstruction now smooth and sleek, no green remaining. Details previously obscured or worn beyond recognition had been restored. The metal had been lovingly crafted in intricate detail. Metal scales lined up with flesh-and-blood scales, but around the eye was a design that did not mirror the opposite side. The dragon's real eye was much larger than Azzakkan's Eye, but the radiating lines and interlocking triangles that filled the space appeared almost natural. It was a masterwork requiring magic—the last magic his people then possessed. Some hated Barabas for that, and he had done it anyway, knowing it would be the case. Now he returned with far greater magic and refused to use it to save them.

True to his prediction, though, those within the Heights must have fought valiantly since the air around the mountain was free of airships by the time it disappeared from sight. When Dashiq slowed, it came as a surprise. Riette had thought she might soar all the way to Sparrowport faster than the most powerful airplane. Instead, she landed on a sizable island that showed signs of being used by humans. Several docks floated within the natural harbor, but no ships were moored there. The few buildings scattered along the shoreline were dark, and no smoke rose from chimneys. The air smelled of salt and the distinct odor of the shoreline.

"Why are we stopping?" Riette asked.

Barabas shrugged. Dashiq turned back to look at Riette and made it clear she was to disembark. Riette owed the dragon her life, but under such scrutiny, she felt small and weak and feared she might become lunch. It was an unrealistic fear, but she did not want to risk a dragon's wrath either way and hurried to get herself and Emmet unstrapped. The reddish clay shoreline was uninviting, but Riette wanted nothing to do with the buildings there. She'd much rather be back in the sky than remain in this place another moment. It gave her the crawls. Emmet stayed close by.

Barabas and Tuck did their best to tend to Dashiq, whose needs were not entirely known or understood by Riette. The cloudiness of the stones embedded in the saddle was an indication their time and resources were limited. Perhaps some magic remained in the atmosphere, as the tales said, but that required one to believe the tales of gods and goddesses were at least in some part true. It was a difficult thing for her to reconcile, yet she had the results before her. If the tales really were true, then what remained was a mere shadow of the power that had once been and would someday be again. Even those who believed true magic would return along with the goddess agreed it would be thousands of years hence. Hardly something that would help in the current circumstances. They had found a small well and already threatened to run it dry. It was a terrifying realization. They had faced but half the Zjhon strength. Barabas was right; this wasn't over. Previously the full extent of the change in the saddle had been hidden. Now she understood.

Barabas was a man who made difficult decisions and did not appear to second-guess himself. Riette envied him. So often she questioned her decisions and actions, and for a great portion of her past, she had been very wrong about so many things, it was difficult to trust herself to make the right decisions going forward. No matter how much she had hated him not so long ago, she found herself wanting to understand Barabas, to know what he thought and what he would do. She felt safe with him, even though the entire world was falling apart. People had said it was an exciting time to be alive with so much innovation and change going on around them, but Riette would have been just as happy for everything to have stayed the same. The cost was far too great.

No matter how unexpected the break, it felt good to walk. Emmet never left her side, and she wasn't certain if it was out of fear or something else. When he spoke, it came as a surprise.

"Dragons," he said, pointing.

Shielding her eyes, Riette scanned the horizon and drew a sharp breath when she realized how close the two dragons had come without their noticing. Though the Drakon should consider them allies, it was disconcerting. Barabas and Tuck calmly watched the dragons approach, which was all that stayed Riette's rapidly beating heart. Even so, she dragged Emmet back to Dashiq's side at a fast walk.

"Do you know them?" Riette asked Barabas.

He nodded.

It made sense that he would, and Riette felt silly, but she was tired of being left out and uninformed. It was time she started to take charge of her own life, and she had to do what was right for Emmet. Wandering around, following a crazy man and his dragon might not be the best answer. It was false but she couldn't stop herself from thinking it anyway.

The dragons that landed were both larger than Dashiq, but they treated the older dragon with a certain amount of deference. Each dragon bore two riders, and Riette's breath caught in her throat when she recognized Keldon. Berigor had saved all of their lives, and seeing Keldon without his dragon seemed unthinkable.

"When you didn't arrive at the Heights, I had to come looking for you."

Barabas nodded. "How is Berigor?"

The man hung his head. "It's not good," he said. "The healers are working with him, but his wounds are grievous. He wanted to be here—" A man who was among the toughest warriors Riette had ever seen cracked at that moment and could speak no more through his grief and worry. No matter how much she hated to see another human being suffer so, it gave her some semblance of hope for herself.

Tarin was among the men who accompanied Keldon. Riette did not recognize the other two. All three remained silent and stoic. "We weren't certain we would find you," Keldon continued. "But I'm glad we did. We need you back. I was wrong."

"No," Barabas said.

"But I cannot be Al'Drakon knowing you are the one of which the legends speak. Dashiq is Al'Drak, which makes *you* Al'Drakon. The choice is not yours. You gave her Azzakkan's Eye. You saved her. And now we need you to save us all."

Riette held her breath, knowing how much it must have hurt Barabas to be cast out and accused of treason.

"No," Barabas said again.

"The choice is not yours," Tarin said.

Turning back to his dragon, Barabas waited. Dashiq watched. Humor dancing in her eye, she snorted and nudged him with her maw. Barabas put his hands in the air and turned back around to face the Drakon. "Fine," he said. "Keldon Tallowborn, I charge you with managing the war effort from the Heights and seeing to your dragon's needs. I order the rest of you to follow him and do as he says; he's not nearly the fool he's made himself out to be."

Tarin had the courage to laugh.

Keldon shook his head. "And what will you do?"

"Exactly what I was already planning to do," Barabas said. "We will go to Sparrowport."

"Then let us go with you," Tarin said. "You decimated the southern fleet! I would not believe it if I didn't see it for myself. Fortunately others also saw it, or no one in the Heights would ever have believed. It's an honor to have fought with you, Al'Drakon."

"You have served well, Tarin. Do me a favor and stay alive until this is all over. I'll buy you a mug of ale."

Tarin's reaction showed he valued the gesture far more than any tankard, and Riette had to once again adjust her notion of who Barabas DeGuiere was. Every time she thought she had him figured out, he changed, and every time, she cared for him more. It was starting to frighten her. All the things in her life she had loved had been taken from her save Emmet. Who would be next? The thought made her tremble.

"When the Heights are secured, you may come find us," Barabas continued. "Until then, you will serve me best by maintaining order and dealing with what remains of the southern fleet, though I suspect they already know they are defeated."

"You are a good man, Barabas DeGuiere," Keldon said. "You embody the true meaning of what it is to be Al'Drakon. Thank you."

Barabas nodded. Nothing was different for Riette and her companions, but the way these other men regarded Barabas had completely changed. The more Riette thought about it, the more she realized things had changed for her as well. Now she needed to understand what it was and what exactly it meant.

CHAPTER FOURTEEN

Dragon Airways. We don't eat nobody. That's our promise.
—Tuck, dragon groom

* * *

Dragonport was unlike other holds they had been to. Rather than a hollowed-out mountain, it looked to have been carved from the cliffs, as if someone had removed a single slice from the mountain like a piece of pie, leaving a perfectly formed plateau, much of which now served as a runway and cargo staging area. Wooden structures stood a short distance from the sheer cliff face. How such a place had been created was a mystery. The perfect right angles and straight lines made it appear man made. Even for mighty dragons, it was a stretch. She'd seen their architecture, and it consisted mostly of sweeping, twisting lines. Only the floors of the hollow mountains were smooth. And how had they even done that? Riette couldn't imagine shaping even soapstone with any level of artistry or mastery, and yet the mountain stood before her, daring her to disbelieve.

The mists evaporated with the morning sun, and Dragonport exploded with activity. Some shouted and pointed at them, but Riette would think the sight of a dragon rider would be a welcome one. Panic was widespread. Many did not even face them, instead pointing out to sea. From the mists emerged a Zjhon fleet. A pair of Midlands diesel props waited on the airstrip below, but Dragonport was otherwise without many defenses. For so long, the place had been the trading post easily accessible to dragons from the Heights but otherwise remote and isolated. Now Dragonport faced a force equal to the one that had devastated a better-fortified hold. Even if they could get word to Forest's Edge in time, it was doubtful sufficient military forces could be mustered at the rear lines to withstand such an invasion.

The Height's supply lines had been severed, and she presumed this fleet had been largely responsible. Argus Kind was thorough in his planning and tactics.

It came as a surprise to many when Dashiq landed not far from the airplanes.

"Help me get the carriage off," Barabas said.

People approached warily at first, seemingly unsure what to make of this sudden arrival and their hurried movements. Busy loosening straps, Riette felt the stares on her back. "Help us," she shouted without turning. "She may be your only chance of survival."

Something in her tone and words must have connected with these people, and they helped get the carriage lifted off Dashiq's shoulders.

"Wait here," Barabas said, and even Tuck remained on the cold stone. Sirens wailed. Aircraft were inbound. With the Jaga swamp on one side and Midlands forest on the other, the chances of help arriving were negligible, and the surrounding landscape made even retreat perilous. People instead stood and watched their doom approach. It was a horrifying sight, but Riette understood the futility of the situation. There was nothing she could do either except join them in silent vigil.

The two airplanes took off on a mission from which they would not return, their cockpits perhaps the loneliest places in the world as they flew out to face overwhelming odds. The best they could hope for was to die valiantly in defense of their people and homeland, but even they must know it would make little difference. The horror of it made Riette feel sick.

A moment later, Dashiq launched herself back into the air and soared after the planes, the metalwork of her face gleaming brightly. Cries rose up from those gathered, a desperate note of hope in their voices. Even with magic, the numbers were overwhelming. Free of the carriage and with the rest of the passengers off her back, Dashiq was in fighting condition. Cheers erupted when she flew past the planes, her speed supernatural. Barabas bowed forward, making himself small. Together they were one, moving in synchronicity, attuned to each other's senses. Never had she heard Barabas speak to the dragon, yet somehow they communicated. At times she'd thought them subject only to the dragon's whims, but she now recognized a balance of control and mutual respect. It became clear from the way they flew together in battle.

Part of her questioned the role of the rider, but intuitively she knew two minds were better than one. At the very least, Barabas was a second set of eyes and ears. He never struck an enemy or used a weapon of his own, other than the dragon. Barabas guided Dashiq through the fleet like a flaming scythe through wheat. The planes followed closely, allowing turret gunners to target passing aircraft on either side. In the chaos created by Dashiq, planes soared past the armada and executed wide turns, preparing for another pass. Dashiq turned much more sharply and attacked the airships carrying additional planes. When the planes from Dragonport returned, no swath was cleared. Airships clogged the air above the naval fleet, and the aircraft they had launched were now headed back toward the fleet instead of Dragonport. Having been largely scattered by Dashiq's attack, the pilots did their best to regroup and defend the fleet. Once the threat was neutralized, the hold would be defenseless.

For those standing along a stone railing, it was surreal. History unfurled before them like a distant play too terrible to actually be happening. Explosions filled the air, and debris rained from the sky. Cheers rose up as chaos continued to give the advantage to Dashiq. The two Midlands planes were now hard pressed, and that had everyone on edge. Then things got worse. Some Zjhon pilots must have realized the futility of their involvement in the sortie since their presence made it more difficult for their comrades to maneuver.

A sick feeling in her gut, Riette watched a handful of planes turn back toward Dragonport. "Get whatever you can throw at them!" she shouted. Those around her did not react at first. "Anything we can throw up in front of them could make them crash."

It must have occurred to the people that they could exert some influence on their fate, and no matter how ridiculous the idea was, at least it gave them something to do. Failure would leave them no worse off than if they did nothing. The heavy guns Dragonport did have began firing along their flanks before the planes were even in range, herding the aircraft closer together.

"They'll come in low the first time and try to take us out with their guns," Tuck shouted. "Wait until they start firing before you throw anything."

Looking around, Riette was proud of what she saw. Those in charge of defending the hold had already done everything within their power, but now everyone chipped in. Children gathered wrenches, nuts, and bolts, all of which could do serious damage to a plane moving at high speed. Two groups prepared nets as a makeshift slingshot. When the firing started, they pulled tight, hurling scrap metal into the air. Not all of it went high enough, but clinks and clanks accompanied the roaring engines overhead.

Planes soared past. In rapid succession, two crashed farther down the runway. The rest started their turn, appearing to have escaped damage. When one started spewing white smoke, a cheer rose up. Those cheers died away when it began to look as if the wounded plane would make another approach nonetheless. Rockets fired just before the three remaining planes passed, and the pilot bailed out of the damaged plane. Wearing a leather suit with wings stretched between the arms and legs, he soared over the Midlands forest before his parachute snapped open and carried him out of sight. His plane continued toward Dragonport, a winged bomb. It struck storehouses with a thunderous collision that sent flames and debris hurtling above even the mountain peak.

The other planes stayed high enough to be out of range to most, but some used bows to target vulnerable engine parts. Farther out to sea, one of the Midlands planes was brought down, and the feeling of hope faded. Dashiq fought like nothing any of them had ever seen before, and even Riette marveled at the power. Seeing it from this vantage gave an entirely different perspective than what she'd experienced from the carriage. Now the planes returned to attack Dragonport. After so many had been knocked from the skies, they targeted Dashiq, who was the clear threat. The dragon came under heavy fire as every part of the fleet set its sights on her. There was no need for accuracy if you could explode the entire sky.

In a single, massive onslaught, the Zjhon managed a coordinated, inescapable attack—for them and Dashiq. Shooting down their own aircraft, which then tumbled down onto the fleet, they also inflicted damage on the dragon. Dashiq emerged from a cloud of smoke, wobbling in the air and looking as though she might simply drop from the sky. A pair of Zjhon aircraft came into view a moment later, chasing Dashiq as she tried to make her way back to Dragonport. Closer the airplanes flew, their speed greater than what the dragon could achieve in her weakened state. Three shots were fired before the final Midlands airplane roared past them on a perpendicular path, its turret gunner taking full advantage of the opportunity. All Zjhon guns were aimed at Dashiq and did not get off a single shot at the remaining Midlands plane. When the first Zjhon plane exploded, Riette wasn't certain if it was debris from the first plane that took out the second or the gunner's fire, but the result was the same. Both planes tumbled downward, their pilots ejecting barely in time to soar and parachute away.

Losing altitude at an alarming rate, Dashiq flew an erratic course. Barabas wove in his saddle. The Midlands plane had circled back and approached from behind, but the pilot could do nothing to help the dragon, save perhaps to offer encouragement. When the dragon reached the landing strip, she almost immediately closed her eyes and dropped to the smooth stone. The impact evacuated the air from her lungs with a whoosh, and Barabas fared not much better. Only the approaching plane kept Riette from running to Dashiq. Tuck took his chances, dashing across the expanse to where the dragon lay motionless. Riette felt like less of a person for hesitating and she followed. Given plenty of landing strip beyond where Dashiq and Barabas had come to rest, the plane landed without difficulty. Moments later, the pilot climbed down and ran toward Dashiq.

Tuck climbed to Barabas and spoke with him. The tall man did not respond. "He's breathing!" Tuck cried, his voice quavering.

Arriving next, Riette went to where Dashiq's head rested, her eye closed but her breath evident. "Dashiq lives as well," she said, though she was uncertain how much longer that would remain true. There was only so much punishment any living creature could endure—even for love. The dragon held on for Barabas, of this Riette was convinced. Both had endured so much and had been so valiant and brave. Riette could no longer see through her tears.

When she did clear her vision enough to make out what was happening around her, she saw the Midlands pilot hugging Dashiq and crying. "They saved us," he said.

Dashiq moaned in response. The gemstones in her saddle were now more white than clear, especially around where Barabas sat. He was moving now, and Tuck helped him from the saddle. Healers came and ministered to him, along with the other wounded. A naval fleet remained offshore but had lost its air support. Much like the naval fleet to the east, its capacity for war had been dramatically reduced. While the Zjhon still posed a threat, it was unlikely Dragonport would fall.

But now what? If Barabas and Dashiq died, what would she do? Where would she and Emmet go? What would Tuck do? So many questions made her weak in the knees. She hated to think of losing her friends, but she knew better than to pretend everything was fine.

"Pardon me, miss," a man in his late middle years said, breaking Riette's train of thought. She stared at him blankly for a moment. "Are you all right?"

"Um. Yes," she responded. "I . . . just . . . need to sit down."

The man, who introduced himself as Finny, put his arm around her and helped her toward a padded bench beneath a nearby overhang. He brought her a mug of cool water, bread, and cheese. For a while he sat in silence and watched her eat. "Do you feel better?" he asked.

Riette nodded.

"Good. I'm sorry to do this to you now, but I need to ask you a couple questions. Is that all right?"

Riette nodded again.

"Are you Riel Pickette's girl?"

The question caught Riette off her guard, and she gaped at him a moment before she nodded, tears gathering in her eyes. She'd tried so hard not to think of her father all this time, having learned so much about the war he'd disappeared into.

"I'm sorry, miss, really I am. He was a good man, your father—a fine pilot and a good man."

"What happened to him?" Riette managed to ask in spite of her quivering chin.

"His squadron went out on patrol and never came back," Finny said with a sniff. "I was his flight mechanic. I can see him in you and Emmet. He was a brave man. When volunteers were needed for long-range reconnaissance missions, he was among the first to go. He went down over the Endless Sea. His plane was found months later. We may never know exactly what happened, but we know he didn't survive. I'm sorry."

Riette sat cold and unfeeling. She'd mourned the loss of her father already; the only difference was that now it was real. There was no longer any chance her father would come walking back into her life and make everything all right. Feeling as if she were being slowly stabbed in the heart, Riette tried to think of what she would say to Emmet. It was easier to worry about him than it was to feel her own pain.

"Is there anything I can do for you?" Finny asked.

Riette shook her head, and tears slid from her nose.

"Then please just wait here and rest for a little bit, and I'll be back. There's something I need to get for you."

Tuck approached a few moments later. "Are you all right?"

Riette nodded, not trusting her voice to speak. Suddenly she felt she knew Barabas just a little bit better.

Tuck sat down next to her. He didn't have to say anything. His presence alone was comforting. "I think they're going to be all right."

In her melancholy, Riette remained silent, not wanting to spread her dark mood. "My father is dead," she said without meaning to.

"I'm sorry," he said.

"It's all right. Finny just confirmed what I already knew." The tremble in her voice didn't lend credence to her words.

When Finny returned, Riette couldn't help but cry. He carried a small square of cloth, but she recognized it. Her father had worn his uniform on the day he left, and she would never forget it; the details were deeply etched in her memory. This was the shoulder patch from his uniform, and it was more than she could bear. For so long she had pushed her father into the realm of stories and legends, things that weren't actually real, things you could lose without being torn into a thousand pieces. But this was real, tangible. It connected her memory to her loss and she sobbed. Emmet had come to see what was wrong, and Riette tried to get herself together for his sake, but it was of no use. Instead, he came and sat beside her, placing his hand on her knee and giving it a pat. This gesture brought even more sobs, and she hugged him hard. Tuck handed her a kerchief, and she gratefully accepted it.

"I'm sorry," she said to Finny.

"Don't you worry about a thing," Finny said. "I don't blame you one bit. But you got good people around you, and you'll always be welcome in my family. You and Emmet are all your dad ever talked about. I feel like I know you already."

"Thank you," Riette said when she'd calmed herself enough to speak.

"There's one other thing. Someone else has been here looking for you."

A cold feeling washed over Riette. Had the Al'Zjhon been here? Were they waiting for their chance to kidnap Emmet?

"He was a big fellow," Finny continued. "Not one you'd want to tangle with in a fight. Had fingers like pickles."

Laughing through her tears, Riette pictured Brick in her mind; the description was not inaccurate.

"He left this for you." Finny handed her a rolled piece of parchment.

Tuck, Emmet, and Finny all looked anywhere other than at the parchment as she unrolled it.

Riette,

You're a hard woman to track down. I wanted to come find you, but the news you sent of a fleet headed for Sparrowport changed my mind. I know you are alive and in good hands. I must go back and make sure our people are safe. I hope you understand. If you do make it back, which I hope you do, I will never let you out of my sight again.

All my love,
Brick

Here was another part of her life she'd been repressing. Brick loved her—always had. He'd come after her, as she'd known he would. Yet he'd had the good sense to go back once he knew she was well cared for. Even if he had been able to track her down, there wasn't much he could have done to help her. She was proud of him for going home to save the people they both cared about, though she wondered how much he could do. Perhaps, as it seemed, their efforts would be futile no matter what. Riette wasn't one to give up easily, but life kept taking things from her. Only the presence of Emmet, and, if she was honest with herself, Tuck kept her from despair. In many ways, the news about Brick came as a relief, and she felt a small bit lighter. When Barabas walked over to where she sat, the burden lifted even more. It frightened her how happy she was to see him.

"Dashiq will recover," he said. "Perhaps not completely but enough to get us back to the shallows. Needs a proper healing."

"Sparrowport?" Riette asked.

"Is in serious trouble," Barabas said. Riette made ready to protest, but he held up a single gnarled finger. "I want to help the people of Sparrowport, but I don't know if we can take on another fleet. This one really took it out of her, and the power in the saddle will be depleted before much longer."

"But we can try?"

"We can try," he said. "We can try."

The pilot who had hugged Dashiq joined them. "Thank you," he said to Barabas with a bow. "I would go with you, if you'll have me. My name is Bronson."

Barabas nodded. "How do you feel about having a very special passenger?"

It didn't take long for Bronson to catch on. "I'd be honored."

Riette couldn't imagine what it would be like to fly atop a dragon atop a diesel prop, but she was about to find out.

"I'll get you fueled up and reloaded," Finny said.

A beautiful red-haired woman approached carrying a tray of travel breads. Riette's mouth watered at the sight. She knew good Midlands food when she saw and smelled it, and these were among her favorite things. Emmet perked up as well.

"I asked Miss Gillian to bring us something to warm our bellies before the journey," Bronson said. Riette liked him already. "As many of you can ride with me as you would like. There's plenty of room."

The offer forced Riette into an uncomfortable decision. Did she accept his offer and risk offending Barabas and Tuck, or did she fly in a rickety carriage strapped to a dragon on top of an airplane and possibly offend Bronson? The fact that she was leaning toward the latter made her question her own sanity. For the moment, she chose not to make a commitment one way or another.

Barabas was also silent on the matter, which could be explained by the steaming travel bread he held. Bacon and eggs by her guess—difficult to execute properly but amazing when done right. Riette grabbed one with the tips of red peppers showing through the bread coating. How she had missed spices other than salt! Tuck finished off his meal and made his way to where vendors displayed their wares. Even in times of war, people had to do business and handle the day-to-day necessities of life. Riette hoped he had the good sense to buy something other than pickled eggs and salted fish.

Deep down, she steeled herself against what they would find upon returning to Sparrowport, never realizing how much the place meant to her until leaving it behind. When living there, she'd felt like an outcast. Now that she had been places where she knew absolutely no one, she realized how much the community meant to her, and there was the familiar sense of surroundings. She longed to once again walk the streets, knowing where she was going and where to find everything she needed. It called to her like a distant dream. If only she could slip back into her old life, as if none of this had ever happened. The thought saddened her, though, since then she would not have known the wonders of magic and the true nature of her brother's existence. She'd learned so many lessons on this journey, no matter how painful the process may have been. There was no way she would wish the knowledge away.

When it came time to board Dashiq, Riette approached with trepidation. The dragon had been largely unresponsive not long before. Seeing her eye open was a good start, but the aging dragon moved gingerly. Riette began to consider flying inside the airplane just so Dashiq would not have to bear her weight. It seemed an unfair thing to ask of a wounded animal. The dragon, though, had a mind of her own. When Riette and Emmet approached, Dashiq reached out to them with her head and guided them to the carriage. The message was clear enough, and Riette was not about to disobey. No other creature in this world commanded more of her respect than this dragon. The valiant beast had more heart than most of the people she knew and had sacrificed herself more than once to protect Riette and Emmet, not to mention Tuck and Barabas. More and more, she thought of these people as her family. Putting her father's patch in the pocket where she carried the kerchief her mother had given her, she drew strength from them. People on both sides of the veil cared for her, which gave her some comfort.

A crowd had lined up to help put the carriage back in place, and Riette found more of the damage had been repaired. Her seat was once again whole and at least somewhat comfortable. If they lived long enough to make the trip back to the shallows, as Barabas suggested, she would be grateful for the added comfort. Nothing could have felt stranger than sitting atop Dashiq while she climbed atop the diesel prop airplane and wound her tail around it.

"Just keep her weight distributed evenly, and we'll be fine," Bronson said.

Barabas nodded.

Black smoke billowed from the engines, which issued a deafening roar. Already Riette was seeing the benefits of dragon flight over aircraft. Rushing air from the props created a turbulent wash alongside the fuselage, leaving Riette to reconsider the wisdom of this idea. No one would have heard her even if she had said something. The engines roared louder, and the airplane taxied down the airstrip. The extra weight required additional lift. Dashiq kept her wings closed. Already she affected the plane's aerodynamics, possibly preventing liftoff. Still the plane hurtled toward the cliffs, where clear skies waited beyond. Emmet had the good sense to scream. Riette joined him. Even Tuck looked to be holding on for his life.

The drop sent Riette's stomach toward her throat. The seas rushed at them as the plane picked up speed. Within moments, they were gaining altitude instead of losing it, and Riette relaxed her grip just a small amount, her knuckles already hurting. Tuck looked back, his face pale and his eyes wide. Seeing Riette and Emmet still strapped in place, he gave her a thumbs-up. Shouts rose up from the remaining Zjhon in the water and along the shoreline. The plane was still climbing and might be within gun range, but no one below was ready in time. Most were busy helping their comrades from the water. Pilots and sailors alike clung to the wreckage of airships and naval vessels. Those who had already made it to shore scavenged whatever they could from the wreckage, braving the deadly surf. Those waves were notorious under normal circumstances but were now filled with debris.

Riette almost felt bad for those who remained. The world had changed in the span of a few days. The Zjhon had gone from being an overwhelming invading force to a group of men and women facing being stranded on the Jaga, trapped between rocky cliffs, the swamp, and the sea. The shoreline was the safest route to travel to the Heights, but even that journey was one no sane person would take.

Few places were more deadly than the Jaga swamp. The land itself seemed to reject the presence of man. Those who did wander into the jungle were almost never seen or heard from again. The rare few who claimed to have survived any length of time in the jungle were haunted by the experience, and none ever wanted to talk about it. These were among the tales Riette had always thought to be little more than stories. Having flown along the swamp's edge, though, she now believed every word. The place oozed evil and hatred, writhing with glossy-slick life large enough to be seen from the air. Riette now had experience with enormous serpents, but she still had difficulty imagining snakes that large. It was as if the swamps were a single creature with a great many arms. The images would haunt her nightmares.

Within a short time, though, the swamp and Dragonport were left behind. Stark cliffs whizzing by at an impressive rate, Riette settled in for what would likely be the shortest leg of their trip. Emmet leaned up against her and fell asleep. They were going home.

CHAPTER FIFTEEN

Most problems can be solved with a hotter fire or bigger hammer.
—Joren, blacksmith

* * *

When the airfield at Sparrowport came into view, Riette's heart sank. They were too late. Debris covered the airstrips, and some were almost completely destroyed, looking as if they had been blown up by massive bombs. Beyond, Sparrowport proper lay in ruin. The sight instantly brought tears to her eyes. The life of every person she knew was now in question. By the looks of things, they might all be dead. A thousand years of architecture had been reduced to piles of rock and plaster.

Bronson made the wide turn to line up with the airstrip. Riette hoped he wouldn't attempt to land. Slowing, the plane soared over the airfields.

"It's one of ours!" someone shouted from below, and a remarkable thing happened. The debris piles began to move—not all of them, but enough to clear a narrow landing strip. Bronson made a wide turn, and Riette scanned the horizon, seeing nothing. While Bronson lined up with the newly cleared landing strip, Dashiq uncoiled her tail and spread her wings. Within the span of a breath, they peeled away from the aircraft. The dragon landed amid the obstructions blocking one of the larger airstrips, once again displaying the advantages of dragons over man-made craft.

Bronson showed his skill and landed cleanly within the narrow strip. People ran toward the airplane and pulled a massive net over it the instant the engines stopped. The need for camouflage gave Riette chills. Once she and the others climbed down from Dashiq, the dragon curled up beside the remains of a downed plane, practically disappearing into the landscape.

Bronson appeared from under the netting, and faces she recognized surrounded her. They might not have run to her with open arms, but it was the warmest reception she'd received since leaving Sparrowport. The debris was moved back into place, much of it on rolling platforms.

From town came a formidable figure. Through trenches and ironworks securing the barrage balloons tied to them strode Brick. The changes in him were immediately obvious. The swagger with which he walked spoke of far more confidence than the boy who'd been afraid to kiss her. A man approached and Riette felt her heart flutter. She'd tried hard not to worry about him all this time, but the concern had always been there, weighing on her. Now that weight was gone. Not only had he survived, but others had too. Though her home looked like a near complete loss, the people mattered far more than the architecture. Buildings could be reconstructed.

"You're a difficult person to track down," Brick said when he got close. Even his voice sounded deeper and more commanding. She liked it.

"So your note said."

"Ah, so you got my note. Good," Brick said, looking embarrassed. "I would have come after you . . ."

"So your note said," Riette responded, but then she smiled and let him off the hook. "You did the right thing."

Brick nodded. "I wish I could've done more. We lost a lot of good people. And town . . ."

"Can be rebuilt by the people you helped save."

The muscle-bound man flushed deep red, but then he looked at Tuck. "Is this the boy you've been running around with?"

Riette hadn't noticed Tuck walking up behind her until that moment, and when she turned, he looked as if he wanted to be anywhere else. "Now, Brick . . ."

The much larger young man approached Tuck, looking him up and down. "I remember you," he said, his face a grim mask. "Welcome home, lad!" Brick swept Tuck up in a bear hug that made the smaller boy's eyes bulge. "You did good. You did real good. She needs someone to look after her."

Riette wasn't certain how to take that remark and considered kicking Brick in the shins. It wouldn't be the first time.

"It's a good thing you're back too, Riette," Brick said with a grin. "We've had no seamstress. People have been walking around with split trousers and holes in their socks. Quite horrifying, really."

Riette could no longer resist that kick in the shins. No matter how he harassed her, though, seeing him soothed her soul. She was home, for what it was worth. Not everyone here loved her or was comfortable around her, but they knew her and she them. They were a community, and when the need arose, they helped each other.

"In truth, you would have been a great help in creating the barrage balloons," Brick said in a more serious tone. "We should get back to the shelters. They'll be coming soon."

"The Zjhon?" Riette asked, her fears returning.

"It takes them longer to get here now that we chased their ships farther offshore."

"How'd you manage that?"

"The Zjhon aren't the only ones who can innovate," Brick said with a note of pride Riette had never heard from him before. "I modified the smithy forge and used parts from downed aircraft to fashion a new weapon. People call it the Ship Sinker. Who am I to argue? The name suits her. She's got triple-walled compression tanks and a barrel twice as thick and longer than anything they could haul across the sea."

"Where is it?" Riette asked.

Brick pointed back the way they had come. She didn't see it at first since it resembled other piles of debris littering the airfields, but then she noticed the circular opening of a massive gun barrel protruding from a downed airship. Sandbags reinforced the structure and were also packed around the barrel. "We only left enough space to sight and aim the gun. They've yet to do any serious damage to her, so they concentrate on grinding the bunkers into dust. They've come a bit closer to success on that account, but we're holding our own. How are things on the other fronts? We've had no news since I left Dragonport."

"The other two fleets have been mostly destroyed," Riette said.

Stumbling, Brick looked back to her, his jaw slack. "What?"

"It's true," Riette said to a crowd of faces who had turned to hear what she would say. "Barabas DeGuiere and the Drakon seized Azzakkan's Eye from Argus Kind." These words brought sharp intakes of breath and incredulous whispers. "Using a magic saddle and Azzakkan's Eye, Dashiq and Barabas eliminated almost all the Zjhon aircraft. The remaining naval fleets are sizable but ill prepared to lay siege on high ground."

"All save the one offshore here," Brick said, rubbing his chin. "We've held them off this long, and we've a few surprises for them today. They may think they've crippled us with their bombs, but they have made us stronger and more determined to survive, if only for the chance to seek vengeance."

"You've done well," Barabas said. "Most would have accepted defeat under the circumstances, but you all have shown the Zjhon what the Midlands are made of. You should be proud."

"No time for pride," an older man said. "Too busy not dying. We should get to shelter before they get here." Riette allowed the man to pull her along and into what looked like nothing more than a pile of rubble. Within, though, she found reinforced walls made from multiple sheets of metal most likely from downed Zjhon aircraft. "They drop it from the sky, we use it against 'em. That's the game we play. Today they'll find out we've been saving up."

"Remember to wait until they are past the barrage balloons before releasing!" Brick commanded.

Not a moment later, aircraft engines approached; it gave Riette the crawls. It was like waiting for death to arrive and hearing it come the whole way. Those around her showed greater nerve, waiting with determination for the chance to make their wrath known. Riette wasn't certain what they had in store but wouldn't have to wait long to find out.

The first wave of diesel planes swooped down over the littered airfield. From what she could tell, no one even noticed Dashiq, the plane, or the location of the big gun. No shots were fired and no bombs were dropped until the aircraft approached the barrage balloons. Not wanting to get tangled up in the purely defensive and passive aircraft, the bombers took aim at the balloons first, which would allow the next wave to come in lower. Still out to sea, they would arrive minutes after the first wave. She wasn't certain how much of this she could take. Waiting for the enemy to drop bombs on her head was perhaps the most nerve-wracking experience she'd had yet.

"Now!" Brick commanded.

A series of loud thrums, booms, and thumps followed. The air above the barrage balloons was suddenly filled with tiny orange spheres that exploded into puffs of smoky dust. There was no way for the airplanes to avoid the cloud of tiny projectiles, but Riette wondered just how effective the munitions were since none penetrated the planes themselves.

"Get down!" Brick ordered.

Metal shutters were lowered to cover the openings through which they had watched. That's when the bombs struck. Never had Riette been so bombarded by sound and pressure; it made it feel as if her head might implode. Emmet had his hands over his ears and rocked back and forth next to her. She did her best to comfort him until the episode passed. In this instance, she could hardly blame him. Most of her wanted to crawl in a hole and hide. This bunker was not far from the mark. Dust and stone pelted them after more bombs exploded, but nothing penetrated the rock and metal surrounding them.

"Reload," Brick ordered. People moved with alacrity, not questioning his commands. Pride swelled in Riette's chest at seeing her friend lead so effectively. She'd always known he was special and would do great things, but this was not what she would have guessed. He was a talented smith in his own right, and she suspected a bright future awaited him—if any of them survived. A late detonation rocked the bunker after the shutters had been raised, reminding them all nothing was guaranteed.

"Listen," Brick said.

The incoming aircraft made their approach, another wave of bombers following closely. Also, the bombers that had just attacked could still be heard flying back to the awaiting fleet, the tone of their engines distinguishable from behind. That tone changed and became intermittent before stopping altogether. People worked feverishly to open the rear shutters in time to see the planes dropping from the sky. Explosions rocked the far end of town, not far from Quarter Yard, where Riette and Emmet had once lived. It was an odd thing to cheer for, but Brick had, indeed, inflicted great damage on the enemy.

"Double flight coming in, people," Brick shouted over the cheers, an edge of panic in his voice. "Get ready! Reload!"

No matter how quickly they worked, it would not be fast enough. With a path cleared through the barrage balloons and no antiaircraft weapons at the ready, these planes would have easier targets to hit. Despite the substantial defenses Brick and the people of Sparrowport had erected, they would not last long. There was no time left to do anything except pull the metal shutters and hope. Unable to take her eyes away, Riette watched the planes approach through a growing gap in the stone walls. These were different than those that had come before. Hanging beneath each plane was a single, massive bomb. The Zjhon continually morphed their tactics based on their enemy's weaknesses.

Brick must have seen this, for he shouted before Riette could get the words out. "Evacuate the bunkers! Scatter! They mean to end us now. Some of us must survive!"

Though she knew he was right, Riette was transfixed, unable to pull her eyes away from the approaching planes. Then movement on the runways caught her attention. At first she thought the people were clearing a landing strip again, but Dashiq unfurled herself. Once the planes passed overhead, she leaped into the air.

"Come on, Riette!" Brick shouted.

Tuck was closer and grabbed her by the wrist, but she remained rooted in place.

"Wait," she said.

Brick opened a shutter enough to see what was happening. He held his closed fist out behind him, a silent command to hold. Many had already fled, but Brick, Emmet, Tuck, and Barabas remained. A pit of fear grew in Riette's gut. If she were wrong, then she might have killed them all. Dashiq, though, had other plans. In spite of her injuries, the valiant dragon took to the air behind the aircraft. No turrets were installed on these planes, which had been modified to carry much larger bombs. The pilots never saw her coming. While the formation slowed for a deadly approach, the dragon used all her speed to reach the lead plane and latch on to its elevator. Tearing it free, she sent the plane crashing into the one next to it. The chain reaction took out three planes.

Looking as though she, too, might fall from the skies, Dashiq winged away. The lead plane struck the ground first, hitting the trenches between the airfield and town. Even from a distance, the explosion rocked the bunkers, and Brick slammed the shutter closed. Riette endured stinging dust that rushed in through the crack. The next two planes struck an instant later. Debris filled the air, threatening the remaining planes. It was Dashiq, though, who did the most damage. Razing the formation with blue-tipped fire, she sent planes in every direction. Most crashed, some fled, but one continued, smoking and sputtering.

"Get down!" Brick shouted.

The sound was horrifying. Louder and louder the damaged plane grew until it struck the bunkers squarely. The initial impact collapsed the roof, leaving Riette staring up at the sky through a now enormous gap in the stone. The airplane remained partially intact and flipped end over end. The following explosion was deafening but lacked the punch of a direct hit, which would likely have killed them all. Even as it was, people screamed in the aftermath, Riette included. Pinned beneath a pile of rock, she couldn't move. Brick lifted the largest piece of debris off of her; the pain almost made her swoon, but she held on to consciousness, knowing it was a matter of life or death. Desperately she searched for Emmet, tears filling her eyes. They should have run—all of them. Her foolishness had cost them dearly. They still might not have escaped in time, but that didn't assuage her guilt. Only when Brick uncovered Tuck did she draw another breath. Her friend was bleeding and covered in dust, but as he unfolded himself, Emmet was revealed. He'd saved her brother, and Riette loved him for that.

A gnarled hand landed on her shoulder, and she let Barabas lead her away.

"It won't be long, and they'll be back," Brick said. "If we don't do something fast, we are defeated."

"The new gun survived!" someone shouted from outside the bunkers.

"We could hurt them with that," Brick said, "but I don't know how we'll get it to the bluffs." Riette's life-long friend and romantic interest turned to Barabas then. "I know your dragon is injured and weakened, but do you think he could help get a cannon to the bluffs?"

"She," Tuck said.

Brick shook his head, momentarily baffled.

"We can try," Barabas said. "How big is this gun?"

"Twice the size of the one on the airfield."

"Have you strong enough ropes?" Barabas asked and Brick nodded. "Gather everyone you can. She won't be able to fly with that kind of weight."

"If you've any strength left, come to the smithy!" Brick shouted.

A distressingly small number of people converged on a spot that looked much like everything else in Sparrowport: rubble. Riette recognized bits of shops and stores she'd frequented her entire life, and seeing the place destroyed threatened to bring tears to her eyes, but she had hardened to the pain. One could suffer only so much loss before the nerves dulled. When they reached the smithy, her will was tested again. She'd practically grown up there.

She tried not to look in the direction of her old home; she already knew it had been completely destroyed. Even if she'd never planned to live there again, knowing it was gone left her feeling lonely and lost. Only when Brick pulled wreckage to one side did she see something that gave her hope.

Beneath all the destruction were familiar tools and implements. The anvil on which Brick had taught her to make horseshoes, the hammers and tongs with handles worn smooth from use. At a modified version of his forge stood Brick's father, Joren.

No longer was the smithy at street level; it now existed in what had once been a root cellar. Massive copper tanks lined the walls, and three strapping lads turned a compressor wheel. Riette had thought them all dead and gone, and seeing them, no matter how much they had teased Emmet, made her smile. Blackened pipes fed air to the roaring forge, which glowed brighter than any Riette had ever seen. Gone were the bellows she and Brick had spent so much time operating. Never had their efforts resulted in such white hot coals.

Brick smiled. "We needed a lot more heat to melt down the metals the Zjhon use. I don't know what kind of forges they have, but they are years ahead of us. Still, we manage."

Joren left the anvil where he worked and embraced Brick. "I thought I might never see you again, my son. What in the world did they drop on us this time?"

"They've abandoned the smaller bombs and now are using massive bombs almost too heavy for the planes to carry. So far they have concentrated on the bunkers, but they will strike here soon. We need to get you out of here."

"And do what?" Joren asked.

"Did you finish the breech?" Brick asked.

His father nodded.

"Their dragon will help us get the new gun to the bluffs."

"Ah, my little Ri Ri!" Joren said, seeing Riette. "I thought the boy might follow you to the end of the world. It's good to see you back. And Emmet?" Riette's brother stepped from behind Barabas and embraced the smith, who was one of the few people in the world he trusted and openly liked. "Ah, there he is. It lightens my heart to see you, but I see my son is impatient."

Brick rolled his eyes. "They'll return soon. We must hurry."

"I know, my son. Sometimes, though, we must remember what it is we are fighting for. Now get over here and help me pin the breech. Then we can see about getting this monster out of here. It ain't gonna be easy, I tell you. I still think we may have gone too far."

"Let's find out," Brick said, visibly annoyed. "If I'm wrong, I'm wrong. It's too late to go back now."

Joren nodded. It took the two men only a short time to finish assembling the breech, and Riette marveled at the size of it. The barrel disappeared into the back of the smithy into a hole dug for that purpose alone. More people arrived and the space was soon cramped and crowded. Riette grabbed Emmet and dragged him back to street level. There she found Tuck tending to Dashiq. The dragon had never looked worse. Her sides heaved with labored breaths. Tears filled Tuck's eyes. That sight stabbed at Riette's heart on multiple levels, and she somehow felt pain again.

"I don't know if she can do it," Tuck said.

"There's nothing left to do but fight," Barabas said. "Dashiq has fought her entire life to keep these people safe, and she won't stop now, no matter what we think. You saw what she did."

Tuck nodded, tears now streaming down his face. "I don't want her to die," he sobbed.

"Neither do I," Barabas said, a catch in his voice.

Hearing his emotion was more than Riette could bear, and she wept openly. Emmet took her hand, and she bent down to hug him, knowing it might be the last time she ever did. The Zjhon would return soon, and the people of Sparrowport had few resources left with which to fight them. The enormous gun was an act of desperation. They would leave the remains of the town and the people still there, undefended, to get the gun to the bluffs. No one worked on reloading the catapults or air cannons and instead worked the ropes coming out of the hole in the ground that now served as the smithy.

Issuing a mournful call, Dashiq committed herself to the effort and allowed ropes to be looped over her muscular neck and haunches. Riette continued to feel useless and did her best to stay out of the way.

"We're ready!" Brick shouted. "When I say, give it all you've got. Now! Heave!"

Like a draft horse pulling a sunken plow, Dashiq leaned into the ropes and groaned from the effort. The ropes creaked and popped but did not budge.

"Help her!" Barabas ordered, and everyone still standing grabbed the ropes and pulled.

Despair quickly began to set in. The massive gun was simply too heavy for them to move. Tears gathering in Brick's eyes threatened to shatter Riette's will. He was the strongest and kindest person she'd ever known. He had stood up for her even when outnumbered, and it had cost him dearly over the years. It had also cost Joren business, but neither had ever complained. Riette had always been grateful for them, and to see them near their own breaking points hurt her in a way few other things could.

"Incoming!" someone shouted.

Despair set its hooks deeply. It was too late. The Zjhon had returned, and the people of Sparrowport had accomplished nothing in the meantime. The planes would encounter no resistance and could choose their targets at will. If the people did not scatter soon, they would give away the smithy's location, which was among the few assets they had remaining, not to mention expose themselves to fire. Without any people left alive, the smithy would mean nothing. Unable to figure out what to do, Riette stood frozen, holding Emmet's hand. If she had to die, at least she could be there to comfort him in their last moments. It was small consolation, but it was something. With sad determination, she turned to face the incoming planes.

When she saw what approached, she drew a sharp breath. A single dragon flew toward them with two riders.

It was Berigor.

Seeing Dashiq in distress, Berigor and Keldon wasted no time. The larger dragon landed not far from Riette, looking not much better than the last time she'd seen him. She half expected Barabas to scold the man, but instead he just took half the ropes from Dashiq and tossed them up to Keldon. The man did not hesitate and asked no questions. Berigor nuzzled Dashiq and the two shared a moment of solace, eyes closed. No one could say exactly what passed between them, but when they opened their eyes again, both began to pull with all their might. The effort tore away the stone atop the smithy and left a gaping hole through which the gleaming gun barrel emerged. Riette had known it would be big, but it seemed to go on forever. When the small end finally emerged, people did their best to guide the massive weapon through the haphazard debris field, which had once been cobblestone streets.

Even with Berigor's help, getting the gun out of town without damaging it was a struggle. Children also helped, working together to move things from the dragons' paths. Upon reaching the trenches, Barabas guided Dashiq to the south. Sloping hills covered in slick grasses made the second part of the journey far easier, and the people struggled to keep up with the laboring dragons. Riette wasn't even certain where they were going until Brick dashed past them, moving faster than Riette had ever seen him go. He ran straight toward a pile of debris that looked like nothing more than a tangle of downed trees. Others joined him and helped clear the brush from what was in actuality a sandbagged base not unlike the one supporting the cannon on the airfield, only this one was half again as large. Copper tanks were just barely visible amid recently constructed berms, and a stockpile of large stone shot rested to one side.

"We've been building this at night for the past week," Brick said with a mixture of pride and anxious anticipation. "Now we'll find out if I was right or if I'm the greatest fool Sparrowport has ever known."

Riette hugged him, unable to do anything more to address his regrettably realistic fears. The dragons pulled the massive gun barrel into place until the trunnions settled into the grooves made for them. The fit was precise and made Riette proud of her friend. He'd come such a long way since the days of making cook pots and door knockers.

People cheered when the air tanks were connected and the first round breech loaded. Once the breech was closed, Brick climbed up to sight the mighty gun. Out to sea, the Zjhon fleet was visible, waiting just far enough offshore to stay beyond the smaller gun's range. Here on the bluffs and with the much larger gun, they would drive the fleet farther out to sea and reduce their ability to launch air raids.

Before they ever got a shot off, though, it became clear it would be too little too late. Somehow the Zjhon must have known they were planning something and appeared determined to put an end to the resistance once and for all. The previous flights had been but a fraction of their remaining strength. The skies above the fleet were filled with aircraft. It looked as if they would send every bit of firepower they had remaining. It was an overwhelming force, and all those assembled quailed. No more cheers rose from the now dispirited group. Within a few minutes, their destruction would come.

"Hold your fire," Barabas barked, and Brick looked at him with confusion in his eyes. "Wait until the planes have moved close enough to town that they can no longer see us up here. Let them attack an empty town, so they have no munitions left by the time they realize we're here."

"He's right," Joren said. "Better to let them bomb empty bunkers than to come here where we are largely undefended. We're only going to get one chance at this. Once they know this gun is here, they'll do everything they can to destroy it, just as they have the one on the airfield."

"They've failed at that so far," Brick argued.

"Won't matter if the gun survives and there's no one left to fire it," Joren said.

Everyone else remained silent, letting the young man's father say his piece. Brick nodded in obvious reluctance. Those gathered on the bluffs watched from concealed positions within a line of scrubby trees, trying to keep from being seen and feeling helpless while a devastating force descended on their home. A pair of young men ran back to town to evacuate those they could, and Riette prayed with all her might the children found their way to safety, despite knowing no place was really safe.

"Open the valves," Brick shouted once the last aircraft disappeared behind the tallest peak along the shoreline. With the shot already loaded and the gun sighted on the largest Zjhon ship, Brick did not hesitate. Taking control of the situation, he fired the mighty weapon. It issued an echoing report like nothing any of them had ever heard before. For a long moment, nothing happened, but then, even from such a distance, the impact was unmistakable. While his shot had flown over the flagship, three smaller ships were damaged and began to sink. "Close the valves," Brick ordered, working to open the breech and reload. Never had Riette been so proud and frightened at the same time.

CHAPTER SIXTEEN

War is a terrible and sometimes necessary thing; avoid it when you can, but fight with everything you have when you cannot.
—Barabas DeGuiere, dragon rider

* * *

Sparrowport died in spectacular fashion under a heavy barrage. The force was excessive, far beyond what was needed to bring the town to its end, but it appeared the Zjhon had tired of the game.

"They've just been playing with us," Brick said, tears streaming down his face while he reloaded the long gun.

"You've fought well," Barabas said. "Every bit you've weakened them will increase the chance of survival for those farther inland. Your efforts have not been for nothing."

Brick did not respond. Instead he sent another round of stone shot into the Zjhon fleet. Already he'd inflicted great damage. No matter how much they had prepared, the Zjhon had not been expecting this. What had been an orderly armada was now chaos. The ships that weren't sinking or too badly damaged to maneuver attempted to turn and sail to deeper water. Brick and those around him did everything possible to prevent that. Smoke rose from the sandbags on which the long gun rested, stone munitions heating the metal with every shot. Unavoidable friction pushed the barrel to its limits.

"Slow down, lad," Joren said. "You're going to stress the metal too much. If that gun fails, it's likely to kill us all."

"If not the gun, then it will be them," Brick said, pointing to the airplanes now soaring toward them, having dropped their payloads on the mostly empty town.

Riette hadn't seen the children or those who'd been in the small field hospital at the end of town, and she feared for their lives. The planes coming toward them posed less of a threat now, but some had not had their turrets removed. Stone shot marched a line across the grassy soil and up the sandbags surrounding the mighty gun. Brick dived behind defensive structures created for that purpose. A moment later, U-jets screamed past, each one taking aim at where Brick lay. Dust filled the air along with Riette's screams. Her friend was the primary target, and the aircraft pummeled the spot where he hid.

Wave after wave passed, not providing any break in the fire. One diesel prop approached with its heavy munitions still in place. Riette shouted in warning. Those who hid amid the sandbags and berms fled the area, knowing the power of even one of those bombs. Riette glanced over her shoulder while running toward a nearby copse of fir trees. Joren dug frantically amid the ruptured sandbags, looking for Brick. A moment later, his son emerged from a spot farther back. He grabbed his father and, despite his limp, did his best to pull the man to the place where Riette now hid. Blood and stone dust obscured most of his features, but he had never been more handsome or heroic.

The bomb released with an audible click, and an instant later, the world exploded. When the smoke cleared, the long gun remained intact but now rested at the wrong angle.

"Help me!" Brick cried, running back to the gun. No matter how valiant his heart, the flesh could endure only so much. Halfway across the field, his knees buckled. He was not alone in his bravery, though; others soon helped him, half carrying him back to the gun.

Close to half the sandbags had been ruptured or completely blasted away. There was no way to rebuild the side that had been destroyed, no matter how hard they tried, the sand simply fell away.

"Lower the far side," Joren shouted. "Take bags from the far side and use them to brace this side!"

Brick orchestrated the deconstruction of the high side. "Don't take all the bags from one spot," he said. "I want the other side built up before this thing decides to move."

As if to prove his words, the mighty gun barrel creaked and groaned while sliding into place. The sandbags held, but the whole arrangement was unstable. Riette sucked in a sharp breath when Brick lost his footing and slid into a gap between the gun barrel and the sandbags. If the enormous weight shifted while he was under there, he could be trapped or crushed. Grunting, he pulled himself free. As he did, he met Riette's eyes, and his face flushed. How he could be embarrassed by slipping while being the bravest person alive was beyond Riette's understanding. Men were unfathomable creatures. Twice more the gun came close to rolling over those trying to repair it. Only Berigor's quick reflexes kept Brick and several others from being crushed.

Riette tended to the wounded. This at least gave her something to do besides watch her friends risk their lives. Some of the townspeople were beyond help, and she tried her best to concentrate on those her efforts might save. Even those who worked around her bore wounds of their own. It wasn't fair—any of it. They had done their best and given their all, and still evil had prevailed. The world made no sense.

Again, the gun fired. No one dared hope it would be enough. It was a noble but futile effort to inflict damage on an enemy who had already won. When she looked back to where Dashiq rested, Emmet was climbing into the saddle behind Barabas. Tuck ran toward her, looking concerned. "We have to go! Now!"

"I can't," Riette answered over her shoulder, no longer looking at him. She cared for Baker Millman, the man who'd always baked the best bread in Sparrowport. He'd been among the few people who were kind to her and Emmet, and she refused to let him die. "I need bandages," she said to Tuck, and he did his best to tear cloth into strips, all the while looking over his shoulder. Riette risked a peek, only to see Barabas and her brother about to fly away. "Go," she said.

"No," Tuck said. "I'm not leaving you."

He was not as big or strong as Brick, but Riette felt safer with Tuck by her side. No matter his strengths or weaknesses, he cared about her, and that meant something. Brick continued to fire into the fleet, hoping to leave the returning aircraft with no place to land. "I need more shot!" he shouted.

"It's too much," Joren said.

Brick ignored him and loaded the mighty gun, screaming as he burned himself on hot metal. When he released the pent-up air this time, Joren's fears came to pass. Rather than sending a projectile into the enemy fleet, the barrel had begun to droop under its own weight, and its tip shattered from the force. People fell and screams filled the air.

Chaos ruled the field, and Riette realized then they should have been paying more attention to what was taking place behind them. Tuck made a choking sound, and Riette turned to see a Zjhon soldier take him down. An instant later, a hand closed over her mouth, stifling her scream. No matter how she kicked and fought, the stern-faced woman she'd seen on the Sparrowport airfield so long ago dragged her toward silent airships hovering above the trees. Within moments, a rope had been tied around Riette and she was hoisted in the air like nothing more than a sack of potatoes. Tuck was similarly tied and met her eyes while they were hauled upward.

"I'm sorry."

"No," Riette said. "I'm sorry."

It was the last thing she said for some time. The woman climbed a rope ladder beside them, her heavy boot landing squarely on Riette's jaw.

Darkness reigned.

* * *

Seeing his sister and Tuck captured by the Al'Zjhon made Emmet want to jump from the saddle and rescue them, but it was beyond his abilities. Already Dashiq moved toward the cliffs, barely able to get herself airborne. Emmet grabbed Barabas by the shoulder and turned him so he could see. Perhaps he would have gone back for them, but the Zjhon pilots returning to the naval fleet knew their fate. Amid the chaos and sinking ships, no place to land awaited. Most now turned back toward Sparrowport. Given the weight of their previous payloads, Emmet guessed they carried just enough fuel to complete the mission. Some pilots ditched and hung in the air, suspended by their parachutes. Others aimed directly for Dashiq and Berigor, who now flanked them.

Only a few planes still carried weaponry. A pair of diesel props and a squadron of U-jets opened fire. Too busy making evasive maneuvers, the dragons had no time to turn back and face the airships departing with their friends. Emmet continued to watch in horror while the first two dirigibles turned east and fled. The third still had ropes dragging on the ground. Brick and Joren ran in pursuit of Zjhon making their way back to the aircraft. Two made it to the ropes, but Brick would not be denied. Through brute force and sheer will, he tossed men aside and gained one of the ropes himself, his father not far behind. Soon the airship soared higher, Brick and Joren swinging in the wind. Fearless, the two climbed and latched on to those above them on the ropes. It was unclear if those on deck even knew they were coming, but their comrades were tossed to the winds. Higher Brick climbed.

Emmet would have continued to watch if not for the fire Dashiq was taking. Shot after shot landed on the dragon, and Barabas was also struck. No one was immune, and pain erupted in Emmet's rib cage. Nothing in his life had ever hurt so badly. Dashiq roared a battle cry and Berigor answered. The dragons took the fight to the Zjhon with unmatched fury. Planes tumbled from the air, unable to evade the enraged dragons.

The skies were afire. Tapping her final reserves, Dashiq tore into the naval fleet and finished what Brick had started. The sinking flagship now stuck up in the air, the weight of it tearing the mighty ship in two; it died with a haunting sound. Few ships remained unscathed, and Dashiq targeted those. Fewer and fewer aircraft filled the skies, but those that remained all targeted the dragons, aware Dashiq was the greatest threat and most likely knowing no safe place existed for them to land at sea or around Sparrowport. Already lost, they wished to do what damage they could to the enemy before they perished. Emmet tried not to think about having had the same feelings toward the Zjhon. How was he any better? He'd seen the desperation in the people of Sparrowport. No one would win this war. All would suffer.

Berigor tore into the planes, doing his best to protect Dashiq, but even he could not prevent her from taking additional fire. Her wing flaps slowed, and Barabas slumped in the saddle. Emmet alone remained alert and relatively uninjured. His ribs hurt but he was conscious. Part of him lamented that. To witness such tragedy was to be scarred for the rest of his days, no matter how few they may be. Watching in horror, he doubted he would ever sleep soundly again. Never had he felt truly safe, but this took his insecurity to new heights.

As the last U-jet struck the bluffs and with the naval fleet in disarray, Dashiq turned back to the east. Emmet's heart soared for a brief moment when he realized she meant to go after Tuck and Riette. He did not know how to save his sister and his friend since knocking the airships from the skies would likely kill all those aboard, but Emmet was ready to give his life in the attempt to save them. Reaching forward, he grabbed Barabas by the shoulder, checking to see if he was still alive. A gnarled hand reached up and patted Emmet's. It was enough.

Berigor flew alongside them. Keldon issued an echoing battle cry. The people who remained on the bluffs responded in earnest. Victory was theirs. None would deny the cost, but Emmet could not blame those who celebrated their very survival. Not so long ago, it had seemed they would all perish at the hands of the Zjhon, and some yet lived. It was a hollow victory for Emmet. Two of the people he cared the most about had been taken from him, and thoughts of what they might endure made him feel small and afraid. Riette had always been there for him. She'd protected him. She'd loved him when no one else had. The thought of her in Zjhon hands threatened to tear his heart to pieces. The pain was physical and as real as his bruised ribs.

Everything changed when a single diesel prop appeared from behind the peaks between them and Sparrowport. The same peaks that had hidden the long gun from the airplanes now worked against them. The gun turret rotated and opened fire. Sluggish, Dashiq was unable to avoid the attack and bore the brunt. Noble and brave, Berigor moved between the plane and Dashiq, taking some of the fire, but the damage was done. Dashiq wobbled in the air, her head drooping low.

With a rage-filled roar, Berigor winged toward the airplane, not looking much better than Dashiq. In good health, he would easily have outmaneuvered the plane, but he was battered and weak. The pilot was not interested in Berigor; the man stared straight at Emmet. Such hatred and intent to kill burned like fire. Reaching out with one claw, Berigor raked the cockpit, collapsing it inward. It was a valiant effort, but he was too late. Even out of control, the plane hurtled toward Dashiq, its inertia too much to overcome. Emmet screamed when the plane careened into them.

Displaying bravery until the end, Dashiq veered, exposing her belly to the attack, sparing Barabas and Emmet the brunt. The impact was jarring, and Emmet tasted blood. Dashiq issued a grunt laced with pain and remorse. Her head was thrown out to one side. Emmet watched, horrified. Going limp, the dragon slumped, her remaining eye rolling up into her head.

The plane dropped from the sky, along with Emmet, Barabas, and Dashiq. Only a moment before they struck the cold waves crashing into the rocky bluffs, Berigor roared, his claws closing around Dashiq. In his weakened state, he was barely able to keep them all airborne. Skimming the waves, they flew south, leaving the Jaga and the Zjhon fleet behind. Emmet's hope of rescuing his sister died in that moment.

* * *

Straining to pull himself up, hand over hand, Brick for once wished he weighed a bit less. His brawn had served him well over the years, but gravity held on to him more tightly than it did others. Only the sight of his father making progress in his climb gave him hope. Riette had been taken aboard a different airship, and he was determined not to let that vessel out of his sight. She'd slipped through his fingers once, and he wasn't about to let it happen again. Meeting his father's gaze, he nodded. The need for silence was understood. So far no one appeared to have realized they were there. The airship moved higher in the skies, making them ever more vulnerable. It would be a simple task to knock them from the ropes and send them tumbling to the rocky shoreline below. Moving east, the three airships lacked the speed of other aircraft, but their flight was stable and their capacity great.

After a brief rest, Joren and Brick resumed their climb, wanting to reach the deck at the same moment. They had spent their entire lives working together, and Brick was grateful for their ability to communicate using few if any words. There had been many times over the years he'd lamented working in a confined space with someone who knew his every weakness. Now he understood just how much his father had taught him. Without that knowledge, he'd never have been able to help save the people of Sparrowport. His father had done his part, no doubt, but it had been Brick who'd rallied the people and come up with a plan. Why the people had chosen to follow his lead, he might never know, but it gave him a sense of pride. Never would he take credit for what the people had done to save themselves, but it was clear his voice had given them direction, purpose, and focus.

It had been Joren's skills that had produced the long gun—skills he'd passed along to his son. He deserved as much credit as anyone, but he was content to let Brick take a leadership role. Even now, his father had followed him to the airship and joined in what might turn out to be complete folly. He had no idea what they were going to do next. There had been no time. Bravery was perhaps about doing what needed to be done in the moment without considering the consequences. If he'd waited to determine the best course of action, he would likely have missed his chance. Only time would tell if his impetuous decision would make him a hero or a martyr. Either way, he'd done what was right.

Riette was among the strongest people he'd ever met, even if she'd always thought herself weak. When her mother died, she'd taken over the family business and kept them from losing what they had. Then her father was called to war. Brick had heard the tales of his bravery and his presumed demise, and he wasn't sure he would have been so brave, even while hanging from a rope suspended above his homeland.

Joren struggled with the climb, and Brick found himself waiting for the sake of his father. No one knew what awaited them on deck, and surely they would be more effective together. Brick suspected that was the only reason his father had come at all. Neither were trained fighters, though both had been in their fair share of scuffles. Defending Riette and Emmet alone had provided Brick with more than a few bruises and scars. It had been his muscles that had gotten him through. No matter how much he'd hated having to work the forge in his childhood, the work had made him stronger than steel. While the other children had played, he'd endured the heat and had become as tough as an anvil. Remembering Joren saying those exact words, Brick smiled in spite of his current circumstances. A single glance told Brick his father was ready to make one final effort to reach the deck.

No matter their plans, Brick got there first. Before pulling himself over the rail, he looked about and saw no one. With a final grunting effort, he hoisted himself aboard. A moment later, he grabbed his father's wrist and helped him over the rail. The older man's chest heaved from the exertion, and he placed a finger over his lips. Brick nodded. He held both hands out to his father, palms first, indicating they should rest for a few moments before proceeding.

After what felt like an eternity, Joren regained his breath and nodded to his son, a look of such pride in his eyes, Brick grew misty eyed. His father was a man of strength—both physical and of character—but he'd never been one to issue easy praise. To know he'd gained his father's respect was overwhelming, but this was no time for sentimentality. Riette and Tuck needed him. He'd just met the boy, but already Tuck had a special place in the smith's heart. Anyone who cared for Riette and Emmet was all right in his judgment.

After a nod from his father, Brick looked around, surprised to see no one on the ship. The deck itself was far narrower than a seafaring ship, surrounding a deckhouse that protruded from the bottom of the giant canvas-covered latticework filled with lighter-than-air gasses. Brick understood something of the construction, having salvaged parts from downed airships to create the weapons used to defend Sparrowport. They weren't far from the galley, and that was where he headed first. The airships had moved out over the water and continued heading east. Brick could only assume they would make for the Firstland and deliver the prisoners to Argus Kind. He was determined not to let that happen.

Before reaching the galley, they passed the weapons hold. Holding up a finger, Brick motioned for his father to keep watch. The door opened with a creak. Brick was immediately met with force. Only a fool left powerful weapons unguarded, and the Zjhon were not fools. Two men in light armor waited within. The first swung a heavy cudgel at Brick's head, while the other made for a handle in the wall that Brick presumed would sound the alarm. Ducking beneath the cudgel, Brick lunged at the second man. After passing the first, Brick turned and shoved him hard in the back, sending him toward the deck where Joren waited. Only the man's scream becoming softer and distant told Brick he would cause them no more trouble. The second man closed his hand around the lever. Brick punched him in the face with all his might. Moments later, the second man went over the rail without a sound.

It didn't take Brick long to find what he was looking for. Stored in crates filled with wood shavings, clay spheres rested, evenly spaced. Gently Brick grabbed two, knowing how potent these weapons could be. Plenty had been dropped on Sparrowport. Though lacking the potency of the massive bombs used to demolish the bunkers, these would be more than sufficient for his purposes.

Luck was with him. Laughter and song emanated from the galley. These soldiers had been spared battle and were headed home. Their celebration would meet an abrupt end. Without any hesitation, Brick yanked the portal open and threw the clay spheres in, slamming the rounded, metal door shut. The weapons detonated with concussive force, most of which was contained within the galley. It took all his strength to yank the twisted portal open again, and smoke clogged the air when he did. At least a dozen soldiers were scattered around the galley in various states of disarray.

Joren charged in first, no longer willing to watch his son fight alone. In a short time, they tossed the stunned, semiconscious soldiers overboard. Surprise was no longer on their side, and the two men made their way to the wheelhouse in wary silence. Brick counted down on his fingers before yanking open the portal. The instant he stepped across the threshold, the pilot opened fire. Pain erupted in Brick's chest, but he ignored it. Still able to breathe and move, he thanked the gods the man was armed with only an air pistol, which lacked the punch of larger weapons. Before his father could say a word, Brick grabbed the pilot and threw him out of the wheelhouse like a hay bale. Joren tried to catch the man but failed. Instead, the pilot went overboard with the rest of the crew.

Sitting down hard, Brick pulled his shirt open and looked at the blood running down his chest. The stinging grew worse as he examined the wounds—two small, red holes in his pectoral muscles. Wincing, he squeezed on either side of the first hole, and a metal pellet emerged. After doing the same with the other, he allowed his father to clean and dress the wounds.

"I think I'll live," Brick said.

"You were well named, m'boy. You're thicker than a brick."

After grinning at his father, Brick winced when he stood. That was going to sting for a while.

"As proud as I am of you, my son, sometimes you just don't think."

Looking at the array of controls before him, Brick didn't have to ask what the older man meant. Throwing the pilot overboard might have been a mistake. He had no idea how to fly this ship, and any mistakes could prove fatal. "I wonder what this lever does," he said.

Joren shook his head.

CHAPTER SEVENTEEN

Pain cuts deeply. Through healing, we grow stronger.
—Marim, hedge witch

* * *

Never had Emmet felt so lonely. Barabas and Dashiq were both unconscious. Berigor held them in his claws, which was far from a comfortable way to fly. Overwhelming emotion was crippling, but the people he cared about most needed him. His heroes had not given up, and neither would he. After taking a deep breath, Emmet placed his hands on Dashiq's neck. Unlike the times he had helped Barabas send healing energy to the dragon, Emmet was in complete control. He moderated the flow, dictated the cadence, and applied the intent, whereas before he'd been but a participant, feeding energy to the existing flow. Now he conducted a magnificent orchestra. All his life, magic had been missing. Like craving a specific food when the body is deficient, magic had called to him. Now he'd found it. Going back would be impossible.

His was the curse of the magic user born after the magic had gone. Only scraps remained—beautiful, delicious scraps. Beneath him, the saddle pulsed with power. The stones were streaked, milky white, and he knew when they went all white, the magic would be forever gone—or at least for two thousand years if the tales were to be believed. The scale of it frightened him. His actions would impact the availability of magic and power for future generations. The saddle and its stones were not his to use as he pleased. Still, he let himself fall into the energy, suspended on the vibrations. It was not for himself he did this, but deep down, he had to admit he relished the experience.

Leaving one hand on Dashiq, Emmet reached forward and placed the other on Barabas. The man did not move, but life force pulsed within him—weak and erratic. Focusing his intention, he let the energy flow through him. He was the conductor. His body warmed and no matter how he wished to send all the energy his friends needed, he could not. Like a wick, he would burn out. Instead, he drew lesser amounts of energy and crafted it into structured waves of intent. Equations revealed themselves in his mind, showing the true nature of the world and the energy surrounding him; he could feel it.

Dashiq was fading, her pain deep and irreversible. Emmet did his best to comfort her, but it was not enough—would not be enough. She was still there, but he didn't know for how much longer. The passage of time had long been the bane of Emmet's existence, and he found himself surprised when Berigor bellowed, about to lower them to a rocky shoreline.

Emmet recognized the place from his first journey to the shallows. No matter how the bigger dragon tried, he could not gently place Dashiq on the rough landscape. Showing she was once again conscious, Dashiq lowered her claws and absorbed the short fall. Barabas, too, showed signs of being awake and alert; his hands fumbled at the straps. Before Emmet reached him, the older man rolled out of the saddle and fell to the ground. By the time Emmet undid the belts and climbed down, Barabas had hauled himself up and retrieved his walking stick from within the saddle.

When he reached the dragon's eye, Dashiq issued a moan ending in a mighty woof. The burst of air made Barabas take a step back. Letting out a low, squealing moan, she closed her eye and nuzzled him. The two stood in a quiet embrace for some time. Inspecting the saddle, Emmet found it distressingly chalky and white—all over, especially around the seats. Along the outer edges, a few stones retained some luster and clarity. He'd done what he could do to heal his friends, and he felt it better to leave the remaining power be, although it called to him.

Berigor landed nearby, and Keldon approached. "I'm sorry I did not arrive sooner."

The apology was enough to express his understanding of the situation. They were in trouble.

"The shallows?" Emmet asked.

Barabas nodded, never opening his eyes or releasing his embrace with Dashiq. It was the dragon who finally broke the bond between them and pulled her head away. She looked down to Emmet and he approached. Briefly she nuzzled him, appreciation and love exuded through the bond. She was so weak. It pained him to see her so and knowing the flight to the shallows was too much to ask. It had taken days from this place the last time, and she'd been in far better health. She would likely perish before reaching the shallows; it was something no one wanted to say. The dragon turned her head to the side so Emmet could see the metalwork comprising much of her jaw and facial structure. There, set into a complex mechanical orifice, rested Azzakkan's Eye—still glossy and slick and pulsing with power all its own. Dashiq pushed her head into his hand, and his fingers came to rest on the release. Scales lining the eye socket rotated outward in succession, until Azzakkan's Eye dropped into his palm, still warm.

The power emanating from the glassy sphere was completely unlike what was stored within the saddle's stones. Where he had drawn raw energy from those stones and crafted it into the form he desired, the energy from the eye was already a symphony of structure and architecture; Emmet could do nothing to improve on that masterwork.

No one spoke.

The choice was Emmet's—the decision his. He did not hesitate. His destiny was upon him, and he owed it to his sister and Tuck and Barabas and Dashiq. Approaching Berigor, he passed Keldon, who remained silent. The man had perhaps learned from his own mistakes. The warrior Emmet had first met would never have let him reach for his dragon's eye. Now, though, he watched in cautious silence while Berigor gazed down on Emmet. The larger dragon had to turn his head all the way to one side for the small boy to reach. Again the mechanism released the glass eye into Emmet's palm. The two looked similar, and perhaps some would find them difficult to tell apart, but for Emmet, it was unmistakable. The one Berigor had just returned to him was a poor imitation of the real thing. No power emanated from it. It had been largely cosmetic.

Reaching up, Emmet inserted Azzakkan's Eye into the socket. The mechanism issued a series of clicks, each scale rotating back into place, securing the eye. Berigor shook his head and took a step back. A moment later blue flames danced along the rims of his nostrils.

"Easy, boy," Keldon said. "Not certain you know what you've just done, young man. Berigor has always been . . . spirited . . . and he's still young. But I also thank you. He, too, is far from healed. Azzakkan's Eye will help him."

As if to answer the words, Berigor snorted, his nostrils flaring.

"She can't fly," Barabas said, and the words came out like nails being driven into his heart. "But she doesn't want to be carried either. She is well enough to get airborne and grab Berigor's tail."

Keldon nodded. "Here are some rations. It's just some dried fruits, meats, and cheeses."

"It's most welcome," Barabas said.

"There really is no time to waste, then," Keldon said before climbing back onto Berigor. The look on his face told Emmet what he needed to know. Al'Drakon felt the magic just as he had. It would take some getting used to. Already Emmet felt cold and bereft of the energy the Eye exuded. No matter how he tried, he could not imagine a wizard skilled enough to craft glass, metal, and magic into a work of art, yet the evidence was overwhelming. Someone had once achieved this level of mastery and created the artifact. It was both humbling and enticing. Given the opportunity, he wondered what else he might learn to do and create. Trying not to let the fact that so little magic remained in the world terrify him, Emmet imagined the things of which he might be capable.

Before he mounted, though, Emmet approached Dashiq with the glass eye. The dragon calmly refused it, pushing him back toward the saddle. Barabas gave him a boost, and soon Emmet was bathed in the ambient glow of the last vestiges of energy remaining in the saddle. Berigor and Keldon alighted, and Barabas strapped himself in.

Never had Dashiq struggled so hard to get herself into the air, but she was still alive, and it was in her very nature. After several long and torturous moments, she gained the skies and skimmed over the waves. Berigor appeared before them in what felt like a short period of time; Emmet was never truly certain. Dashiq grabbed on to his mighty tail and wrapped hers around his. The bull dragon trumpeted. Magic poured over them all as Berigor drew deeply from Azzakkan's Eye for the first time. The metalwork in his face blazed brightly, exceeding even what Dashiq had achieved. When he moved his head, the metalwork flexed and moved, molten and reacting like normal flesh and bone.

The air changed pitch when Berigor leaned into the wind, using it to send them ever faster until their hair flew straight backward and their cheeks flapped.

"No more!" Keldon yelled.

Faster still Berigor flew.

Even lacking synchronicity, Emmet knew time was not on their side. Judging by how many stops it had required, he surmised it had taken weeks to reach the shallows the first time. Speed was called for, but there were limits.

Ducking down behind Barabas, Emmet enjoyed some of the rations Keldon had provided. Twice he tried to share with Barabas, and both times the man refused. Emmet worried about him. The man had become something of a father figure. Emmet's own father wasn't coming back, and Barabas had much to teach and share. The uncertainty of the near future gnawed at him as he ate, and it didn't take long for his appetite to fade. It was probably for the best. Who knew how long they would have to live on the rations they had with them?

Getting low in the saddle, Emmet found a spot where the wind wasn't so bad, and soon he slept.

* * *

Traveling by airship, especially one of such quality, might have been a pleasure under far different circumstances. Constructed of richly grained hardwood, a mountain of the finest brass, thick taupe canvas, and miles of heavy line, the airship *Dominance* was a monument to design and achievement. However, no matter how elegant the lines or how thick the polish, she was first a machine of war. Occasionally strong winds caused the ship to bob and turn, the rigging creaking under the strain, but her flight was for the most part steady and smooth.

The farther they got from Sparrowport, the less likely rescue would be. Riette had no way to know if Emmet, Dashiq, and Barabas were still alive. The order in which she thought of them was not lost on her, but already she missed them all. The questions running over and over through her mind threatened to drive her mad. Everything was wrong. Everything was broken. Quite possibly everyone she loved was dead—save one. Being imprisoned in the same cabin as Tuck was all that kept Riette from utter despair.

"They'll come for us," Tuck said. "You know they will."

"That's what I'm afraid of," Riette admitted. Neither needed to say more on the subject. Both understood why they had been captured.

"There's a chance we can escape," Tuck said softly. "There are parachutes and jumpsuits aboard. I've seen these ships crash, and the crew don't hardly never go down with the ship."

"We've got to get out of this room first."

The cabin itself had obviously not been designed as a prison, which could potentially work to their advantage. It was a long voyage, and the Zjhon would have to feed them to keep them alive. Each time would present an opportunity. Few things had been left in the cabin for their comfort, but Riette began to inventory the items they might use to their advantage.

"We might could throw the blankets over the poor sap who brings our food," Tuck said barely above a whisper. "And then we can hit 'im."

"With what?"

Tuck shrugged and raised his fists. Riette wouldn't say it to him, but she didn't hold out much hope for taking on armed guards. Deep wooden benches for sitting and sleeping lined the walls. Not much else presented itself, in spite of a thorough inspection. With nothing more than blankets to arm themselves, the odds of escape were impossibly small. Still, it was at least some hope, and it was perhaps the only way they could get out of this without endangering those they loved. It was the unspoken truth that drove them both. Words were not required. Emmet would be proud.

"No matter what happens," Riette said. "I'm glad we're together."

"Me, too," Tuck said. "If things had been different—" His voice caught and he left the words unspoken.

Perhaps it was the time spent with Barabas and Dashiq, but Riette needed words less and less to communicate. Between her and Tuck, things were just understood, which frightened her like nothing else. She cared for him. Everything else she'd ever cared for had been taken from her. It was a thought that brought tears to her eyes. If not for the cabin door opening, she might have said more.

Burly men in full armor entered the room as if they feared the two young people. The woman they now knew was named Casta Mett followed them into the cabin.

"I hope you're comfortable," she said with a wicked smile. There was no warmth in her eyes. "We've brought you some refreshment." The woman did not wear a coat, and she rubbed her arms. "It's cold in here. I hope you've not been uncomfortable. We wouldn't want our passengers to be unhappy, now would we?"

Riette and Tuck said nothing, both knowing her concern was far from genuine. The woman took pleasure from torturing them with her words.

She smiled at their sour expressions. "Don't worry. Barabas will come for you." This was the first time a smile reached her eyes. It was out of place and made her even less attractive. "Who knows? Maybe even your brother will come. We'll be ready and waiting for them when they arrive; you can be assured of that. And once we've disposed of them, we'll have little use remaining for you. At which point, you'll be free to go, of course." The wide grin she now wore made it clear the words were not true.

Casta Mett might be the most deplorable person Riette had ever encountered, and she hoped one day to find vengeance. No matter how unlikely, she held on to that grim desire.

A young man not much older than Riette and Tuck came then carrying a wooden bowl filled with a greasy-looking liquid. He handed it to Riette, who looked back, confused.

"I hope you enjoy it," Casta Mett said with her most evil smile yet, and she nodded to the guards, who grabbed Tuck in spite of Riette's cry and dragged him from the room. The woman then turned to leave but stopped and looked back to Riette. "I almost forgot." Walking over to the benches, she took the two blankets. "Can't have you attacking the crew, now can we?"

When the door closed behind her, Riette wept. Outside, Casta Mett laughed.

* * *

Only once more did Berigor land before they reached the shallows. Emmet barely remembered the stop, having spent most of it in a sleepy fog. When the shallows came into view, however, he was awake and alert. The first things he noticed were the missing pillars. From the mighty circle where Dashiq had once hovered, two pillars had fallen and one stood at an odd angle, leaning away from the others. The landscape was completely surreal. Deep blue waters ended at a shelf of land topped with white beaches, scrublands and a not-so-distant mountain. The shallow waters now contained jagged, luminous rifts, some of which emitted bubbling gasses. Emmet wondered if the damage had been done by the meteorites, but it seemed unlikely given how far they were from the impact craters—one on land and one in the shallow waters farther inland.

Dashiq uncoiled herself before they reached land and soared free. For a short time, she enjoyed the act of flying, turning in lazy circles over the sun-drenched landscape and bathing in reflected warmth. The land had magic of its own, and here that power was more prevalent than anywhere else

Emmet had been. He was happy to be back in spite of the circumstances.

Berigor soared to where Dashiq had once hovered, and his partially lidded eye gave the impression of bliss. Dashiq landed near their previous campsite, and Emmet was surprised to realize someone else had been there since. It was strange to know they shared this place with others. The Zjhon had been in the area, but it did not look like a force of that size had made camp there. The evidence spoke of a small group. This place was so remote, it was difficult for him to reconcile. It also made him anxious about anyone who might return.

Barabas climbed down, remaining standing by virtue of his walking stick. Emmet made it down on his own, not needing the assistance Barabas might otherwise have offered. Though his ribs still hurt if he moved the wrong way or coughed, he and Keldon were the healthiest among them.

"The trees," Emmet said, pointing, and Barabas nodded. He made no move toward the water. Emmet was on his own. Walking to the shoreline, he reminded himself of the dangers he faced. Saltbark leaf was precious and did not come without risk. Wading into chest-deep water, he had second thoughts. Perhaps it would be better if Keldon went after the leaves. Still, the trees called to him like old friends, and he could not resist. The current pulled more strongly than the last time, tugging at him, relentless and persistent, ready to drag him out to seas where monsters waited to swallow him whole. Emmet shivered at the thought of being forced into the deep, frigid waters beyond the pillars. A fallen pillar blocked part of the way, torn by unyielding currents. Wandering vortices swirled in the waters around it, making loud sucking noises.

Even if the waters were not terribly deep, Emmet wanted nothing to do with those whirlpools. Fish scattered closer to the far bank where the saltbark trees grew. Keldon, now shirtless, waded toward him. It gave Emmet some comfort to know the man was close by. What crushed his hopes, though, was the state of the trees; they had been picked nearly clean.

Only a fool would treat such a precious tree this way, and Emmet was outraged. Now he hoped the fools did return so he could tell them what he thought of this practice. Even so, he was tempted to take at least a couple of leaves since the need was so great. How was he any better than they? he asked himself. It was the kind of question his sister would have asked, and the thought of her made his heart ache. Life did not always offer fair choices. Sometimes every option available was terrible in its own way. It was something that troubled him deeply but about which he could do nothing. The feeling of powerlessness was all too familiar.

Keldon shook his head when he saw. It meant they would have to take their search farther inland. Before they did, though, Emmet had something he needed to do.

"Friends," he said. It was then he noticed the slender tendril of new growth along the shoreline farther inland, at the place where he had planted a new tree. Knowing he had helped bring a new life into existence thrilled him, and for a time, his heart soared. Even amid all the sorrow, anxiety, and fear, he'd been able to do something good in this world. That made him feel more like a hero than anything else he'd done. Mostly he felt like a scared little boy, but that was beginning to change.

Wrapping his hands around the tree that had previously given him a seed, Emmet did the opposite of what he'd come to do. He'd come to ask more of the land, to take, as humans always did. Now he wanted only to give back, to lend these trees the energy they had been deprived of when stripped of leaves. He felt the need and yearning for the sun's energy. Without the surface area of those green leaves converting light into nourishment, the trees would slowly starve. Using all his might, Emmet connected with the tree and let his life force flow into it. He had no idea how long he'd been connected to the tree, but he felt a hand on his shoulder, which gently pushed him away. Emmet opened his eyes, confused. When he looked to Keldon, the man stood out of arm's reach at a respectful distance. Emmet looked back to the tree but saw no one there. What he did see, however, were dozens of tiny green buds now springing from where leaves had once been. When he pulled his hands away, three brown-and-white-striped seeds rested in his palms, though he'd not felt them being placed there.

Keldon stared in silent amazement, appearing content to watch whatever it was Emmet chose to do.

"Friends," Emmet said, pointing inland.

Keldon grabbed him and hoisted him up onto his shoulders. Together they moved against the current. The far coast was covered in low, twisted scrub that would not allow for easy traversal, and the channel grew wider and more difficult to cross farther inland. Keldon stayed close to the far shore, where the current was not so strong, though the water did sometimes become deep. Emmet remained above water most of the time, but Keldon needed to swim for it on two occasions. What troubled Emmet even more were fevers of giant manta rays floating past and terrifying eels darting in and out of holes in the seafloor.

Along the way, Emmet felt urges to drop seeds in specific places, and he did so in the hopes of repaying the trees for their kindness. They had healed his friends at their own expense and had been abused by others. He could only hope to make up for the damage done.

When they next encountered a tree that had not been picked bare, it was surrounded by tangled vines. No wonder the careless people had ignored this one; it was all but impossible to get to. Keldon almost passed it by, knowing he would have difficulty getting through the branches.

"I can fit," Emmet said. Dashiq, Barabas, and Berigor all needed healing, and it was worth whatever he had to do to get it.

"It's dangerous in there," Keldon said. "Be careful."

Slipping back into the water, Emmet grabbed the vines and pulled himself into their tangled web. Slick and slimy under water, they were coarse and prickly above, but Emmet endured. Sparkling leaves waited within, and he forced himself deeper into the foliage. Reaching forward, he sucked in a sharp breath when a hand grabbed his wrist. Involuntarily he drew a sucking breath and pulled away, now seeing a snake coiled on the branch he'd been about to grab. A woman more beautiful than any he'd ever seen waded within the foliage. She glittered with sparkling facets that covered her skin. Her warm smile made Emmet feel protected and loved. Considering she had saved him from a potential snakebite, he instantly trusted this strange woman. She held a finger to her lips.

"Are you all right in there," Keldon asked.

"Fine," Emmet said.

The woman smiled and silently giggled.

For a moment the two regarded one another, each one looking as if they had found the greatest treasure. The woman cupped Emmet's cheek for a moment, longingly. Aching loneliness flowed through the bond, and Emmet promised to visit again if he could. A tear slid down the woman's smiling face, and she squeezed Emmet's hands. When she pulled away, Emmet's palms filled with sparkling green leaves.

With great reluctance, Emmet left the woman behind and forced his way back out to where Keldon waited. He did not encounter any snakes on the way out, but he was far more watchful.

Not long after he emerged, Barabas shouted across the water. "Hurry! We're losing her!"

Keldon hoisted Emmet back to his shoulders and walked out toward the center of the channel. A pair of rays split and passed them on either side. Keldon was close enough to reach out and touch them, but Emmet was glad he didn't. He hoped they didn't encounter many more. Seeing such massive sea creatures was terrifying. He would make but a morsel for such monsters. Keldon had a plan, though. In deep water he treaded, and they were pulled swiftly back toward the pillars by the current. Before they reached the downed pillar, Keldon swam toward the shoreline, still being pulled out to sea. Emmet feared the current might be too much, but Keldon was a strong swimmer. Still, he was breathing hard when they gained the shoreline.

Emmet ran to Dashiq and held his hands out to Barabas. The dragon's breathing was labored, and she barely responded to Emmet's presence on his return. Berigor now rested nearby and whined while looking over to Dashiq.

"Thank you," Barabas said with overwhelming gratitude. Taking two of the larger leaves from Emmet's palms, he walked to Dashiq's head. She accepted the first leaf on her tongue and closed her mighty jaws. Barabas tried to give her more, but she refused, keeping her jaws shut and nudging him back toward Berigor. The big dragon was hesitant but accepted the five leaves Barabas offered him before curling up and settling in for a nap.

Emmet ran his hands along Dashiq's flank and began removing the saddle. Dashiq stopped him, nudging him from behind and lifting him up. He swung a leg over the saddle and wrapped his arms around her. The dragon issued a contented woof then dragged herself to the shoreline. Like a giant crocodile, she slid into the water, flattening a wide swath of brush.

With serpentine movements, she swam to the pillars. Once there, she spread her wings, gradually ascending until she hovered just above the rushing current. Emmet let the sun warm him, the water evaporating from his clothes. Below him the amber statuette still glowed; no one had dared disturb it. No longer did Dashiq have the magic of Azzakkan's Eye, but power still emanated from the land beneath them, and Emmet did his best to tap into it. While the saddle held precious little magic, it conducted natural energy flowing from the land. Emmet couldn't be certain, but he suspected the energy here could replenish the magic in the saddle given time. Even the sunlight itself held power, though it was far less potent. Perhaps, with patience, he would find power anew.

Providing comfort and empathy, Emmet communed with the dragon. Dashiq had done so much for him and all of them. He understood perhaps better than any other that the dragon had remained alive mostly for the sake of Barabas. Without her, the man would have had very little for which to continue living, and she refused to allow that to happen. In some way she communicated this to Emmet without words or sound, he simply knew. Squeezing her tighter, he told her he didn't ever want her to go away. There was sadness and truth and empathy and hope. All of it flowed into him and Emmet cried.

The dragon nudged him then, breaking into his meditation. She stared at him with one eye and an empty metal socket. It made him sad. He had never seen her in the prime of her life, but he could imagine it and he did. That was how he wanted to remember her. In his mind he fashioned a vision of her when she was younger with Azzakkan's Eye, wearing the sparkling saddle with Barabas and Tuck aboard. Never had they all come together in that way, but it did not matter. Emmet fixed the vision in his mind forever. When he inspected the saddle, he thought the stones might have just a bit more luster.

I must go now.

Sadness and acceptance overcame him. It was the closest anything or anyone had ever come to speaking in his mind, and the words were physically painful. Time compressed. The light blinded. Sound overwhelmed. Putting his hands over his ears, Emmet rocked forward and back in the saddle. She touched him then, sliding her muzzle under his hand, which glided across the scales and came in contact with metal. A spark leaped to meet his finger, and her magic connected with him once more.

Soon.

She broke the contact, and Emmet was left to guess what she meant. Time stretched back out, and he pulled his hands from aching ears. Dashiq turned and headed in the opposite direction of the campsite. On the far shoreline, she landed and nudged Emmet out of the saddle. Once he was on the ground, she hauled herself through the trees. In the distance, he could hear something else crashing through the brush. Climbing the tallest tree he could find, Emmet looked out across the mostly flat landscape to the east. Trees and bushes shook, giving evidence of Dashiq's passage. In the distance, a far larger swath of vegetation moved, and Emmet lost his breath when a mighty serpent reared up, towering above the trees. It let out a terrifying roar then continued.

Across the channel, Barabas and Keldon made their way toward him. He probably should have gone back to them, but something drew him on. After climbing back down from the tree, he followed the trail of downed foliage Dashiq had left in her wake. The closer he came, the louder the dragons grew. What sounded like a terrible battle erupted up ahead, and Emmet froze in place. Barabas and Keldon shouted his name as they crossed the water. The world otherwise grew still, and Emmet moved forward with a sense of dread anticipation.

When he reached a place where a giant clearing had been created from all the brush getting knocked down, he found Dashiq at its center, curled into a ball but with her wings extended forward, forming a small tent. Slowly lifting her head, she looked him in the eye. Sadness and acceptance were conveyed but also hope and a sense of fulfillment.

The dragon did something unexpected then. Snake quick, she struck out at him. Magic built up within the metalwork. Fire danced as Dashiq tapped into the saddle she still wore. Time stretched, her attack slowing, but he did not move. He could have run all the way back to the shoreline before she finished her thrust, but he did not fear her.

Time compressed.

Dashiq's closed maw slammed into his breastbone—hard. Pain erupted, running far deeper than flesh and bone, as if his being had been rung like a bell. The frequency at which he vibrated changed as a result. He felt strange and even more disconnected than he had his entire life, but now the rate at which time moved felt . . . constant, stable. Something foundational within him had changed, but still the world was far away. He felt like a piece of the background, unable to fully engage with reality.

Dashiq pulled her head back, the magic building into a blazing inferno drawn from the saddle, the air, the land, and the dragon's own life force. All his life he'd yearned for magic but had never known exactly why, now the dragon's maw raced toward him, glowing and pulsing with blue plasma.

No longer could he stretch time, which left him no way to get out of her path. Whatever her intent, it was too late to protest, too late to reconsider. Her choice was made, and she slammed into Emmet, knocking him backward. His world exploded, feeling as if his spirit had been knocked free from his body. The frequency at which he vibrated remained the same, but he could see it now. He existed as waves, with crests and troughs. The world around him was the same, except his waves were out of synchronization, his crests lining up with everything else's troughs. He vibrated at the same frequency but was ever so slightly out of time. It was the force that had defined his life, but never had he been able to see it so clearly. Dashiq's second blow knocked Emmet back into rhythm with time and space. A resounding click shook his very soul. It was deep, fundamental, and permanent. He felt it in his bones.

An overwhelming sense of rightness filling him, his knees buckled from the enormity of it. Never would he sense the world in the exact same way his sister and others did, but Emmet Pickette was, for the first time, truly connected to the world around him.

Still reeling from the change in his reality, Emmet watched Barabas approach, speechless. Dashiq's sides heaved; even at the very end, she waited for him. Keldon was a step behind, but the dragon never even glanced at him. Her one eye was focused on Barabas and Barabas alone. He opened his arms, tears running down his cheeks. Whining, she nuzzled him. After a long sigh, her head dropped to the matted brush.

Barabas wept.

CHAPTER EIGHTEEN

Friends come in all shapes, colors, and sizes.
—Tuck, dragon groom

* * *

Slowly the dragon's body relaxed, and her wings opened, revealing the treasure she'd been protecting. Emmet sucked in a deep breath when he saw the first shiny, metallic egg within her final embrace. Keldon scouted ahead to make sure the mighty serpent did not return, and Barabas was no longer fully aware of his surroundings. Emmet shared his sorrow. Feelings and emotions that had been abstracted for so long washed over him. All he could do was stare and concentrate on breathing. Farther Dashiq's wings drew open, and the true magnitude of her gift became clear. Twenty-four eggs huddled together, gleaming with life. Dashiq was gone, but her legacy remained.

"By the gods!" Keldon said.

Barabas looked up then. Despair turned to shock and realization. Emmet could not say what emotions the old man experienced, but he himself had never felt so strongly or deeply. The pain made him ache. Joy and grief merged into a strange soup that manifested in tears and sobs.

A not-so-distant roar brought the group to attention.

"We need to get out of here," Keldon said. "Now."

No one argued, but some things were too precious to leave behind. With speed born of need, Barabas and Keldon removed the saddle from Dashiq and began loading the eggs into the saddlebags. Reaching out, Emmet grabbed an egg and held it to his chest. Within, something stirred, and the egg jumped in his embrace, tapping him on the breastbone. Again Emmet felt pain, and again he was changed. He had been chosen.

Barabas cast him a quick glance, as if ready to ask the boy to help, but instead his look softened. With a sigh, he lifted Emmet into the saddle. Holding the egg to his chest, Emmet was thankful for Barabas and Keldon; the two men carried the saddle, and thus him, over their heads the entire way back to the campsite. Berigor issued a low whine at seeing the saddle then cooed when he saw the egg in Emmet's arms. The dragon sensed the rest of the eggs and snuffled around the saddlebags. His trumpeting call was unexpected. Emmet hoped it didn't draw the sea serpent back. The creature had been majestic and beautiful but terrifying. When the egg shifted in his grip, Emmet's imagination ran wild.

Barabas and Keldon hastily modified the arrangements of straps used to secure the ancient saddle to make it fit behind the one Berigor already wore.

The bull dragon now put his weight on both legs and appeared to be feeling a good bit better. Emmet's heart hurt so badly, he didn't think anything could take the pain away.

Once again, Barabas put Emmet in the saddle and strapped him in. Neither man said anything about the egg Emmet clutched. He was thankful. Barabas did give the boy an extra blanket, which he used to wrap the egg and keep it both warm and safe. When he saw Barabas wrapping the other eggs tightly and packing them around where he would sit, he smiled. Keldon did the same then packed the area around where Emmet sat. Life force pulsed in the eggs, and he loved them all, but Emmet kept that first egg closest.

Golegeth.

The name came like a scent on a breeze, transient yet inescapable. Emmet smiled. His life would never be the same. Every day from there forward was a new kind of gift in a new kind of world. No longer would the same old patterns prevail or the same feelings define him.

"She gave me a gift," Emmet said. "She changed me."

Barabas turned to look at him, and then nodded with a grunt of affirmation.

"Thank you for everything you've done for me—and Riette—and everybody."

Barabas grunted again.

"Can we save them now?"

This question made Keldon turn as well. Barabas nodded. "If they can be saved, then we'll save them. If not, we'll avenge them."

The man had not lied to him. He'd not tried to pretend Riette might not already be dead. He did not assume Emmet was stupid or daft or incapable of understanding the world around him. This was going to take some getting used to.

"I have a gift for you, for what they are worth," Keldon said to Emmet. He reached for the pocket holding the two cache stones within their wooden box. Emmet knew exactly where they were and that the energy in them had been largely—but not entirely—depleted. He accepted them with a grateful bow and slipped the box into the hem of his coat.

Keldon and Barabas mounted, and Berigor leaped into the air from a standstill. It was something Dashiq had struggled to do, especially when bearing a heavy load, but the much younger dragon now did it with ease. The restorative power of this place was like nowhere else, and Emmet, in many ways, was loath to leave. But staying here would not save his sister or Tuck.

Power coursed through Berigor, and the mighty dragon allowed himself full access for the first time. Before he'd been wounded and somewhat tentative. Now he was on the mend, and his confidence grew with every passing moment. Energy washed over Emmet like a lullaby. Holding Golegeth tightly to his chest, he slept, dreaming of a new kind of dragon unlike any to have come before. Already he knew Golegeth and his brethren would be different. Emmet could relate.

Tap. Tap. Tap.

At first Emmet thought he imagined it, but then it happened again.

Tap. Tap. Tap.

Emotions flowed from the egg he held—insistence, impatience, and perseverance were all overshadowed by gnawing hunger. Emmet found himself reaching for the rations Keldon had provided.

Crack.

A tiny jaw bearing razor-sharp teeth protruded through a gap in the shell. Legs pushed at the shell, forcing the crack to expand and the shell to open. A long neck uncoiled, followed by what looked like fresh-grown leaves. They unfolded into webbed wings. When front and hind legs emerged from the shell, Emmet drew a sharp breath; no longer were there any questions regarding Golegeth's lineage. Berigor trumpeted, somehow sensing the new arrival, but he did not slow. Emmet thought the large dragon might actually have sped up a bit. Barabas and Keldon turned back in time to see Golegeth fully spread his wings for the first time. Rushing air caught the wing membranes, and the tiny dragon was whipped out into open air. He did not flap his wings or glide; instead he fell like a brick. When he struck the water, Barabas, Keldon, and Emmet all jumped. Berigor did not overtly react, but he did slow a little.

Bursting from the water a moment later, Golegeth flapped his wings and hauled a fish just smaller than himself from the water. Berigor dipped lower, and Golegeth returned to Emmet's lap. On his way, he called out, sounding almost as if he scolded the larger dragon. Berigor appeared to take no offense, though he did speed back up once the baby dragon was safely within the saddle. Looking pleased with himself, Golegeth devoured the fish. It was a messy and noisy process, and Emmet tried to convince the dragon to eat somewhere other than in his lap, but there weren't many other places to offer except the empty seat behind them. Either way, the dragon did not take him up on any of his suggestions.

Five more trips he made to the sea below, each time returning with a different kind of fish. After the fifth, he lay distended and exhausted. The boy took the blanket that had been in his lap and stuffed it in the seat behind him. While Golegeth slept, Emmet considered the rest of the eggs, all of which were showing signs of life. What would happen when the rest hatched? Panic set in. He would be covered in fish. Golegeth burped, adjusted himself, and went back to sleep.

Berigor either took them ever faster for the fun of it, or he, too, sensed the hatchlings' impending arrival. Emmet suspected it was both. The mighty dragon reveled in his newfound power, the might of the ancients at his disposal. No longer was he a dragon missing an eye; now he was practically Azzakkan reborn—and he knew it. He was the very thing Argus Kind had sought to prevent.

Golegeth's early existence consisted of fishing and sleeping. Never had Emmet known such a voracious creature, and never had he seen a beast grow so quickly. He could almost see the great oaf growing larger while he watched. Berigor maintained a grueling pace and made no stops. Only when Golegeth fished did he slow. When the Midlands shoreline came into view, it felt too soon, as if they had somehow skipped part of the journey. Seeing the edges of the Jaga swamp, it was apparent they were far east of Sparrowport but still on the western side of the swamp. To the north would be Dragonport.

Berigor did not slow. Those who lived in the few settlements they passed along the way cried out and pointed to the skies at the sight of them. Around Emmet, life stirred. Golegeth slept, but the eggs grew restless, as if sensing something. When Dragonport finally came into view, movement within the eggs had grown feverish and insistent. Emmet was tempted to help the baby dragons escape the shells that bound them, but somehow he knew they wanted to be left alone. It was a rite of passage. Such a thing should not be taken away.

People in Dragonport scrambled when Berigor was spotted, and many lined the airstrip where he landed. A few aircraft were in various states of restoration, but no other flying ships could be seen. Finny approached from the crowd and might have said something. Emmet would never know.

Crack. Crack. Crack.

Golegeth was annoyed at being awoken and flew from the saddle. People cried out on seeing him, and he turned a wide circle overhead before making his way to the cliffs. Once over the edge, he dropped from sight like a missile.

Crack. Crack. Crack.

All around Emmet, dragons clawed their ways out of shells. Barabas and Keldon, too, were surrounded by hatching eggs. Wings spread. New voices called out to the world. Baby dragons filled the air. The people of Dragonport stood with their mouths agape. Despite the name, their home had not hosted dragons for centuries. Long had the Heights been the place of dragons, and only when the trade fleets came did the people ever see the majestic creatures. Now strange, four-legged dragons flew among them. Some knocked down children and sat on their chests. Another coiled around a middle-aged mother of two's neck and hissed at anyone who came close. The woman looked ready to faint. The people of Dragonport were hearty and brave, though, and did not scare easily—not even the young. Twenty-three hatchlings claimed people. Most were left in complete confusion when the dragons flew to the cliffs and dropped from view. Children ran to the ledge, adults rushing after, warning them to be careful.

"They're fishing," Emmet shouted. "You might want to get a towel or something."

Not everyone took his meaning, but quite a few made a run for linens before the dragons returned. When they did, chaos ensued.

Barabas and Keldon counseled those bonded to dragons and their families. People's lives had quite suddenly, unexpectedly, and irrevocably changed. Children reveled in their newfound friends, and even those approaching middle age found themselves with dragons eating, sleeping, or preening on their laps or shoulders.

In the following days, Emmet did his best to help others, but nothing mattered more to him in that moment than a saddle. In spite of the changes in him, people still assumed he did not listen to what was said around him, but Emmet had keen ears. Preparations were being made, and the message was clear: Emmet would be left behind. He understood children were not actively used for acts of war, but he no longer felt like a child. He'd already proven himself valuable and capable, even if in the body of a nine-year-old. The people of Dragonport, for their part, had been generous and kind—especially those now bonded to dragons. They looked to Emmet for guidance and understanding. It was a totally new experience for him, and he liked it. Golegeth was a matter of days older than the rest of the hatchlings, but that experience was invaluable for all those going through it for the first time. Even if they did not personally have the things he needed, they managed to find someone else who did. Leather, rawhide, awls, knives, and heavy needles all surrounded him now while he worked.

Golegeth watched from nearby, napping with one eye half open. Emmet had not grown up in the house of a seamstress without learning to stitch, sew, mend, and fold. He'd watched his mother teach Riette all these things and lacked only the muscle memory of having performed the steps so many times, they became second nature. His mother had been able to stitch a quilt, tell Riette what she was doing wrong, and watch Emmet at the same time. He felt a connection with her while he worked and took pride in what he created.

Having no idea how big Golegeth would get—a thought that terrified him—he designed a saddle capable of growing with the dragon. Taking a cue from the Drakon, he created a saddle that would wrap all the way around Golegeth at first then later expand along with his girth. After that, he would just need longer and longer straps. Keeping this in mind, he filled one saddlebag with long strips of leather and buckles.

Finny checked on him often and offered to help if he could. Looking over his handiwork, Emmet decided to take the man up on his offer. After showing him how he wanted the straps routed, Emmet asked Finny to lift the saddle into place. Golegeth wasn't sure about the whole thing. Emmet had fashioned a halter and lines, which Golegeth already wore, that would at least give Emmet something to hold on to while flying. Finny held the lines while Emmet secured the girths. Donning his new flying hat, goggles, gloves, and scarf, he was thankful for the generosity of the people in Dragonport.

"You're not planning to go anywhere, are you?" Finny asked.

"No," Emmet said. "I just want to make sure the stirrups are at the right height." It was the truth. The urge to fly was great, the desire to rescue his sister and Tuck even greater, but he was not yet ready. Every hour that passed was a reminder they were still lost to him. He tried not to think about what being prisoners must be like, but his imagination would not relent. Only the stitching soothed him. It gave him something to work toward. Soon he would fly.

"You're needed here," Barabas said. Emmet hadn't even been aware the man was beside him. "Flying off to the Firstland and getting killed will do no one any good."

Emmet nodded. He'd heard it before. He understood. People could think what they would of his saddle and his intentions. Eventually those bonded to dragons would all need saddles, and he was just ahead of the game. Deep down, he did want to fly straight to the Firstland and confront Argus Kind and the Al'Zjhon. It wasn't right for someone else to go and do that for him. He felt a deep and personal need to tell these people what he thought of them, but even more, he wanted his sister back. She would be so proud of him and what he'd done—what he'd become. Things between them would never be the same, and that made him smile. He'd been a deciding factor in her life for far too long. Now he had found his purpose. Most waited until of marrying age before striking out on their own, but most did not have a dragon and a saddle and the ability to sense—and use—magic.

The last part was unreal to him still, but it was a part of him, deeply ingrained within his existence. Magic was not a learned skill; it was a state of being. It connected him more closely to the world around him, and if he were truly honest with himself, he could not resist the lure of so much magic gathered in one place. The thoughts shamed him, but he did not have full control over what popped into his head. He could influence the direction of thought, but the yearning for magic was unrelenting. His skin itched for it.

Flying with Golegeth would be amazing when the time came. Most people agreed riding him too soon could potentially cause problems in his development. Given the dragon's rapid growth, Emmet understood their concerns over soft bone structures and ligaments. Those thoughts in mind, he began unstrapping the saddle. Immediately Golegeth became agitated and flapped his wings in Finny's face. To his credit, the man held on to the lines. Using his closed mouth, Golegeth struck Finny in the chest, and the man let go. Barabas reached out to grab hold of the lines, but the dragon was quick. Turning toward daylight, he fled the shelter, Emmet on his back. The lines flew freely, smacking the dragon, which frightened him into running faster, which made the lines hit harder and more often. All Emmet could do was hold on. Bursting into the open, Golegeth took flight. Emmet had flown on dragons before but nothing like this. He had no idea what Golegeth would do. If he decided to go fishing, Emmet would be in real trouble.

The dragon did not fly toward the sea, though. Stretching his wings, Golegeth flew east, toward the Firstland. From behind, Barabas shouted. Perhaps unaware of the dangers, Golegeth flew over the twisted Jaga swamp, giving Emmet a view of just how corrupted the place really was. Deeper into the vast wilderness, movement was everywhere. Patches of the swamp escaped its fetid embrace, springing into the air. Dragons. Wild and free, these creatures were nothing like Berigor or Golegeth. These dragons gleamed like black snakes with fearsome beauty all their own. Reflecting the light, they were sometimes blue or green, depending on the angle.

Higher the beasts climbed, and Golegeth gained speed, now aware of the danger. Emmet's dragon was young and inexperienced; he hoped it didn't cost them both their lives. Despite his smaller stature, Golegeth proved himself a capable flier and dodged swamp dragons' advances, which seemed more curious than anything. Still, the swamp itself reached out to Emmet with magic of its own—ancient magic, steeped in anger and hatred. The closer they came to the center of the great swamp, the stronger the sensation grew, and Emmet did everything he could to convince Golegeth to change course. Still flying unerringly to the east, the dragon must have had some destination in mind. Eventually Emmet managed to grab the lines. Using them and his knees, he expressed his desires to the dragon. While Golegeth did not turn around, he did angle to the north. Swamp dragons swooped past them, drawing ever closer, as if testing Golegeth and Emmet to see if they were dangerous. To Emmet's relief, the much larger dragons soon lost interest and returned to whatever it was they had been doing.

Along the northern edge of the swamp, the corruption was less evident, and the place began to appear almost natural. The smell of brine was a welcome change from the foul emissions emanating from the morass below. Emmet had never liked the smell of the coastline, but it was a spring breeze in comparison. This, at least, was part of the natural order, whereas the swamp had been twisted and subverted by some unknown force. Emmet was glad to leave it behind.

Golegeth largely ignored his input and flew over the waters just off the northern coast, still heading generally eastward. Their speed was greater than Emmet would have expected given his previous experiences adragonback, and they passed the towering peaks of the Heights before the sun dipped below the horizon. The place looked magical against the backdrop of the sunset, the skies cast with oranges and blues. No dragons flew out to meet them, and no armies camped below. It was as if the war had never taken place. The ships, too, were gone, and Emmet basked in the peaceful beauty. It helped keep his mind from the future and where they might be going. If the dragon had read his mind and his desires, then they were destined for perhaps the most dangerous place in the world. The only thing that conquered his fear was the desire to rescue his sister and Tuck—or avenge them. With every fiber of his being, he hoped it would be the former.

No matter how brave he tried to be, he was but one little boy in the face of an evil madman and what remained of his armies. What chance did he have of succeeding where so many had failed? Magic. It was the thing that separated him from the rest. Magic called to Emmet even across the great expanse of the Endless Sea. Perhaps it was a misnomer since he'd seen the lands across the sea, but it did *feel* endless, and that must have been enough for those who'd named it.

The world had changed even since Emmet's birth, and distance was not what it had once been. Planes, airships, and even steam-propelled sea vessels crossed vast distances previously impossible. So much change in such a short time made the world a dangerous place. Nothing was certain, permanence itself an illusion. Sparrowport had been the entire world to him for most of his life, and now it was gone, a pile of rubble and a few cannons in its place. The thoughts made Emmet feel small and afraid.

Golegeth trumpeted as if in response to his rider's morose thoughts. The dragon experienced no fear. Through the physical bond, Emmet sensed his dragon's state of mind, if not his thoughts, and he suspected Golegeth could do the same in return. Up until that point in his life, Riette had been the only one capable of reading him in such a way. Thoughts of her brought tears to his eyes. She was the only family he had left, and he loved her more than anything else in the world. Knowing she might already be dead made his heart ache.

Only Golegeth's and Barabas's caring for him gave him any consolation in that moment, and when Berigor trumpeted from behind, Emmet smiled. Beneath clear, star-filled skies, the older dragon came like a meteor, streaking through the sky with thunder and fire.

"Hold on!" Keldon shouted.

Emmet did as he was told. Golegeth cried out like a petulant child deprived of getting his way. Berigor bore down on them, his mighty claws clamping around them, gentle yet inescapable. Golegeth bit the larger dragon, not hard enough to do any damage, but with enough force to make his displeasure known. Dragons were strong-willed creatures and did not respond well to having their freedom taken away.

Emmet half expected the larger dragon to turn and take them back to Dragonport, but instead Berigor continued speeding east. When islands became visible below as pools of darkness amid the shining waves, they circled lower. To the south, Emmet saw something he'd never seen before. Like an errant star, a ball of light rivaled the moonlight and blotted out the stars. Behind it stretched a sparkling tail that shone a myriad of color. Everyone had heard the legends of comets, and Emmet couldn't help but wonder if the goddess had returned early. Perhaps he was the one foretold by legend as the Herald of Istra. His access to magic lent credence to the notion, but it would mean the tales were off by thousands of years.

When he concentrated on it, the comet called to him more strongly than the magical items on the Firstland. This was no ancient artifact holding remnants from the last age of power; this was the very source of magic itself. It was so beautiful, it brought tears of joy, his heart swelling with the feeling of it. He also suspected the saddle and other artifacts exposed to the light absorbed the magic. Closing his eyes, he wished for the rest of the comets to come, the fabled storm to return and flood his world with the magic he craved. Something told him it would not, that this was the only comet that would come in his lifetime, which pained him deeply. It teased him and would soon be gone. It was the nature of comets to disappear for eons. Part of him wanted Golegeth to fly into the night sky and capture the celestial beacon, to keep it from fleeing back into the vast darkness from which it had come. Golegeth was not in control of their path, though, and Berigor continued toward the islands below. Just before he landed, he released Golegeth and roared at the younger dragon. For the moment cowed, Golegeth did as the larger dragon instructed; he landed.

Moments later, Barabas was at his side. "Are you hurt?" he asked.

Emmet shook his head but did not speak. His mind raced with so many possibilities, and he could not find the words to express his thoughts. So many ideas and notions rattled in his mind, he wasn't certain exactly what he thought or wanted. He had always done what others had asked of him, at least to the best of his ability. Now he wanted to chase his own desires but was unsure how to go about it. No matter what he did, he had to depend on others who had needs and desires of their own. Even Golegeth was a free creature who did as he pleased.

Berigor roared at the smaller dragon again, hurting Emmet's ears, and Golegeth had the good sense to appear remorseful.

"Dragons," Barabas said, shaking his head. "It's a wonder they haven't been the death of us all."

"Sometimes I wonder if they don't have plans of their own," Keldon said, "and we're just along for the ride."

Barabas chuckled at this, and the tension in the air lessened. After helping Emmet unstrap, he lifted the boy from the saddle and placed him on the rocky shoreline. On unsteady legs, Emmet tried to get his balance. So much time in the saddle made the land's firmness seem strange and foreign, but it did not take long for normality to return.

"What are we going to do with you?" Barabas asked no one in particular and none answered. Keldon gathered wood and lit a fire, and the group sat around the flames in silence. Golegeth leaped into the air, making Emmet fear the dragon would abandon him and continue to the east, but he returned moments later carrying a fish not much smaller than himself. Berigor, too, fished, but he also brought fish for his human companions. Keldon used a stick to dig a hole in the glowing coals and placed the fish inside. Sizzling and popping, the fish issued a cloud of steam when Keldon raked coals over it. It did not take long to cook, and Emmet soon realized how hungry he was. The more the excitement faded, the deeper his hunger grew. When Keldon uncovered the fish and pulled it from the hot coals, an alluring aroma filled the air.

Beneath the ash-coated scales waited delicate white meat more delicious than anything Emmet could remember. He and the others ate their fill, and soon, beneath the light of a single, magical comet, sleep claimed them.

CHAPTER NINETEEN

If you expect the wind to catch you, then you will fall.
—Keldon Tallowborn, Al'Drakon

* * *

"We're lost," Joren said.

"I know," Brick replied, giving his father a withering look. They had been over this before.

"I told you this was a bad idea."

"I know," Brick said—again.

"You really shouldn't have thrown that chap overboard."

"Yes. I *know*." Brick ground his teeth, trying not to snap at his father. The man was right, but that was not exactly helpful at the moment. What good were the lessons if neither of them lived to act on the knowledge? What he needed at the moment was silence or, at the least, help figuring out how to safely land the airship. They had tried to follow the other two ships and pretend nothing had happened, but not understanding the controls sent them far off course. Now they soared over ubiquitous waves with no land in sight. Even if they did find land, neither had any idea how to safely get off the massive aircraft. From what Brick had seen at Sparrowport, docking an airship involved dozens of people on the ground, not to mention skilled hands at the tiller. They had neither of those things.

"We've about a day's worth of coal left," Joren continued. "When we run out, this thing is going to come down whether we like it or not."

Brick refrained from responding, afraid he'd do nothing but shout at the man he loved. His father had never been an easy man to live with, but he cared for Brick like no other. He wanted to teach his son everything, and his methods had always seemed harsh. The older Brick grew, though, the more the things his father taught him had become his greatest assets. Even so, now was hardly the time to pound lessons into his thick skull. Right now he needed a plan. The charts and sextant within the wheelhouse might have been knitting needles for all the good they did him. From what Brick could tell, they were sailing in the right direction. Given the distances involved, even the slightest deviation in course would put them off by hundreds of nautical miles. They might never see land again. If the airship went down in the water, they could do little but cling to the wreckage and hope someone found them. It was a thin hope.

Trying not to think of that eventuality, Brick held on to the belief they would find the Firstland. He'd seen people jump from planes and airships alike with parachutes, and they had plenty aboard. He'd also seen people soar through the air like flying squirrels wearing strange leather suits with flaps extending between the arms and legs. Few things were more terrifying than falling. Even the idea of a parachute was ludicrous. He and his father both were solidly built men and had trouble jumping even a small distance in the air. Gravity had far too tight a grip on them for a thin layer of canvas to keep them aloft. Surely they would plunge to their deaths. Shaking his head, he tried to chase the images away, but they persisted, taunting him.

"I'm going to shovel coal," Joren said. "Not making much progress here anyway."

Brick couldn't argue his father's sentiment. Keeping the ship in the air would require continued effort from them both, and shoveling coal was a big part of it. It was exhausting but necessary; without the fires they would lose both propulsion and the hot air that kept them aloft. As they depleted the stores of coal, they had to carry it a greater distance, which made the task increasingly difficult. These ships normally carried a much larger crew. Brick tried not to remind himself he'd thrown most of that crew overboard. His father regularly made sure he didn't forget it nonetheless.

Leaving the wheelhouse unattended felt strange and dangerous, but there really wasn't anything for them to run into so far out to sea, and their course had been set long before. All he was really doing was babysitting gauges he really didn't understand and second-guessing himself. With that in mind, Brick left the wheelhouse behind and headed for the galley. The one advantage of having thrown the crew overboard was they had plenty of food. Thankfully the explosion that knocked out the crew happened in an eating area and didn't much affect the food stores. The only thing Joren had spent more effort teaching Brick than blacksmithing was cooking, and he put those skills to use. Soon Joren returned from the boilers, allowing them at least a little bit of pleasant time together. His father had a much more difficult time complaining with his mouth full, and Brick did his best to keep them both well fed. They needed their strength to keep the fires burning and would at least die with full bellies if it came to that.

It hadn't taken long to find the stashes of whiskey and wine used to keep the crew happy during such long flights, but the two men drank sparingly. They needed their wits about them. Still, a little wine with their meals didn't hurt.

When Joren did arrive at the galley, he was covered in soot. Even after he washed, only his hands and face were truly clean, which made him look strange. "What have you cooked for us today?"

"Salt-cured ham and spicy red potatoes," Brick said. "Will you cut us off a wedge of cheese?"

Joren nodded. Brick had learned long ago the best way to keep his father from lecturing him was to keep him busy. He enjoyed the respite while it lasted. Together they ate in amicable silence. Though Brick had already sworn never to board another airship again, he did have to admit it wasn't the worst way to travel. Such luxury he'd rarely seen, and perhaps if someone who knew their business had been at the helm, he might have actually enjoyed himself. This, of course, reminded him that his father was right about throwing the man at the helm from the ship. He'd always been too impetuous for his father's taste. He hoped it wasn't the end of them both.

"I've been thinking," Joren said when he finished his meal. "Perhaps the best thing to do is to build ourselves a small boat and toss it overboard before we end up in the water. If we go down with the ship, we might not be able to get away from her when she sinks. She'll likely take us down with her."

Brick didn't like the idea much, but he couldn't argue with his father's logic. There was no guarantee the airship would float.

"I pulled the largest of the parachutes from the storehouse," he said, and Brick looked at them dubiously. "And then there were these . . ."

Laughter burst forth from Brick. His father held two of the leather jumpsuits they had seen people use when leaping from aircraft. The suits did not so much allow people to fly as enable them to fall in a directed fashion. "You don't think we're going to fit into those, do you?"

His father laughed as well and shook his head. "I know, my boy, I know, but we should at least try." He tossed one of the suits to Brick. Knowing better than to ignore his father, he stripped down to his undershorts and pulled the suit on or at least made the attempt. The legs rode up to the tops of his shins and the arms to his elbows. There was little chance he'd ever get any of the many straps buckled, and he felt like a fool.

His father's eyes twinkled with mirth. "You look like an overripe melon wrapped in twine."

"You don't look much better," Brick said. "This is a terrible idea."

"I know. I know."

Brick thumped his head against the polished wood walls. Then he looked at his father with new hope.

"Did you bang an idea into your brain?"

Brick nodded. "Can't we mix wood in with the coal?"

Joren looked around at wooden benches, tables, and countertops. "I'm going to need a hammer."

* * *

Prevailing winds chilled the air. Cold stone leached whatever warmth Riette could find save what emanated from the fireplace behind her. Turned around backward in her chair, she huddled before it. Arms outstretched, she warmed her hands. Tuck did not seem to mind the chill. Agger and

Grunt watched over them in uncomfortable silence. She and Tuck communicated with their eyes and expressions. Talking was strongly discouraged. At least they were together again. The flight had been torture. Not knowing why they were now allowed to be together wasn't much better.

They certainly had little to fear at this point. It wasn't as if they could just walk home. They were trapped in a foreign land, held hostage by a tyrant and his madwoman. Casta Mett frightened her the most. Riette remembered seeing her in Sparrowport. She was the woman Emmet had said was mean, and he couldn't have been more correct. She never smiled, apparently ready to kill them at any given moment. The marks on her face and residual puffiness spoke of how poorly she'd fared against the hornets Emmet had used against her. Casta Mett would showed no kindness without some reason. When she returned from deeper within the hollow mountain, Riette turned and sat in her chair properly, wondering how the woman would further turn the situation against her and Tuck.

The mean-spirited woman pretended not to notice but still glared at them with open contempt, her scowl itself seeming to suck the warmth from the air. "Have these things been fed?" she asked. "Argus wants them fed. Bring them fish."

Grunt nodded and retreated into the hold.

"Perhaps you should fetch them some water," Casta Mett said to Agger before turning back to Riette. She waited until they were alone before speaking again. "If it were up to me, I wouldn't waste the food or water. The only reason you're alive is because I want your brother dead."

Riette kept her eyes averted, trying not to provoke the woman.

"Have you ever been fishing?"

Riette nodded without ever looking at her. She knew better than to ignore a direct question. She could still feel the sting on her cheek.

"Did you slide a worm onto a hook?"

Riette nodded again.

"How does it feel to be the worm?"

Tuck shifted in his chair, and Riette hoped he did not once again try to speak up in her defense. Some of Casta Mett's reprimands might have already left him with internal injuries. Riette wasn't certain how much more either of them could take. Even if her friends did come to save her, they would be flying into a trap. Two airships loaded with heavy cannon and exploding rounds awaited them. She'd heard Agger and Grunt talking about having repaired the damaged cannons. The city of Ri once again bristled with weaponry.

Casta Mett was well defended herself. In one hand she carried a glittering staff embedded with thousands of tiny crystals. In the other, she carried the sky stone. She had gloated to Riette and Tuck about her intent to use it against Barabas. "I can't wait to see him again. I'll be sure to welcome him properly this time."

It made Riette squirm. She did not want Barabas to come to any harm, but she knew he would come. He would not leave her and especially Tuck there to die. The boy was like his son. She was not foolish enough to think herself equally important to him, but she did think he would have saved her nonetheless. There had been a time when she'd hated him, and now she wondered how she could have had such opposite feelings for the same person. He'd done much to prove himself in spite of his betrayal. Riette had still not completely forgiven him for putting Emmet in such danger, but he had saved them both multiple times. And Emmet had thrived. In many ways, he was her only hope of survival.

When he arrived, it was a shock. Riette wondered how the woman had known and stood armed and ready to meet him.

When Berigor approached in near complete silence, the wind stretching his wings all that announced his arrival, it didn't seem real. Keldon and Barabas rode in silent readiness, looking prepared to spring from the saddle at any moment. A thrill ran through Riette, and she allowed herself a moment of hope. When the smile on Casta Mett's face widened, hope faded.

No weapons fired on the incoming dragon. Riette could not understand why they would let the dragon approach after so much effort to arm against them. Realizing they might only want to trap Berigor made Riette feel sick. Being held captive was the most terrifying thing ever to happen to her, and she did not want to think of what Argus Kind and Casta Mett would do to Barabas given the chance. All along he'd been their target, and he would not get any of the courtesies afforded to her and Tuck, no matter how flawed those courtesies might have been. Casta Mett had hinted at what awaited Barabas, and Riette tried to block the words from her mind.

Now he was here, like a light in the darkness. Blazing with power, Berigor looked ready to tear the mountain to pieces. He landed hard, clinging to the broken stairway alongside the entrance in which Riette and Tuck sat.

"Oh, do come in," Casta Mett said. "Your friends are waiting for you."

All Riette could think about was being a worm on a hook. Barabas was about to bite. He undid his straps and started to get down. Keldon remained where he was, appearing ready to leap into the fray if needed. Riette and Tuck were close enough to the front of the chamber that they could conceivably escape. Grunt and Agger returned and dropped the trays they carried, drawing air rifles instead. Casta Mett stood deeper in the chamber.

Meeting Tuck's eyes, Riette got ready to run. Grunt backed away. Agger, too, retreated, looking as if he'd seen his own death approaching. Both men held their ground but clearly wanted to be as far from Riette and Tuck as possible. A terrible knot formed in Riette's stomach; these men must know something she did not.

Laughter echoed through the valley. Behind Berigor, atop a nearby ridge, waited a terrifying sight. A dragon twice Berigor's size was ridden by Argus Kind and one of his henchmen. Lines of lightning and metal connected to a gleaming headpiece restrained this wild creature. It slithered with exaggerated serpentine movements and was missing one eye. Unlike Berigor and Dashiq before him, the wild dragon did not appear to have suffered massive facial trauma in battle. This dragon had only a ring of unadorned metal around a lifeless glass eye, as if Argus Kind had carved out the dragon's natural eye just so it could use the ancient Azzakkan's Eye. Such cruelty gave Riette physical pain.

Argus Kind sat behind Deacon Rex, the Al'Zjhon who held glowing lines that seemed to bite into the creature with lightning and fire whenever he yanked on them. Crying out in impotent fury, the wild dragon seethed. The self-declared king was armed with something that looked like a crossbow with a luminous bolt nocked, but he held it to one side. In his other hand, he held a metal horn that amplified his voice. Clearly he'd thought this through. This was a devious, hateful man bent on revenge who had set a deadly trap. Again, Riette squirmed.

"You always were a sentimental fool, Barabas," Argus said, his voice booming through the valleys. "And now it will be the end of you. I told you long ago kindness was your greatest weakness. That and willful foolhardiness. You knew I would be waiting for you. And now you are not the only one with a dragon. How do you like my pet?"

"Beautiful creature. Deserves to be free, not enslaved by magic," Barabas said in response, his deep voice carrying well, slurred speech loud and evident.

Argus Kind laughed. A moment later, he spoke without a trace of humor. "You have something that belongs to me. I want it back. And I have something you might want back. Make me a trade, and I will let you leave in peace. But I know you won't do that. Therefore we must face the alternative, where I kill you all."

The wild dragon thrashed the air and reared up beneath Argus. Deacon Rex yanked on the lines. The mighty giant roared in pain. Its tail twitched. Bile rose in Riette's throat.

"You just have to break their spirits," Argus said afterward. "Just like people."

With those words, he raised the strange crossbow and aimed at the table where Tuck and Riette sat. He smiled at her a moment before pulling the trigger. Everything happened so fast, Riette had no time to react.

A bolt of blue light raced toward her and slammed into the table. Her chair toppled over backward, and Riette felt the sting of shrapnel. Dust filled the air and obscured her vision. Pulling herself up, she was still uncertain if she were hurt. On trembling knees, she looked over the dust and the wreckage of the table to see Tuck pushing out from under his chair.

Whirring sounds began to echo in what must have been intentional silence. Argus Kind was a showman. Even before he'd killed the rightful king and named himself successor, he'd been a spectacle, known for criticizing society's fascination with executions then carrying out those very executions. Now his airships were about to close off any possible routes of escape. How Argus Kind must fear Barabas DeGuiere, Riette thought, to have planned such a massive and inescapable trap for an old man who appeared to have lost his dragon. Riette knew Dashiq was gone. Even in a moment of such imminent danger, her heart broke with the knowledge. She thought of Tuck and how he must feel, even as two airships came into view. Argus Kind laughed.

A third airship appeared a moment later traveling at a different trajectory. Shouting echoed within a narrow point in the valley. The airships were already dangerously close together. From the third dirigible, someone jumped.

Agger and Grunt came up behind where Riette crouched. They did not assault her but did prevent her from seeking shelter deeper within the mountain. Bait. When Tuck made his way to her, no one tried to stop him.

"Give me Azzakkan's Eye, and I will let you go," Argus Kind said, his crossbow pulsing with blue light and aimed directly at Riette and Tuck. They had played right into his plan, giving him a single target.

Berigor turned around, clinging to the mountainside, his wings spread and neck coiled in an aggressive posture, ready to strike. Hissing like a cornered viper, he exaggerated his size. The wild dragon above issued a low, guttural growl like rolling drums Riette felt in her bones. There was no panic, no posturing, only the secure knowledge he was the more powerful of the two bull dragons present. The air reeked of aggression and fear.

Another person jumped from the third airship just before it struck one of the first two broadside, the attacking airship radiating steam and fire. Constricted by the valley walls, all three airships collided. Even the wild dragon retreated when the explosions began. Suddenly the air was filled with debris, shrapnel, and people leaping from airships. Most immediately deployed their parachutes, but some skimmed through the air on wing flaps sewn into their flight suits, including the two from the attacking airship.

Berigor wore his war saddle, which seated two people, but he also wore the ancient saddle Dashiq had once worn behind it. It was further confirmation the dragon had died, and Riette continued to mourn the loss. Never had she known she could love a creature such as a dragon, that such true friendship and loyalty were possible. She was proud to have known

Dashiq the battle dragon.

Her body tingling with adrenaline, time slowed, leaving Riette disconnected from the events around her. She and Tuck could not simply climb into the saddle and escape, even with the airships destroyed. Argus Kind had assembled an overwhelming force, and perhaps rightfully so. Berigor did not appear ready to go down without a fight.

Looking back into the cavern for a split second, Casta Mett's face was illuminated by the fiery explosions, shock and panic registering in her expression. Moving toward Riette and Tuck, she leveled her staff and them, the light around her taking on a bluish green hue. Thunder rumbled within the chamber, low and deep as the woman's temper got the better of her. The promise of death filled her eyes. Then Riette's view was blocked. Tuck stepped between them.

"I've had about enough of you," Tuck said, and it was perhaps the bravest thing Riette had ever seen. He was no match for this powerful woman now wielding ancient magic, yet he stood tall and strong. The woman did not smile or laugh but instead continued forward, the light emanating from the tip of the staff growing brighter with each step. She wanted Riette to know what was coming, to know how she would die. Casta Mett was no better than Argus Kind. She was a killer and a performer, and it made Riette sick.

Time compressed.

Events moved so fast, her thoughts could not keep pace. Berigor leaped away from the mountain and attacked the wild dragon. Another soon filled the space. Far smaller than Dashiq had been, a four-legged creature bearing Riette's brother landed within the cavern.

Emmet met her eyes, and she saw something that had rarely been there before but that she'd always known existed deep down within him—connection, synchronicity. At that moment her own connection with time felt tenuous, the flow of events accelerating and decelerating, stretching and compressing. It was almost what she imagined Emmet must have felt, which overwhelmed her with fear and compassion. Emmet trapped her in his gaze and communicated with her.

It's going to be all right. I've come for you, his eyes said.

Casta Mett released her energy, no longer aimed at Riette but now at the smaller dragon. Emmet had no magic, no defenses. The dragon he rode looked so young and inexperienced. Riette could barely keep up with all the input. Sounds amplified and sights rushed in. Soon she found herself in a ball on the floor with her hands over her ears and her eyes squeezed shut. This had happened to Emmet so many times that she'd become desensitized—perhaps at times lacking empathy for his condition. Now she understood and it shamed her. Tears in her eyes, she rocked.

CHAPTER TWENTY

First rule of dragon riding: Never pretend you're in complete control.
—Barabas DeGuiere, dragon rider

* * *

Emmet Pickette watched in horror, realizing his sister had fallen into what looked like one of his episodes. Knowing all too well the overwhelming sensation, his heart raced in empathy. Always before he'd thought there was nothing anyone could do to help him during his episodes, but now he understood better. From the hem of his coat, he pulled the two stones Keldon had given him, each containing a small reserve of energy—one slightly more than the other. Using the very last magic available to him, Emmet soothed his sister and ignored the Al'Zjhon. He was defenseless and Golegeth was no match for ancient magic, but neither was Emmet. In the end, he was compelled to do for his sister what she had always wanted to do for him.

Emmet Pickette let the magic flow through him until it was gone. Now chalky and white, the stones depleted. Not wanting to destroy them as he had his first stone, he would draw on them no more. With trembling hands, he put them back in the wooden box and into his jacket.

Light erupted from Casta Mett's staff, and Golegeth cried out in pain. He thrashed the air, his tail whipping back and forth, and Emmet was taken along for the ride. No matter how brave coming here may have been, he stood no chance against the Al'Zjhon.

It shamed him that he could not save his sister the way she had always done for him. She looked back with understanding and gratitude, though. At least she was conscious and able to act in her own defense now. Perhaps hope still existed.

Golegeth hopped awkwardly, not putting any weight on his right front leg. Casta Mett aimed at him again, the light growing brighter. When a dark shape flashed through the air and slammed into her, Emmet didn't know what to think. One moment she'd been standing there, and the next, she was gone. Two bodies collided—one moving at high speed and the other standing still. The air leaving their bodies was painful to hear, and they tumbled to the back of the hall, one looking like an overstuffed sack about to burst. Behind him came ropes and a small explosion followed by a wall of canvas. Perhaps not in the way it had been designed, the parachute caught on the broken table and did slow the man down some. Emmet had to shake his head when he thought he recognized Brick. It seemed impossible, yet there he was, out cold on top of Casta Mett, who also did not move.

Emmet heard the terrifying battle behind him and turned to see, unable to resist the need to know what took place outside. Too powerful was the instinct to watch his back. Objects within the cavern called to him, but they would have to wait a moment longer. Berigor reached Argus and his dragon. The two beasts now clung to each other in a deadly embrace, tails wrapped around each other and massive jaws open and ready to make the kill. Barabas and Keldon were helpless as the larger dragon overwhelmed Berigor, and though he issued dragon fire, the wild dragon was able to physically dominate him and direct the deadly fire into empty air.

His friends were about to die. Golegeth cried out, lunging toward Agger and Grunt, who now moved toward Riette and Tuck with malicious intent. Striking each in the chest in rapid succession with his closed mouth, the dragon knocked them backward, the air rushing from their lungs. Brick now stood behind the two men, caught them, and knocked their heads together. Casta Mett remained still, beside her a staff radiating power and a stone that sucked the light from the room. When Emmet was filled with power, the stone was like a deep hole in space into which he might fall and never been seen again. He found it disturbing yet alluring. He knew what the sky stone was and what it could do. Casta Mett would use it to make herself immune to magical attacks, and that was an advantage Emmet wanted to take from her—permanently.

Golegeth must have understood his desire or responded to his movements within the saddle and his input through the lines. Taking him closer to Casta Mett's still form, the dragon leaned down low, allowing Emmet to reach the stone without having to leave the saddle. No sooner had his fingers closed around cold stone than the air around him exploded. Magic, lightning, and fire erupted around Emmet but mostly struck Golegeth.

The dragon reared back in shock and pain, his heart racing hard enough that Emmet felt it. Gleaming lines issued sparks and filaments of light, each biting into the dragon, reaching in behind tough scales and inflicting acute pain. Casta Mett stood smiling in spite of the blood that ran down her forehead. In her hands were lines like those Deacon Rex used to control Argus Kind's dragon. Emmet and Golegeth had fallen into their trap. It was then he realized it might have been him they wanted all along. Though Argus Kind may have had a long-standing feud with Barabas, the man was long past his prime and would not pose much of a threat without his dragon.

Azzakkan's Eye was indeed a prize worth fighting over, but Emmet could be so much more. His ability to sense and locate magic made him the most valuable thing of all. And he'd foolishly flown right into their hands, bringing with him a young, impressionable dragon. Barabas had told him to stay back, but Golegeth read his deepest desires and brought him here anyway. Emmet could not blame the dragon since he truly wanted nothing more than to save his sister and his friend. How could he blame the creature for being brave enough to come here and try to fulfill his wishes? He could not. Now, though, the dragon was already paying a price. The thought of Golegeth's life being spent in captivity and denied free will was physically painful—a fate perhaps even worse than death.

There was a difference between the relationships he and Barabas and Keldon had with their dragons and what Argus Kind had done to the poor creature he rode. Golegeth stayed with Emmet not because he was constrained by magic, but because he cared about him. One might even say he loved Emmet; they were family. What Argus Kind did was to enslave a creature and destroy its spirit.

This was the fate Golegeth now faced, and Emmet tried to release himself from the saddle, to find some way to reach Casta Mett and stop her no matter the cost. Struggling, he held on to the sky stone, despite its making his skin crawl while leeching energy from the air around it. Lightning arced between the outstretched stone and the magic lines over Golegeth's head. For an instant, the radiance pulsing through the lines was interrupted. Ordinary metal links making up the chain were revealed. Golegeth turned back toward Emmet until the sky stone and the lines touched. The previously glowing magic lines went dark.

Golegeth swung his head violently, the chains still wrapped around Casta Mett's wrists. Cast along the smooth floor, skidding to a stop just before the entrance, Casta Mett slowly toppled over the edge. The metal lines snapped tight, and Golegeth stumbled forward, pulled by her weight.

Just outside the cavern, Berigor's neck was exposed, and the wild dragon lashed out. Emmet watched in stunned horror, his mind failing to process the information quickly enough to save his valiant friends, but his sister had been watching. Released from her episode, she had seen what the sky stone did to the lines, and she did what he could not. After snatching the sky stone from Emmet's grip, she threw it with all her strength just as massive jaws came close enough to buffet him with a rush of wind. The sky stone flew, tumbling end over end, striking the wild dragon in the jaw, connecting solidly with the lines restraining the majestic beast. The force of the impact not only interrupted the energy flowing through the lines but also sheared through the metal rings on one side. Even when the energy did begin to flow once again, it was greatly diminished.

The dragon collided with Berigor but did not bite down on his neck as he could have. Instead he thrashed his head from side to side, yanking the lines from Deacon Rex's hands. The man sat in his saddle, stunned. When the towering dragon turned and gazed down on him, the lines still dangling from his head, Deacon Rex screamed. In an instant, he was gone.

Argus Kind had already realized his fate and aimed his light bow at his own dragon. The beast glared at him, daring him to discharge the weapon. The usurper king pulled the trigger. A bolt of light and fire struck the beast in the jaw, just below its artificial eye socket. It staggered back, pushing away from Berigor. Before the larger dragon could get away, though, Berigor had an opening. Lashing out at the larger dragon's throat, he did not go for the killing blow as Emmet had expected; instead, he latched on to the still glowing lines. With a single tug, he freed the mighty dragon from its chains. The giant roared and chuffed, shaking its head and rattling Argus in the saddle. Having been violently whipped back and forth, Argus Kind was still trying to return to his senses when the light bow was yanked from his limp grip. When he did come to, he screamed. The dragon tossed the ancient artifact into the valley and flew out to sea, apparently not yet finished with Argus Kind, whose screams gradually faded.

Emmet slumped in the saddle for a moment, overcome with emotion and pride for his sister, who stood in the entranceway, her hands over her mouth. Golegeth peeked over the ledge. Casta Mett still held on to the lines. She dangled above a terrace; the fall probably wouldn't kill her, but it was unlikely to leave her uninjured. The lines remained wrapped around her wrist, but her other hand was free and still held the staff.

Golegeth began pulling her up. Without ever changing the expression on her dour face, the woman reached up and unleashed an attack on the lines themselves, which snapped under the assault and sent her tumbling to the stone below. After shaking off the remains of the lines looped over his own neck, Golegeth leaped down to where Casta Mett had fallen. Within a sandy garden, they found the staff, but the woman was gone. When they returned to the upper chamber, Agger and Grunt were also gone. Berigor rested on an adjacent portico, his saddles currently empty. Barabas and Keldon waited inside with Riette and Tuck.

Emmet climbed down from Golegeth's back. The dragon immediately launched himself into the air and flew away. Emmet prayed he would not get himself killed.

When Emmet looked back to Riette, she met his eyes. No words were exchanged between them; none were required. Tears welled in both their eyes, and he ran to her, wrapping her in a tight embrace. "I'm so sorry," he said. "I'm so sorry for everything."

Riette sobbed. "I've always loved you. Even when I behaved poorly."

"I know. I know."

"And now I might understand a little better myself," she said. "Thank you for helping me. How . . . did . . . this happen?"

"Magic. Dashiq used her last magic to knock me back into synchronization with time."

Riette chewed on those words. "That's what it was like for you all the time, wasn't it? What I experienced was one of your episodes, wasn't it?"

"I think so."

"I'm going to have to keep an eye on you," Tuck interjected. "Nice throw, by the way."

Riette laughed and elbowed him. Tuck winced in pain. "I'm so sorry!"

"Oh," Tuck grunted. "Don't worry. It'll heal eventually."

Berigor sniffed at the group then chuffed in satisfaction. None of them were seriously injured, and for the moment, no one threatened them.

"We should get out of here," Barabas said.

Keldon nodded in agreement.

Emmet pointed to the back of the chamber, "Magic."

Barabas appeared torn but was unable to resist the temptation. He and Tuck had searched the rest of the world for magic without ever finding a fraction of what Argus Kind had in his collection. The man had not had a lick of magic in him yet hoarded the greatest magics remaining in the world. "How much are we talking about here?" Barabas asked.

"It feels like a lot," Emmet said.

Riette continued to stare at him. "I'm sorry, my brother," Riette said. "You are far more intelligent than I had given you credit for."

"It wasn't your fault—or mine."

Keldon went first, moving deeper into the mountain. Tuck and Barabas did their best to reinforce the man in case they encountered trouble. Thus far the halls had been empty and silent, but no one let down their guard. Emmet let the magic draw him onward. He moved in selfish interest, though he knew it would serve them all. Even with Argus Kind gone, such magic still threatened the world. It occurred to him that simply transferring the possession of such a collection would not necessarily ameliorate the danger. When the magic washed over him in waves and the light shone so brightly, he had to cover his eyes, Emmet was thrilled to see a collection not so different from the one they had destroyed, albeit smaller. In some ways, destroying the stash of magic items had been against his own self-interest, but such were the consequences of war.

Seeing an array of glass spheres suspended on delicate stands made his heart race. Without actually meaning to, he picked one up. It was warm and slick in his hands. Power pulsed through the object, honed and refined by the form and structure of the glass. Swirls of color backed one side, but the other half revealed a translucent world of chaos. It swirled and danced within as he turned it in his hand. Another contained a blooming flower— springtime forever captured in glass. Emmet marveled over its beauty and tried to figure out how one could capture a flower in molten glass and leave it perfectly intact, looking fresh as if still on the vine. Six staves filled a rack on the wall, and one broken light bow remained. For Emmet, even a single glass sphere was a treasure beyond reckoning.

"Let's load up what we can and get out of here," Barabas said.

The group bundled up as much of the valuable collection as they could and packed the priceless and potentially dangerous items within saddlebags, pockets, and anywhere else they could manage. Emmet still sensed magic within the mountain and even on the island surrounding him. It was a powerful place, but he left confident he had enough magic to last the rest of his life. He almost felt a little bad for taking the treasure from those on the Firstland, but they had proven poor stewards. He promised to do better and accepted his selfish desire never to become disconnected from the world again.

Golegeth returned not long after Berigor was loaded. The young dragon struggled to reach them, most likely due to the large man on his back. Joren looked terrified and still wore his leather jumpsuit. Brick helped him down after Golegeth landed.

"Are you all right?" Brick asked, guilt and concern evident in his voice.

His father nodded. "That was a terrible idea."

"I know," Brick said.

"I mean a really terrible idea."

"I know." Brick grinned.

* * *

Walking through Sparrowport with Tuck holding her hand was perhaps the happiest moment of Riette's life. In many ways it was also sad, but she concentrated on the good parts. The debris had been cleared from town, and ambitious reconstruction was under way. Those of the Zjhon fleet, stranded in the Midlands, were not themselves evil. Some had refused to integrate with the local peoples and were last seen making boats from wrecked airships, but most had stayed. Progress moved a little more slowly in the world, but that suited Riette just fine. It was unfortunate the decrease in the popularity of traveling by airship or airplane also meant an increase in demand for dragon-based transportation. She would not allow herself to cry.

Tuck held open the door to the smithy, and Riette slipped in. Joren sat to one side, watching Brick fabricate a gear.

"You've got to get the curvature just perfect," the old smith said.

"I know. I know," Brick replied, smiling the whole time. Never before had he been so content. In their younger days, he had longed to do anything but work in the hot, sweaty smithy, but he'd seen his share of adventure now, and the people counted on him to make so many of the things they required. It was good to feel needed.

"Well, well. Look at the two of you lovebirds walking around, trying to make an old man jealous," Joren said when they walked in.

Brick looked up from his work and grinned at them. Then he frowned. "Just a moment," he said and quenched the gear.

"How do you know it was perfect?" Joren asked.

"I know."

"Did you check it?"

"No," Brick admitted.

"Well, then you don't know, and what you don't know you don't know. You know? Always check it."

"I always check before they leave the shop, Dad."

"You're supposed to check it before and after. If you just check it after and it's wrong, then you have to start all over again. What sense does that make?"

Brick stared at his father for a moment before looking back to Riette and Tuck. "I suppose you've come to pick up your gift."

Riette nodded sadly, pursing her lips.

"It really is a lovely gift," Joren said.

Brick shot him a look, and the old smith rolled his eyes. "You know I don't usually work in wood," he said, and he presented a short staff of polished cedar topped by a bronze dragon's claw holding Emmet's favorite chaos sphere. He said it was as if he could see all of creation within its depths, and Riette wondered how much of it was true. It was beautiful and complex indeed, but the universe did not swirl for her the way he said it did for him. It was something she might never understand. If Emmet said it moved, it moved. Thoughts of him were painful, and she took a deep, shuddering breath.

"Well, aren't you going to give her the one you've been working on when you were supposed to be sleeping?" Joren asked.

Brick glared at his father but did not respond. He turned back to Riette. "I made something for you too." He took a moment to stare down his father again before he presented Riette with a staff, her favorite flower marble mounted at the top. Brick had constructed a smooth, straight staff with sweeping lines forming a perfect stem and leaves for the flower trapped in glass. He handed it to her with a grin. Her mouth hung open. Tuck had said he was having a nice box made for it. She had never expected something so perfect. When she closed her hand around it, magic streamed in through her fingertips, and she could no longer hold back her tears. "Thank you," she said. "It's beautiful."

"I talked to Emmet and Barabas this morning, but you tell them I said good-bye," he said, still unwilling to accept a compliment.

Riette nodded. Part of her wanted to drag her feet, as if that would stop him from going. He'd grown so much, so fast, it scared her. But mostly she was grateful for what Dashiq had done. She had given Emmet a chance to do things he might not otherwise have been able to do. Dashiq had helped

Riette find understanding and compassion and even forgiveness. It had been difficult, but she had accepted the truth. Having Tuck at her side made it a little easier to bear.

"Thank you both for everything," Riette said before leaving. "We should take some sweet rolls."

Tuck gave her a look that said he knew she was delaying the inevitable, though he did eat two sweet rolls. The walk to the airfield was the completion of a strange circle in her life. There waited a dragon and her brother and Barabas. Tuck squeezed her hand.

She'd come for a proud moment to see her brother off on his journey, but things didn't appear to be going terribly well. An enormous Golegeth, who continued to get bigger with each passing day, dragged Emmet across the airstrip. Bigger did not necessarily translate to more mature.

"He'll be fine," Barabas said while eating a sweet roll. Then he shouted to Emmet, his speech continuing to improve. "Bring him on over here, and let's get this thing on him!"

Golegeth continued dragging Emmet around the airfield, by the looks of it chasing butterflies. The dragon would stop for a moment, wait, wiggle his hind end, and spring into the air using all four legs. Emmet was getting better at predicting when the dragon would jump, but he still had little control over where they went.

"Is this normal?" Riette asked, becoming sincerely concerned for her brother's safety.

Barabas nodded. "Bring him back over here!" he shouted to Emmet.

Riette glared at him when the dragon pounced on the same butterfly for the fifth time.

"All right. You're doing good. Wear him out," Barabas said. He turned back to Riette. "Sometimes you just gotta let them get it out of their system. This one likes butterflies. It'll pass."

"And Emmet?" she asked.

"They're bonding," he said. He laughed from his belly, no longer able to contain his mirth. "He'll be fine. The dragon won't hurt him. That dragon loves that boy, and that boy loves that dragon. We'll get the tierre on him when he's ready. Things like this aren't supposed to come easy."

Riette shook her head and turned her attention to the thing Barabas called a tierre. He'd said it was an ancient word and that Golegeth was the first dragon large enough to warrant one since the last war of power. Rather than a saddle, the tierre was wood and leather construction forming a cabin atop the dragon. It would seat three rows of three on each side of a central aisle. At the front were a pair of comfortable seats and thick, heavy lines with loops of reinforced leather forming handholds.

Emmet approached a moment later, his chest heaving from exertion and his clothes grass stained but a smile on his face. Golegeth followed him, panting. Riette held back a giggle, not wanting to embarrass her brother, but he didn't appear to care. He'd been denied so much in his life, it warmed her soul to see him get to do the thing that made his heart sing. She was going to miss him.

"I brought you this." She handed him the staff.

"You didn't have to go and do that, but—ooh. What is it? Lemme have it. Mine, mine, mine." His eyes went wide when he held the staff in his hands for the first time. "Brick did this?"

Riette nodded.

"He outdid himself."

"He made this one for me," she said, showing him the staff she'd already grown entirely too attached to. She couldn't help it. It made her feel more complete.

It had been Emmet who suggested the lily marble would help make sure she never experienced an episode again. "Perhaps our smith friend has missed his calling. I never pictured him a whittler."

"I'll be sure to tell him you said that," Riette said.

"Wait until I've left if you don't mind."

She nodded, not trusting her voice.

"I'm glad you're here," Barabas said. "I hope you didn't just come for the refreshments. We need some help getting this tierre on our big friend here. You got him this time?" Barabas asked Emmet.

He had to be joking, but it was at times difficult to tell. In the end, Tuck and Barabas did most of the heavy lifting, and Riette, her best to guide them. Golegeth snorted the entire time, watching them without blinking, but he allowed them to slide the tierre into place and secure the straps. It was not so unlike the saddle to which he was already accustomed.

Once the cabin was secured, Emmet climbed the rope ladder for the first time and entered the place where he would be the captain. In control of his own destiny, the world was an open canvas. A tough teacher Barabas may be, but he cared for Emmet; of that there was no doubt. It had been a difficult thing for Tuck and Barabas to end their partnership, but things had worked out for the best. Barabas would look after Emmet and Golegeth, and Riette would look after Tuck. She giggled at that thought.

People had begun to arrive at the airfield and watched the events transpire. Soon a balloon drifted toward the airstrip, the pilot using thrusters to steer against the wind. Emmet sat alone in his tierre and had just buckled himself in when Golegeth spotted the balloon. Bouncing on all fours, he looked back at Emmet. His pupils wide, he turned and leaped into the air from a standstill.

"Whoa!" came Emmet's shout from the tierre.

"Uh-oh," Barabas said with a chuckle.

Riette gaped.

"He won't eat anybody," Barabas continued with a lopsided grin. "But I bet they don't know that."

After three times approaching the balloon, Golegeth tired of the game and landed back where he'd started. He looked back at Emmet again, his pupils still wide, as if he found it all immensely amusing.

"You probably shouldn't have let him do that," Barabas said, and Tuck couldn't contain his laughter.

Riette elbowed him in the ribs.

Emmet climbed down, and despite looking a wee bit squeamish, he took his proper place as both barker and pilot—just as Barabas had started out. People disembarking from the balloon cast a wide berth around the dragon who had greeted them. "Fly Dragon Airways," Emmet called out to the first person who passed. "We don't normally scare folks like that."

Emmet smiled at Tuck, who smacked his forehead.

"Fly Dragon Airways," Emmet said to the next man, who grumbled in response. "At least we're friendly, even if perhaps too friendly."

Barabas groaned.

"Fly Dragon Airways. We don't hardly never crash."

Tuck gave Emmet the thumbs-up on that one. Barabas shook his head.

CHAPTER TWENTY-ONE

Magic and light are one. Some shine more brightly than others.
—Gemino, sorcerer and artist

* * *

Emmet Pickette was afraid. He was just a boy, and one only recently synchronized with the rest of reality. Always before, Riette had looked after him. She'd taken all responsibility for their lives. He'd wanted to participate but had been prevented by the severity of his former condition. He was free now. The world was wide open, and with Golegeth, no place was too far. It was exhilarating and terrifying. Having Barabas with him bolstered his confidence. The man could have gone anywhere, could have done anything, and yet he'd chosen to remain with Emmet and Golegeth.

The tierre had been constructed by the people of Sparrowport. Everyone had contributed something. The memory misted his eyes. The construction was simple but sturdy and of high quality. Nails, straps, and other fasteners made by Brick and Joren mated sewn leather Riette had stitched. They had even included a flap, which allowed Emmet to reach down and have physical contact with Golegeth. It was something he missed from flying with Dashiq. Flying with his own dragon was not better or worse, but it was different. Sitting in the tierre was more like being in Dashiq's carriage, only sturdier and larger. Pulleys and tensioners at the front of the structure kept the lines from binding or going slack with the movements of the dragon's head. The lines did not control Golegeth in the way magic lines had controlled Argus Kind's dragon, but they did allow Emmet to convey his intentions to his enormous friend.

Golegeth still did not know his size and often acted like a mere hatchling. It had taken a great deal of effort to break him of the habit of eating in Emmet's lap. There were times, though, when he did exactly as Emmet asked, and he seemed to understand when he could get away with misbehaving. Dashiq had taken control of events on numerous occasions, which colored some of Emmet's fears. What if the dragon decided to go somewhere he didn't want to go? It was an uncomfortable feeling, even if Golegeth was currently behaving himself and following Emmet's input.

Barabas helped. He understood the landscape and showed Emmet how to use maps, landmarks, and even the stars to navigate. When Dragonport came into view, the sight was distressing. The port through which most Midlands trade came was in complete chaos. The detritus of war had been cleared away, but twenty-three dragons perched upon rooftops and milled about in seeming disarray. There was no clear spot to land. Only when horns sounded, announcing Golegeth's arrival, did some sense of order prevail. The skies above Dragonport erupted with dragons not much smaller than Golegeth. Emmet's dragon had grown quickly, perhaps because of need. His clutchmates, who were collectively and lovingly known as Dashiq's Revenge, were all just a little bit behind him developmentally. It was among the reasons they had come here first. If not for the other dragons and their chosen, he would have gone back to the shallows—perhaps permanently. It was tempting but it didn't feel right when he could possibly help so many people. Barabas was a wealth of information with regard to rearing dragons, and the word from Dragonport was that they needed all the help they could get. The thought that someone might need Barabas more than he did also gnawed at his resolve.

He was Emmet Pickette, war hero, magic user, and dragon rider. He'd always dreamed of finding magic, but the other parts were still difficult to believe. Should not someone who'd achieved such things have also left fear behind? Apparently not. The dragons approaching only added to his concerns. There was no order, no collective will. Dragons whipped past them, roaring in greeting. Screams grew louder then faded when a dragon flew past, his chosen dangling from one claw. Emmet shouldn't have laughed. Even Barabas had difficulty restraining his mirth. What were they getting themselves into?

More dragons streamed past, and two now flanked them, looking almost giddy to see their slightly older brother. Golegeth radiated excitement. When he turned back to look at them and roar, his pupils were wide and his nostrils flared. It was an uncomfortable feeling, being atop a dragon who was hurtling through the air and not watching where they were going. Golegeth proved he was in complete control and made Emmet's fears once again seem unfounded. It was a lot of change to adapt to all at once. Barabas must have sensed his unease and gave him a reassuring pat on the knee.

When Golegeth landed, he displayed inherent grace and innate skill. That did not mean his passengers disembarked without event, though. The other dragons landed all around, far closer together than seemed wise, and Golegeth turned in place to greet them. Dragons snuffled at the tierre, blowing Emmet's hair with excited bursts of breath. Without parents to guide them, these dragons had to learn how to be dragons mostly on their own and it showed. In the excitement, a storage building was knocked over, along with several clotheslines. The people of Dragonport took it in stride and set about cleaning up the mess. Already they had grown accustomed to the chaos, but Emmet wondered if he would ever do the same. Eventually Golegeth stood still long enough to allow Emmet and Barabas to climb down.

Finny came to greet them. "Thank the gods you're here!" Emmet couldn't help but laugh again. Finny took no offense but looked haggard. "It's like raising toddlers as tall as oak trees," he continued, gesticulating.

"You've done well, my friend," Barabas said. "Some things we must simply endure and see through."

"I'm not sure I can do it," Finny admitted. "I love Lodiarch, but I think she might be the death of me. Just yesterday she took me fishing. It's not as much fun as it sounds. Believe me."

Barabas didn't laugh but came close.

"You're the first ones here. Can I get you something warm to eat?"

Barabas appeared as if he might decline, and Emmet kicked him lightly in the shin.

"Say no more."

Before Finny returned with steaming fish pies, the horns sounded again. Dragons—including Golegeth—took to the sky. Emmet hoped the dragons would be careful and not damage the tierre, but he couldn't really do much about it. Even if they had thought to remove the tierre, it was unlikely the dragons would have made it easy for them. The air still sang of excitement, and Emmet found his own hands shaking when he accepted a fish pie. When he glanced back up, Berigor approached. Al'Drak was now smaller than all of Dashiq's get. These would be the largest dragons anyone alive had ever seen—legends in the flesh. So many of the old tales continued to prove themselves true, Emmet could only imagine what the future would hold.

Berigor did not share the younger dragons' enthusiasm, and his roar sent the others scattering to the wind. In the ensuing silence came diesel engines. Larger than any aircraft before it, the eight-engine plane had a wingspan larger than any dragon. This was a plane capable of flying from the Firstland to Sparrowport without ever refueling. News of its construction had reached them long before, but seeing such an impressive and historical engineering feat was an experience none would soon forget.

"Eat your pie before it gets cold," Barabas said.

Embarrassed for gaping like a fish, Emmet did as he was told and didn't regret it. The pie had reached the perfect temperature to be eaten without burning his tongue and the roof of his mouth and where the flavor was at its richest. This was not everyday fare. The people of Dragonport had prepared a reception fit for a king even if that was the very thing they sought to make sure was relegated to the past. If the people aboard the airplane upheld their promise, Argus Kind would be the last king.

Escorted by dragons, the plane slowed its approach and lined up with the landing strip. Only when the plane moved over the airstrip did the dragons veer off. They landed a moment later, giving the plane much wider berth, unsure what to make of it. When the delegation for the Firstland emerged, the people looked pale and afraid. Emmet understood their fears;

he was still trying to quell a few of his own. No matter how Finny tried to reassure them the dragons were friendly, the Firstland delegation stayed huddled together, trying to appear regal and failing. Dragons snuffled around them and the plane.

"Just let them get a good whiff of you," Finny said. "Or they'll never leave you alone. They won't hurt you, but I definitely do not advise running away."

Berigor landed a moment later, and his roar sent the younger dragons scattering. Golegeth hid behind Emmet. This was a battle dragon. There could be no doubt. He stood tall. His wings partly extended, he dared anyone to challenge him. He was Al'Drak and everyone knew it. Keldon sat, steely eyed in the saddle, looking as if he'd aged a decade since Emmet last saw him. The older dragon tilted his head and acknowledged Golegeth, who then danced around the older dragon with unrestrained glee, wiggling his hindquarters.

Keldon let the excited dragon get it out of his system before climbing down to greet Barabas and Emmet, who had moved closer. "It's good to see you, my friends."

"And you," Barabas said.

Emmet gave Keldon a hug that clearly made the man uncomfortable.

"Someone is going to have to teach these dragons some discipline," Keldon said with a look of disapproval.

"You're just the man for the job," Barabas said, and they both laughed.

"Are you sure you won't take the position back?" Keldon asked.

Barabas shook his head. "Not for all the gold in the Heights."

Though they joked, the toll the position had taken on Keldon was plain to see. His hair was graying rapidly, and the lines around his eyes had grown deeper.

"I've already tried to get the clutch moved to the Heights, but the dragons refuse to leave Dragonport. What use is it being Al'Drakon if no one listens?"

Chuckling, Barabas nodded. "What use indeed."

"You do agree that Drak are Drak regardless of their breeding, though, correct?"

Barabas had done his best to avoid involvement in politics—especially Drakon politics. "It is not my opinion that counts," he said after a long moment. "It is the opinions of those dragons and their bonded that are important. Without their hearts and minds, it will make no difference what words you use. In truth, if you win them over, it still won't matter what you call them."

"You are wiser than I ever gave you credit for."

Barabas nodded again. "Wisdom comes at a cost. Don't rush it. When at last people tell you that you're wise, you'll long to have back the innocence you lost. It can be a bitter reward. After all, ignorance can be fun, albeit dangerous at times."

"If you will aid me, perhaps I can have the benefit of both?" Keldon asked.

It took a long moment for Barabas to respond. "I will be your friend, Keldon. I can promise no more than that. If you find my counsel helpful at times, I'd welcome it, but I fear you'll have to forge your own path."

"I suppose we should greet our new allies," Keldon said. Barabas walked beside him in silent agreement. Emmet followed unbidden.

Golegeth watched with concerned interest. It was clear he did not trust these people. But then, the dragon did not really trust anyone other than Emmet and Barabas. It was something they would have to work on.

A bald man with a short white beard approached a place on the plateau that had been cleared, at his arm, a young woman. "I am Rodram. I stand for the people of the Firstland. This is my granddaughter Lienna. She will attend me if you will allow the indulgence. I'm not so weak that I cannot walk, but her presence brings me comfort."

"You are welcome here. I am Fineous Wermer, and I've been asked to speak on behalf of the Midlands."

"I am Keldon Tallowborn, Al'Drakon and representative of the Heights. I welcome you in peace."

Barabas said nothing but took Emmet's hand in his own. Pain and memory flowed between them. Barabas had lost everything he held dear to the war with Argus Kind and the Firstland. Dashiq was gone and they had hastened her demise. So many friends, fellow soldiers, and Drakon had been lost in a pointless war. No one had gained a thing. These were not easy things to let go, and tears streamed down the old warrior's cheeks.

"I see you, Barabas DeGuiere," Rodram said unexpectedly. "We all know who you are, how well you fought, and what you've lost. I won't claim to know your pain, but I will tell you that it hasn't been for naught. No more will our lands be divided by petty hatred." From within his robes he pulled a rolled parchment. A table and benches were brought to the clearing, and Rodram seated himself. "We have read the treaty you've proposed, and we find it not only acceptable but very gracious. We thank you for not punishing us for the actions of the one who has been deposed."

His unwillingness to even speak the name Argus Kind illustrated how he felt about the man, which suited Emmet just fine. He suspected those around him felt the same based on their reactions. Even the dragons were quiet and respectful, as if the solemn nature of this meeting were known to them. Golegeth watched intently while all three men signed multiple copies of the treaty and affixed their seals. Those assembled watched in silence. When the last seal had been pressed into glossy red wax, Berigor issued a trumpeting call. All at once the dragons took flight. How they managed not to collide and knock each other from the sky was a mystery, but they soon scattered. It was a sight that gave Emmet chills. Such majesty and might, and one belonged to him. Emmet couldn't help but remind himself it was the other way around. Golegeth had chosen him before ever escaping his shell.

Food and wine was brought to the table, and the atmosphere became a bit more relaxed. Emmet reached for a sweet roll at the same time as Lienna. Their hands touched. She met his eyes and smiled shyly. Emmet wasn't certain which of them blushed more furiously.

"Perhaps relations between our lands are already on the mend," Finny said with a sly smile.

Rodram raised his eyebrows and looked at Lienna, who now averted her eyes, turning an even darker shade. Keldon Tallowborn laughed from his belly, and it was the youngest Emmet had ever seen him look. It would have made him feel good if the laughter were not at his expense. Even so, he dared a glance back at Lienna. She must have sensed his gaze, for she looked up and giggled.

"There are less pleasant matters that must yet be dealt with," Rodram said. "All those listed as war criminals within this treaty have been captured save three. Agger Dan, Casta Mett, and the one they call Grunt have thus far evaded capture. I can assure you the people of the Firstland will scour land and sea to find them, but we also request your assistance in this matter. Our access to the air is . . . not what it once was."

That last remark made some in attendance shift uncomfortably. The aircraft they now lacked had not so long ago attacked this very place. Not much damage was still evident, which was among the reasons Dragonport had been chosen as the location of this meeting. The devastation of the Heights and even the reconstruction of Sparrowport were perhaps too stark a backdrop for the makings of peace.

"There is nothing we can do to take back the harm done to you and your lands," Rodram continued. "Though we lost many lives at the hands of a failed ideology—if you can even call it that—we've caused even greater damage to your lands on top of lives lost. To show our commitment to enduring peace, I've brought with me some of our best engineers and aircraft designers and their families. Perhaps we can, at least in some small way, be a part of rebuilding that which has been lost and make a better future."

"This is most appreciated," Keldon said. "Casta Mett, on the other hand, proposes an ongoing, long-term threat that must be neutralized. Given her ability to locate magic and her companions' survival skills, we cannot consider ourselves safe until they have all been brought to justice."

Finny nodded in agreement, as did Rodram. Barabas patted Emmet on the knee, now wearing a sad but peaceful smile.

"There is one final matter with which I will ask your assistance," Rodram said. "This young man was found in the Firstland wilderness, where no one in their right mind would go. It took a brave crew to rescue him. He says he's from Sparrowport."

A young man Emmet suddenly recognized stepped forward. Destin Brightwood had aged well. No more was he the skinny, pasty kid the others picked on; here was a young man who'd survived in the wilderness and no longer feared death. Emmet could see it in his eyes. They both had changed.

"Thank you, Rodram," Finny said, "for bringing him home. Perhaps we can convince one of the dragons to fly him back to Sparrowport."

At the mention of dragons, roars filled the air and a stream of dragons returned from a successful fishing expedition. Finny went pale. "Just stay here and everything will be fine," he said, contrary to the look on his face. Lodiarch spotted him and roared in excitement. Finny ran. He made it only a few steps before the huge tuna Lodiarch had been carrying struck him full in the back. A moment later, Lodiarch landed, looking proud. Finny pulled himself from the ground, but before he could scold the dragon, Lodiarch licked him from toe to hair.

Lienna giggled.

All over the plateau, dragons found their bonded humans and showed them their catches. No one was safe.

"Is it always like this with dragons?" Rodram asked.

Barabas chuckled. "Give 'em a couple decades. It'll wear off."

Emmet stood, watching the chaos around him.

"Can I come with you?" Lienna asked, meeting his eyes for only a brief instant. "Grandfather doesn't really need my help at the moment."

Rodram said nothing to contradict her.

"You might want to stay here a moment longer," Emmet said, hearing Golegeth's roar. Though he'd mostly broken the dragon of trying to sit in his lap while eating, excitement was clear in his dragon's voice. His brethren were not exactly setting a good example.

Emmet ran. Behind him, Lienna giggled. Golegeth swooped and scooped Emmet up in his free front claw. In his other he held some kind of fish Emmet didn't recognize. The species mattered little at the moment. The dragon did not land; instead, he circled above Dragonport with Emmet dangling from one claw, his fish from the other, bragging to his brethren. Only when Berigor issued a deep roar did Golegeth return to the field. He placed Emmet gently enough on the ground but held his human in place while he ate. There was little doubt who was really in charge.

Without fear, Lienna approached. "Are you all right?"

"I'll be fine," Emmet said, struggling to break free of Golegeth's grip. "He's not normally like this. He's just excited to see his kin."

"He's beautiful," Lienna said.

Golegeth released him and turned to regard Lienna. He sniffed her twice, sending her hair and skirts flying, then licked her across the face. Embarrassed, Emmet feared she would be upset, but she just laughed. The sound lightened his soul, and he'd never be the same again.

Barabas came to Emmet's side, putting a hand on his shoulder. "I've spoken with your grandfather," he said to Lienna. "He thought you might like to take a ride on a dragon."

"Really?" she bounced with excitement.

"If the conditions are right," Emmet said. "We're going to see a man named Tellymore. People call him Telly. Brick told me so."

Emmet could not have been happier. Perhaps flying within the tierre would allow him the appearance of having some control over the situation. Before he helped Lienna into the tierre, though, a family from the Firstland approached. While the mother and father weren't all that remarkable, Emmet could not look away from their son, an awkward boy with ears a little too large for his head. He shone like a new star.

Nodding to Barabas, Emmet pointed. "Magic."

Be sure to check out *The Dawning of Power* and the rest of the *Godsland* fantasy series to find out what happens when the goddess finally returns. For more information visit BrianRathbone.com.

CPSIA information can be obtained at www.ICGtesting.com
Printed in the USA
LVOW08s1343270616

494270LV00005B/191/P